UNSEEN ALLIANCE

The Hidden Realm in World War II

Vicky Fox

Copyright © 2023 Vicky Fox
All rights reserved.
ISBN:979-8-8639-5968-9

DEDICATION

The brave men and women who sacrificed so much in the fight against totalitarian regimes in World War II

CONTENTS

    Acknowledgments

    Prologue

1. Land Girl
2. Pitdown Hall
3. Greyfolk
4. Birth
5. Hermitage Theatre
6. St Jude's
7. The Fall
8. A King
9. Doctor Dee
10. Abomination
11. Blitz
12. Reckoning

ACKNOWLEDGMENTS

Friends who read drafts.
Podcasters who provided inspiration

PROLOGUE

In the summer of 1940, while the Battle of Britain was being fought in the skies, two men walked through a dimly lit corridor behind the scene-dock of a minor London theatre.

The shorter of the men said, 'I needn't tell you that no one must know of this visit.' He stopped and lit the cigar he was carrying. 'It will be a lacuna in the records, as though it never happened. If this becomes public knowledge the government will be a laughingstock.'

They stood contemplating his words, then he continued, 'Unless, of course, the German Army crosses the Channel. If that happens, we will need them.'

In July 1940 the fear of an invasion by German forces was at the forefront of every British mind. It had been unthinkable that France, with its superior numbers and highly mechanised army would be crushed in six weeks and sue for peace. British expeditions in Europe and Norway had been disastrous and the country stood alone against a seemingly unstoppable Nazi Germany.

The smoke from his cigar hung around the bare light bulbs. Further along the silent corridor a woman appeared in a doorway. The taller man stepped forward, his hand inside his jacket.

'It's alright Walter. I believe this is the theatre's cleaning lady. No need for firearms.'

They saw an elderly woman of dark skin with a long silver plait hanging down her back, dressed in tunic and trousers under her overall. The older man recognised her as a child of the Empire, he thought she must be from India, and he smiled and touched his hat as they walked past her. He was disconcerted by the smile that was returned. It was more than recognition; it was a look of knowledge and experience and not what he expected.

If Winston Churchill was worried by the meeting he had just attended and not keen to have its contents made public, she was even more concerned. What was the Prime Minister doing in a second-rate theatre in the middle of a war with only his bodyguard for company? Where were the private secretaries and cabinet ministers?

Mariel McKinley was a woman who had lived a long time and seen great changes in the world, and she suspected that Winston Churchill was a man open to dangerous ideas that would not have been considered by other world leaders. Although these were desperate times for the country, she was familiar with the occupants of the Hermitage Theatre and knew what secrets might be found there. She was aware they had become dissatisfied and restless and was afraid that their primitive morality would thrive in the maelstrom of total war.

A few weeks later a land girl working on her uncle's farm in Hampshire received an unexpected visitor. She was invited to participate in one of the most extreme measures that Great Britain's government would consider to ensure its sovereignty and that of its empire. She would, of course, accept the invitation.

1 LAND GIRL

Friday 19 July 1940

One of the regular labourers approached as she topped up the oil in her uncle's new tractor, his pride and joy.

'Miss James, there's a lady waiting for you in the farm office. I hope you haven't gotten into trouble.'

'Waiting for me?'

'I'll have to mention it to your uncle.'

'Of course you will. I'd expect nothing else,' said Rosalyn.

She was thinking what a snitch, but she had to deal with his resentment regularly. A lot of them struggled to accept women doing the same work as men. Perhaps he was also dreading getting his call-up papers. His essential occupation wouldn't be quite so essential if women were able to farm in his place.

Rosalyn James had been working on her uncle's farm near Winchester since the outbreak of war and it was work she was used to, having spent many holidays on the downland with its abundant sheep and excellent riding country. She had been sent here many times to stay with her aunt's family as a child after her mother died. Rosalyn had been two years old when her Jewish mother had died in the Spanish flu epidemic of 1920. She had no memory of her, but she knew that marrying outside the faith had earned the displeasure of her own people, and the little family had been ostracised. But the love match between Albert James and Hannah Levy, nurtured among the antiquarian books of the British Library could not be denied, and the years they spent together had been happy.

She strode over to the farm office pausing briefly to visit the lavatory and wash her hands at the pump. If she was to shake hands with a lady, they had better be clean. Her breeches were passable, and her shirt freshly laundered. She scraped back any errant strands of hair and brushed herself down. At five foot eight

Rosalyn was tall for a girl and had always been able to stand up for herself against her brothers. They never made allowances for their sister's sex and teased her for being the youngest, presenting her with challenges she was unable to resist.

The woman standing in the farm office was aged about fifty. She wore a tweed skirt and jacket, brogues and a robin hood hat. She was slim and wore no make-up and, despite the warm weather, had on gloves that she didn't remove. They shook hands and Rosalyn closed the door. The woman closed the window. This was surprising because it was a warm day, and the office was stuffy and always smelled of engine oil although none was kept there.

'How can I help you?' Rosalyn said gesturing for her guest to take a seat.

'It's your country that needs your help Miss James,' the woman said.

'And you are?'

'I'm not at liberty to give you that information and what I am about to tell you must not be disclosed to anyone. Effectively if this meeting continues you will be bound by the Official Secrets Act. Anything you learn must be kept secret for the duration of the war and for thirty years afterwards. If you want to terminate our discussion, now is the time to do so.'

Rosalyn had always thought she was doing useful war work, what more could she contribute? If she didn't hear what the woman was about to tell her then she would never know, and she had the feeling she'd regret it for the rest of her life. Her brothers had enlisted as soon as war broke out and one of them had been engaged in the naval evacuation of Dunkirk earlier in the year. Now in July 1940 Britain was standing alone against a German army that had conquered most of Europe. The shocking speed with which Europe had fallen and years of under-investment in British armed forces meant the country was ill-prepared. It was only the English Channel that had prevented the Nazi Panzer divisions from continuing their momentum and rolling into Britain.

The James children would be classified as Jews and all three siblings had been appalled at the antisemitic rhetoric and the violence of the Nazi regime during the 1930s and were determined to fight it wherever possible.

As she considered this, the strange woman said nothing.

Rosalyn thought about Winston Churchill's words in a radio broadcast a few weeks earlier: that the Battle of France was over, and the Battle of Britain was about to begin. Rosalyn wanted to do more. Unconsciously she sat up taller.

'If you've done your homework,' she said. 'You know that I'll do whatever I can to help defeat the Nazis.'

The woman said, 'Your father lives in London and works for the British Library and your brothers are in the armed services. I understand you're not courting.'

Rosalyn nodded. She said, 'That's correct.'

'We'd like to move you to a different location. In fact, it's an estate that's been left derelict for about twenty years and has now been taken over by the War Department.'

'I'm to assist the farmer?'

'Some of the time. In addition to farming, other duties will be added.'

'Can I ask what sort of duties?' Rosalyn said.

'You can ask but I am not able to tell you except to say that you would be deployed only in the event of an invasion by Germany. You will be helping your country in her hour of greatest need.'

'Why me?'

'Your name was mentioned by an influential participant in the project. That's all I can say. I can't allow you any time to think about it Miss James. Either you will join and be inducted into the unit, or you must forget that we had this conversation.'

Rosalyn wondered what sort of unit. There had been rumours about undercover workers being trained to harass and disrupt the enemy should the Germans land in England.

'Did you choose me because my mother is Jewish, therefore I will be a target if the Nazis invade?' she asked.

'No,' the other woman replied. 'There is a reason for your selection that I cannot disclose now. But I can tell you that we know you have lived near the estate. It's close to Guildford and you were at school there until you were sixteen. You were considered a promising pupil …'

'I was expelled from that school.'

'And led them a merry dance I believe.' She said it without a trace of humour. 'You are able to think for yourself and make decisions. We're not looking for rule followers, we need mavericks, rule breakers, men and women who have physical courage.'

Rosalyn knew she could never turn down something like this. It was the stuff of her childhood dreams, adventures with men, on equal terms. She felt a rush of excitement and tried to control it.

'There will be training I presume?'

'Yes, that will start at the Pitdown Estate where you will be classed as a land girl, but you will have a greater value in the long term. I understand you have an interest in shooting.'

'It was simply a matter of keeping up with my brothers. Although I must admit I am competitive,' Rosalyn said.

'And exceeding them when it came to equestrian feats.'

'Will we be mounted?'

'No.' The woman looked at her curiously. 'This is an experimental unit. One more thing. Do you suffer from claustrophobia?'

'I don't think so.'

'Good. Now I must go, and you will speak to no one, not your uncle and not even members of your family who are serving in the armed forces. Do you understand?'

'Absolutely,' Rosalyn said. She didn't really understand but she knew that nothing would deter her from such a venture.

Paperwork was produced and Rosalyn signed it without any clear idea of what was involved except knowing it was dangerous.

'If anyone asks, I am a civil servant making an assessment of the health of female farm workers.' The woman stood. 'Your uncle will receive a letter transferring you to another farm.' She held out a gloved hand. 'Goodbye.'

'Goodbye.' Surely good luck would be more appropriate, Rosalyn thought. Luck will have everything to do with it.

She let the woman out and saw the farm worker scuttle round the corner. He was too far away to have heard anything, but it made her think about the posters exhorting the British public to keep its secrets. There were people who sympathised with the Nazis, fifth columnists they were called, and she shuddered to think what would occur if the Nazis were fighting their way across the country. Who would be the collaborators? She closed the door and sat in her uncle's office chair and allowed her imagination to run. Waves of emotion passed through her until she realised she was smiling. She knew it was foolish, and she ought to be afraid but at twenty-two anything seemed possible, and she would be part of it. She just had to behave completely normally until it came about, and keep the silly grin off her face, because no one could know the secret.

*

Friday 26 July 1940

A week later her uncle called her to the farmhouse and handed her a formal letter from the Ministry of Agriculture and Fisheries requesting that Rosalyn report to Pitdown Estate office the following Sunday. He was annoyed at losing an experienced worker, and a member of the family. He suggested appealing against it, but she reasoned with him and said that she was ready for a new challenge, and they would soon send a replacement. He grumbled that a new girl wasn't likely to have Rosalyn's experience.

In the ensuing days she wrote to her father with the new postal address and wondered what he might be doing. The national collections of art and books had been moved out of London the previous year, so he was spending his time between town and the National Library of Wales in Aberystwyth where some of the rarest antiquities were being stored. He would inform her brothers when the opportunity presented itself.

Saturday 27 July 1940

Rosalyn had a comfortable bedroom to herself in her uncle's farmhouse, and it was a matter of regret to realise she might not see her aunt and uncle and little cousins for a long time. She tried not to think that it might be forever, but she took every opportunity to hug them. Packing essential items into a small case she thought about the sacrifices that so many young men had already made when the British Expeditionary Force had been defeated and brushed the feelings aside, determined that she wouldn't give them any cause to believe she was not going to another farming job.

'I don't know why they chose you,' said her aunt at the big dinner held in Rosalyn's honour the day before departure. She was cutting up the meat of her five-year-old and helping the three-year-old to handle his spoon.

'She's got experience of farm work and they're recruiting more town and city girls so they have to spread the knowledge I expect,' her uncle said. 'We have to produce a lot more food at home now that the country is cut off from the dominions.'

He had evidently come to terms with Rosalyn's reassignment.

'That place you're going to, Pitdown Hall near Guildford, I heard it hasn't been run properly for years. The War Department have requisitioned it to help with the war effort, there was a big fuss in the House of Commons, questions being asked,' he said.

'Why did the owner allow it to get into such a state, surely he could have found a tenant?' Rosalyn said.

'There's no money in farming my girl,' her aunt said. 'So much cheap stuff brought in from abroad, that's what the Empire has done for farmers.'

'Yes my love, I daresay it is cheaper to grow it abroad and ship it in, but I believe in this case there has been some dispute on the ownership of Pitdown Hall. An eccentric gentleman has been living in it, but the legal title is held by a trust. That means lawyers get involved and they can knit fog when they want to. Heirs were lost in the Great War, then this chap turned up and he seems to have established some right of occupation, so he moved in. The estate has plenty of game but not much in the way of cultivation. Well, the War Office aren't going to stand for that. Got to get as much land under wheat as we can.'

'Is the eccentric gentleman still alive?' asked Rosalyn.

'If he is then he's away with the faeries,' said her uncle.

'Don't talk like that,' said her aunt. 'It would drive anyone mad to lose their family in a pointless war. And now we've got it all to do again.' She looked tearfully at her two little boys.

The older boy immediately began making aeroplane noises, flying his fork as far as his arms would reach.

The three-year-old shouted, 'Spitfire.'

'Messerschmidt,' shouted the other and raised his knife.

'Stop it!' cried their mother, too late to stop the German plane being shot down onto the white tablecloth and upsetting a glass of milk. At this the little one wailed, and chaos ensued until mopping of tears and the tablecloth had been achieved and they had been stowed in their bedroom with toys and comic books.

'You should never have let them watch that dog fight,' her aunt said to her uncle when she came back to the table. 'We'll never hear the end of it. Just think, the Spitfire pilot might have been killed, imagine the effect that would have had on their young minds.'

'Well, they both missed,' said her uncle. 'So they flew off in different directions. I shouldn't have minded seeing the Gerry get shot down. Coming over here and bombing our airfields.'

'Still be a horrible thing to see,' his wife said, after a pause.

'They might see worse than that if the invasion happens. Shelling and bombing and bullets flying everywhere. Dead bodies in the fields. I suppose we'll have to decide what to do, stay here or move up country, assuming they invade along the south coast.'

'We'll have to stay for the animals,' said her aunt.

'Me and the workers will, but I'd be happier if you and the boys went north.' Her uncle said, looking at his wife sternly.

Rosalyn remembered photographs she had seen in the newspaper.

'In France they were dive bombing columns of refugees with Stukas,' she said. 'You might be better staying here. Food is bound to be scarce and at least here you can grow vegetables and keep chickens. Assuming they don't requisition everything as they move through.'

'Good point,' said her uncle. 'We'll have to find some hiding places on the farm. Disused wells, things like that. Make sure they're invisible.'

They sat in silence for a while contemplating the great unknowns of the day, would the Germans invade and if so, when? The boredom of the early months of the war had led to frustration and then it seemed impossible that France, Belgium and the Low Countries would fall, but they had. The occupation of Norway meant bombers could reach Scotland, and Aberdeen had been recently attacked. Rosalyn steered the conversation onto more cheerful matters and a letter she had received from her father announcing that her older brother was engaged to a girl he had met in Portsmouth. It was a shame she would miss the party, but they all held out hope for a get-together at Christmas.

'I hope she's not in the family way,' said her aunt.

As her uncle grumbled platitudes about short lives and living for the moment Rosalyn reflected that these days getting engaged was almost an acceptable way to have sex before marriage. He might be posted away and never make it back. No one would blame them, and speedy weddings were becoming more common as the reality of war on the home front faced them. The Germans seemed unbeatable and, despite Churchill's rhetoric, there was a great deal of pessimism underneath the outward facing optimism.

They spent the evening listening to radio programmes and then Rosalyn finished her packing. She would take only things she needed and leave her trunk at her uncle's farm. She leafed through treasured books and decided to take just one, of poetry. She would burn her diary. There should be nothing to link her with this family except her aunt being her father's sister and her work as a land girl. She hesitated over the few photographs but decided to keep them in the trunk, she could hardly ask her aunt and uncle to destroy theirs. Tomorrow she would take a train to the Pitdown Hall Estate and the next phase of her life would begin.

2 PITDOWN HALL

Sunday 28 July 1940

The train journey was uncomfortable. These days there were more passengers and fewer services, and Rosalyn was glad she had only a small suitcase to lug around the platforms in addition to her handbag and gas mask. It was crowded with forces' personnel in uniform and particularly sailors with their big cylindrical kit bags that never fit properly in the luggage racks but got under your feet. Everybody smoked and Rosalyn, who had not taken up the habit, was offered so many 'gaspers' she thought she might have to accept out of politeness. It wouldn't have mattered. She reckoned she had smoked several cigarettes simply by breathing the air. The sailors' Capstans were the most noxious of them all. By the time she reached the little station she felt as though she'd been 'kippered'.

As the steam train pulled out, she checked her clothes for smuts and then took stock of the little station. One other person had dismounted at the same time. A thin man in corduroys and a knitted sweater. Everything about him seemed shabby, even the slouch hat he wore low over his face. She stood next to her suitcase and waited for the smoke and noise to die away, and when no one else appeared she picked it up and walked to the ticket office.

It was empty. She rang the handbell and waited. Eventually there was the sound of flushing and an irritable man came into the office adjusting his braces. She had obviously interrupted him in the middle of a major bowel movement.

'Sorry,' she said.

'What's there to be sorry about?' he replied huffily.

'Is there a taxi service? I was expecting to be met but there appears to be no one here.'

'Where are you going?'

'Pitdown Hall.'

He glanced at her dress and appeared to decide she was a member of the re-formed Women's Land Army, and not a fifth columnist. He pointed to the road.

'If they haven't met you, it'll be a walk of about four miles. Hope you've got a pair of sturdy shoes.'

He turned away and began riffling through some papers. Assistance had been provided and the interview was over.

She thanked him and hefting her case went through the door to the dusty roadway. There was no sign of the thin young man, so she began the walk. It was a glorious day; birds were singing, and the breeze had a cool easterly aspect. The station was some way from a hamlet comprising a few cottages, a church and a post office that looked as though it sold everything. It was next to a delightful river crossed by a stone bridge. Rosalyn decided to double check the directions she'd been given. All signposts were reputed to have been removed or swapped around to deliberately mislead the enemy and she had never been to Pitdown Hall. Her school was located on the other side of the forest and although she had explored on horseback many of the green lanes and paths in the country, she had never chanced upon it.

The postmistress was friendly, confirmed the directions and she set off with renewed vigour. A few hundred yards further along the road it entered the shade of dense woodland with steep banks on either side and became narrow with occasional passing points. It was silent except for her footsteps and breathing.

'He insisted on going back for you.'

Rosalyn stopped and looked around but there seemed to be no one. He chuckled and lit a cigarette so she could see him. The man who had been at the station stepped out from behind the tree that had hidden him and jumped down to stand several feet from her.

'That was good of him,' she said. 'He must have missed me when I was in the post office.'

He looked at her with disdain.

She said, 'And you must have told him about me.'

'Only when he asked. I didn't know who you were, or that you were expected. I daresay he thought you'd missed the train or changed your mind. It would be a good idea to do that you know. Change your mind.'

They stared at each other. He was tall with deep set brown eyes, his nose long and chin strong, but part of his face was hidden by the hat. The sound of a car prevented further exchange and Rosalyn was able to put on a neutral face to meet the driver who jumped out and loaded her bag into the boot. He was apologetic and tried to treat her as a lady, obviously expecting the other man to get into the back allowing her to sit in the front but after an awkward pause she climbed over the seat and settled in.

'I'm sorry miss. When you weren't on the platform, I assumed you'd been held up.' He spoke with a country accent in contrast to the clipped tones of the first man.

'Chickened out you mean,' said the first man as he stubbed out his cigarette. She did not respond but found his patronising manner infuriating.

'This isn't going to be a picnic,' he continued. 'You don't know what you're in for.'

'For God's sake shut up – sir.' The driver looked at Rosalyn in the mirror. His eyes were blue. 'My name's Farrell and this is Julian Brent.'

'How do you do. I'm Rosalyn James.'

She looked at the driver's sturdy shoulders as he started the car. He was strong and muscular, his hair neatly cut, and he was clean shaved. She found herself admiring the contours of his cheekbones and, because his sleeves were rolled up, his forearms were visible as he held the steering wheel and changed gear. She noted the curve of muscle beneath the suntanned skin and then admired the neatness of his ears. They left the woodland and came into the light. The open window pushed the smell of fresh masculine sweat into the back of the car and she found it intoxicating.

A hen pheasant wandered into the road and the car hit her.

Farrell stopped the car and got out. He walked back to the fluttering bird and quickly broke her neck.

'Find that exciting, do you? I expect he's good at breaking necks. He's a gamekeeper.' Brent had turned in his seat and was studying her as she watched their driver.

Rosalyn assumed her neutral face and looked at him. With a shock she saw him clearly for the first time. The left side of his face was puckered with scar tissue. It would be rude to ask about it, so she did.

'What happened to your face?'

'Well, I wasn't attacked by an angry pheasant,' he said, but nothing more as Farrell got back into the car.

'Begging your pardon Miss, but would you mind keeping that down by your feet?'

He handed over the warm carcase. She smiled and took it and tried not to show any pleasure at the touch of his hand. His eyes met hers again, and there was a hesitation, a recognition. Brent had turned away in disgust. Rosalyn sat back, the thrill of it must be the strange circumstances, and the promise of danger. Poker face, she thought, watch, and analyse, get over this crush, if that's what it is.

There was no small talk for the remainder of the journey, and she was dropped at a lodge a short walk from the Hall. Farrell removed her case and took it to the door which was unlocked. He touched his cap and their eyes met again. She tried not to look after his departing figure but registered Brent's scowling face in the car.

It was a very small cottage, comprising a kitchen with a table, settle and a range, and a butler's sink at the window. The other room on the ground floor was stocked with china and glass, and furniture that looked out of place. It must be a storage area for things removed from the Hall that they would not be needing for the duration of the war. A squint-eyed Major from the time of the Crimea was propped against a wall, a dust sheet hanging off the frame, and a pale lady with bulging alarmed eyes was blocking the fireplace. It was difficult to walk into the room, so she closed the door and went upstairs.

There were two bedrooms with tiny windows under the eaves and a double bed in each with army issue blankets, a towel, and a pillow. She left her case on one of them and went back down to the kitchen. An envelope on the cold range was addressed to Miss James. The letter read:

28 July 1940

Miss James

Report to the main house at 1700 to receive provisions and to meet your commanding officer for a briefing. Bring your ration book. Dinner will be at 1800. Dress informal.

Yours etc

Lt G R Greaves

Rosalyn drank some tap water, would have killed for a cup of tea, and regretted not being able to enjoy a cigarette. There was something comforting about smoking she had never appreciated before. It was a habit that anyone could acquire, a leveller and a reminder of home. There was nothing in the cottage that reminded Rosalyn of home. None of the rooms had any books in them. The lights were oil lamps or candles, and she felt the less time spent here the better, so she went outside and explored the cottage garden. It was in front of the property, the back was untended scrub, and woodland was close by. There were overgrown vegetable beds, a few fruit trees and shrubs and she found an earth closet and a woodshed.

*

An hour later she was walking to the main house along a twisting drive through tall cedars and enjoying the quiet of the place. As she passed a hedge a rough arm grabbed her around the neck and another hand covered her mouth. She managed to take a breath then bent double so that the body behind her slid over her shoulder and she bit down hard on the hand.

She thought if that's how they like to play and took the advantage throwing herself on the man with her hand on his throat. He was stronger and would soon have her off, but he just laughed.

'Ow, that hurt.'

'Good. Now that I'm on top, who are you and why am I kneeling in the grass?'

'Not bad Miss James. Good instincts. Perhaps we can do something with you after all.'

He pushed her off him and got up. Then he extended a hand.

Before she took it, she said, 'No funny business.'

'Promise.'

They shook hands.

'I'm Gerald Greaves and I'll be heading up this unit.'

So he was the Lieutenant who had written the short formal note. He was slim but wiry, wore battle dress but without insignia, and sported the type of thin moustache favoured by film stars.

'Is it usual for land girls to learn how to fight?' Rosalyn had her suspicions, but nobody had explained it to her and she was just beginning to grasp the full implications.

'You're the only woman in this unit, and no one will show you any favours so be prepared for a rough ride.'

'What a surprise. I'm sure the Germans will go easy on me if they catch me,' she said.

He smiled.

It was a shock to realise there were no other women. Despite growing up with brothers Rosalyn enjoyed the social company of her own sex as respite from the rough and tumble of male egos.

She choked back her misgivings of impropriety; what if she was required to do something immoral? An odd disconnect happened in her mind as she realised learning to attack people would be morally acceptable but having sex would not, and she dared not ask the question.

They walked to the Hall. Rosalyn was impressed by the chimneys and the imposing Tudor façade; there were steps up to the front door and a row of large windows looking southeast. But an air of decadence and authority hung over it so she was reminded of her old school and the power struggles that always existed in institutions.

'Three of the men you are about to meet have just returned from training and after tonight's meal they will return to their homes in the village. Their families have no idea. I don't know exactly what you've been told but in a special auxiliary unit secrecy is of the utmost importance.'

'The woman who recruited me said this unit is experimental. Can you tell me what that means?' Rosalyn said.

'We have a woman member, of course,' he avoided her eyes. 'As with other units we must be deeply embedded in the community and training is usually carried out at night or weekends. Our activities relate to what will happen if there is an invasion, and after the Germans have fought their way up the country.'

'Assuming they invade from the south.'

'Exactly. The speed of the German advance in Europe has led some to suspect they may have had assistance from cells of sympathisers,' Greaves said.

'Fifth columnists?'

'If you like. Anyway, we will take out possible Nazi sympathisers and sabotage the supply network and communication channels the Germans set up. Basically harry them in any way we can.'

'So why are we different?' asked Rosalyn.

'We have this house as a base, and we have a member of the women's land army.'

'I still don't understand.'

'None of us have close family,' he said. 'Around here, at least.'

For a pleasurable second Rosalyn reflected that Farrell didn't have a family, no wife, but she pushed it out of her mind.

Greaves continued. 'You'll understand, eventually. At least as much as any of us do.'

They mounted the steps and he showed her the refectory and meeting rooms and then took her into the sitting room where five men were smoking and drinking tea. A couple of them stood when she came in and she was introduced to the group.

Brent and Farrell were there, and she noted that the gamekeeper looked uncomfortable. She saw the tea urn and made a bee line for it.

'Thanks love, I'll have three sugars,' a man said. She looked at him quickly and saw a muscular man with a beer belly, badly shaved and with bad teeth. She tried not to let any hint of disgust show on her face, it wouldn't do to appear stuck-up. Any one of these men might have her back at a critical moment.

There were a few guffaws and she forced a smile. She helped herself to a mug of tea and enjoyed it as Greaves offered her a cigarette. Tempted, she declined and perched on the window ledge.

'Been rolling in the hay, Lieutenant,' someone said. 'You've got grass stains on your back.'

So that would be the other line of verbal attack, Rosalyn thought. She was the skivvy or the tart.

'Miss James is not to be underestimated,' said Greaves. 'She was demonstrating her combat skills and shows promise. Now as we are all here, we might as well begin. As you know we are classified as a special auxiliary unit tasked with harrying the enemy from behind their lines.'

He brought up a large plan of the estate.

'At some point this house will be occupied as a British army unit headquarters. You will be in situ among the local essential workers and deployed only when the Germans have control of the area. It will be a grim business, fighting without the benefit of the Geneva Convention if we are captured.'

A few men exchanged glances, but nothing was said.

'In this unit we have a vicar,' Greaves continued. A slim red-haired man stood, he was wearing a dog collar and introduced himself as Davies and said he would be based at the parish church where he would hide the radio and be responsible for communications.

'We have a gamekeeper,' said Greaves. Farrell stood up and nodded. 'A man of few words but knows these woods like the back of his hand. There is a farrier, Mr Osgood; as well as shoeing horses he can make just about anything in metal. Mr Claff here is a farm worker and sometime poacher I've heard.' Claff and Farrell glared at each other. 'Today we have added a land girl, Miss James.'

All eyes turned to Rosalyn and she smiled at them. Their faces were mainly curious, as though they could not understand what she was doing in their midst. She did not notice any outright hostility.

'What about him?' The farm worker gestured to Brent who lounged off to one side, barely engaging with the group.

'This is Private Brent and he will be finalising our training and will join the unit. For reasons best known to himself he's refused a commission. He has experience of guerrilla warfare behind enemy lines and, with the knowledge of explosives you have recently acquired and his specialist expertise you will be able to strike effectively at strategic targets.'

There was a ripple of excitement from the people in the room. Who was he and why was he scarred? He slowly turned and looked at each of them so that they could see the full effect of the puckered skin and damaged ear.

'He will not be answering questions about his past,' Greaves continued. 'You are each here for a reason and that will become clear. Training will continue tonight after we've eaten. Our gamekeeper will lead us around the estate in the dark. Mr Claff also knows the land so between them we should acquire a thorough knowledge of the area. As a matter of interest our farrier, Mr Osgood, is also a practising warlock. For some reason he and the vicar do not see eye to eye.'

Rosalyn looked around expecting someone to laugh at this. No one did and she saw that Davies and Osgood studiously ignored each other. Surely, he couldn't be a male witch? She then remembered they had no families, and wondered if something tragic had happened at Pitdown and remembered her uncle's misgivings about the owner and his fate.

'The unit must be secret,' said Brent. 'The lieutenant will rejoin his regiment if the Germans invade, but I will remain. Once we are deployed and after the Germans have overrun the area there will be no chain of command. We must work as a team.'

He stood and went to the fireplace, his lean figure surprisingly commanding and his voice compelling. 'You know your chances of survival. Units like ours will only exist for a few weeks and it will be preferable to commit suicide than be taken prisoner and interrogated by the Gestapo.'

Although Rosalyn expected something like this it was a shock to hear it stated openly and she felt weak for a moment. They were looking at her, she knew, but she strained every nerve not to show her feelings.

Greaves said, 'For the benefit of Miss James; our leaders have decided that targeted missions by trained operatives behind enemy lines will be an effective resistance force. We will not wear uniforms as we are not regular servicemen and women. If we are caught, they will torture and kill us. You have all signed the

Official Secrets Act. You must be clear that you can never tell anyone of this venture. The enemy expects our government to sue for peace, but as Mr Churchill says, we will never surrender.

'You have had a little time to learn the basic skills needed to spy on and harass the enemy should he land in the South of England. We will disrupt supplies and provide information on German troop movements to enable our forces to regroup further up country. We will collect information and pass this by radio to the defending forces. We will destroy German transport lines and communications.' He paused and continued quietly. 'If required, we will assassinate key individuals. Not always the enemy. Are there any questions?'

It was obvious all the men were aware of the suicidal nature of the mission facing them. As she thought about it, Rosalyn realised that for her it was less a choice and more a destiny. She could fight the Nazis and likely die, or not fight them and likely be enslaved. The only real alternative was to flee to America, and she would not consider that.

Greaves continued, 'If the Nazis invade and gain a foothold, we will be using everything at our disposal to disrupt them. For many people of faith that will include prayer, for others such as ourselves it will be guns and bombs. For Osgood here it will be the ancient practice of witchcraft.'

'Don't underestimate his powers,' said Claff. 'I've seen him turn a panicked cow into a calm and biddable creature and there's nothing he don't know about horses.' He looked questioningly at Osgood. 'There's a rumour he - '

'That's enough,' said the farrier. 'I will do what I can to disrupt them. Mark my words.'

'Then I suggest we eat,' said Greaves. 'There is a hot meal in the refectory. Go on through.'

*

A subdued group went into dinner, and conversation was sparse and functional. The news was that there had been a raid on Dover and we'd lost some aircraft but our boys had shot down more of theirs. Rosalyn heard someone mutter we'll need to, they've got so many more planes and pilots. She'd handed over her ration book to the cook who dished up pie and vegetables. At least there was jam roly poly afterwards. She sat between the Reverend Davies and Lieutenant Greaves and observed the subtle tensions that were already apparent in the unit.

'Are you a churchgoer Miss James?' asked the vicar.

'Not really. I've dabbled in the faiths of both of my parents. My mother was Jewish and my father Anglican. I was baptised but not confirmed. I'm still trying to decide.'

She became aware that everyone was gathering intelligence around that table. She caught Farrell looking at her and blushed. So much for the poker face. It took all her willpower not to look at him again.

Davies continued, 'I have a small congregation from the village and the estate. In fact, there's a chapel attached to the Hall and it is reputed to have been unaltered for decades I believe.'

'There is a chapel,' Greaves said, 'but it's used for storage. Perhaps we should explore the house more thoroughly. The Germans may decide to occupy it as a command centre utilising its good road and rail links, so it would be useful to have a working knowledge of every back staircase and exit.'

'What happened to the man who lived here?' asked Rosalyn.

'You should ask Osgood,' said the farmworker and smiled tapping his nose. 'He put a spell on him, and he ended up seeing faeries everywhere and started talking to them.'

The blacksmith stared at Claff. A frisson of excitement ran through the group and even Brent looked interested.

'If you really believed that, Mr Claff, you would do well not to bait him, so I assume you are just passing on tittle tattle.' Rosalyn said as she sliced into the roly poly looking for jam. It was stodgy and not to her taste, but she ate it and pretended to enjoy it.

Osgood looked down at his food and the atmosphere subsided. She took the chance to assess him. Not tall but strong looking and about fifty years old. His hair was fair and his eyes almost turquoise, fringed with red-blond lashes either side of a broken nose. He had a trim beard and crooked teeth. He caught her looking and she quickly turned back to the bowl of stodge she was struggling to eat. She felt his stare but did not look at him again.

The Reverend Davies wiped his mouth with a pocket handkerchief.

'The man who lived here was a libertine who used the house for extravagant parties and is now somewhere in London, an asylum I assume. He claimed to have seen and spoken to faeries and other magical creatures and became very insistent. It was probably a case of dementia exacerbated by his use of recreational drugs.'

'He is quite elderly I think,' said Greaves, glancing at Brent.

'Something like that,' said the vicar. 'But he had strange ideas, and because his ravings were so public he became an embarrassment to the royal family and the well-connected people of the county.'

'The royal family?' Rosalyn asked.

'One of his guests was convinced that he was Edward VII's love child and declared it at every opportunity. Anyway, he brought actors and actresses and other unsavoury characters from London for weekends of wild parties and orgies. They ran around scantily clad in the woodland.'

'He and his friends seduced as many women as they could get their hands on,' Claff said.

'That's enough,' said Osgood. He was very still, and his face had lost its colour.

'It's why you cursed him and addled his brains. He had your wife and your daughter.'

Osgood launched himself at Claff and the other man rose to meet him, but Brent had grabbed his left arm and spun him round so that the haymaker swung into open air. He kicked the back of his knee and brought him down onto his right side. Farrell had grabbed Claff in a bear hug and dragged him away from his prey. Rosalyn was impressed that a man as insubstantial as Brent could neutralise the blacksmith so rapidly and with apparent ease.

'If you can't work together you're no good to us and one or both of you will be shipped out,' Brent said. 'Which one is it to be?'

He looked between them with an impassive coldness and as Rosalyn read their faces a realisation dawned. She knew that if one of these men left the group with bad blood then Brent might simply kill him. The unit she had joined was an endgame and there was no way back. His words cooled their tempers and after a breathless moment there seemed to be a palpable sigh.

'Sorry. I should have had more control,' Osgood said.

Claff stood up and offered his hand to Osgood.

'No mate, I was out of order and I'm sorry, really. He was a bastard and we're well rid of him. You did good.'

They shook hands and Osgood clapped the other man on the back. It appeared they both had grievances against his lordship and were men that frequently clashed and then made up.

'You've got half an hour for coffee and then we begin,' said Greaves glancing at Brent who nodded stiffly. They quietly took their coffee and, in most cases, smoked either cigarettes or pipes. Rosalyn noted that Brent smoked some foreign brand that smelled like cigars. Farrell smoked a pipe. She sat a little further away and tried to observe impartially, but her eyes drifted back to Farrell.

*

Four hours later it seemed as though their peaceful coffee drinking had occurred in another time. They had been led around the estate using the most obscure paths, ditches, and sunken lanes. When the going was good Farrell led them off at a tangent through tunnels and drainage pipes. They used no lights and everyone except she and Brent had a good knowledge of the area. She was determined not to fall behind and often stumbled, catching her shins, and scratching her face and hands on branches. They made no allowances for her, and she knew that Brent was watching her and looking for weakness.

Eventually they stopped at a ridged and tree-covered area and the gamekeeper knelt and fished a line out of the ground, then he pulled up a hidden trapdoor and told them to descend a ladder.

Only when they were all inside and the cover was replaced were they allowed to turn on a lantern. In front of them was a blast wall, behind that, an underground shelter, equipped with the most basic furniture, but was already stacked with boxes in the furthest reaches.

'This is the OB – Operational Base - and it may be necessary to spend a long time in here. It's tight and claustrophobic with limited sanitary provision,' said Greaves. 'There are two exits that can be used in an emergency. One of them is very long and narrow.'

'If the Germans find the main entrance, they'll drop a grenade down the hatchway. If we're lucky enough to have made it through the escape tunnels then the explosion should block the entrances and give us some time to hide in one of the two other bunkers,' said Brent.

'Assuming they don't want us alive to interrogate,' said Greaves.

'But we are not to be taken alive, and believe me, you won't want them to take you alive,' said Brent.

'How much food will we have if we 'go to ground'?' asked Rosalyn.

'Two weeks' worth. We don't expect to survive more than three weeks once we're activated,' said Greaves. 'We have a job to do.'

'What about dogs?' asked Claff. 'Won't they be able to scent us?'

'There are ways to confuse dogs,' said Osgood. 'Farrell and I know what they are.'

When they had explored the bunker, they began to climb back up the ladder. Rosalyn was left with Osgood and Claff. They rounded on her.

Osgood said, 'I understand why we're doing this, we're middle aged and have had most of our lives and they've been hard. But why is a young woman with everything to live for staying behind to engage in a hopeless fight?'

'And we've been preparing for three weeks already yet suddenly you're thrown into the mix, why?' said Claff.

'Three weeks?' said Rosalyn, shocked.

'Been at Coleshill,' said Claff.

'Shut up,' said Osgood.

'She don't know,' said Claff.

'I'm prepared to do the same things you are,' she said.

'You're late in and a woman. There's something fishy going on.'

'Perhaps it's an experiment,' said Rosalyn, feeling panicked.

'She don't know,' said Claff again.

Osgood gave her a hard stare.

Rosalyn said, 'And, if you must know, I'm Jewish so I don't have anything to lose. Do I?'

She tried to sound positive but knew she sounded afraid.

Greaves called down. 'What's taking so long? Get up this ladder.'

Claff went next and when he had neared the top Osgood whispered to her. 'They've asked for you 'specially.'

'Who's they?'

He looked meaningfully at her, and she found his closeness repulsive. Could he really be a male witch?

'Go on,' he said nodding to the ladder.

He pushed her to it and Rosalyn climbed, trying to control her shaking legs, and wondered what the hell he was talking about. Who had asked for her? How could she find out? It was a dangerous situation to be thrown into and it was clear she did not have all the information. There was no chance to talk to him once they were outside. She had to focus on the group's exploration of the estate and memorise everything she could sense about the area, its sounds, and smells. There was no moon, but the starlight gave a little illumination once her eyes had adjusted. Most of the men had excellent night vision, only she and Davies struggled to keep up.

Eventually they were back at the house and given cocoa and biscuits and a nightcap of rum before retiring for their beds. It was clear that most of them were staying at the Hall.

'It's 0200 hours. Well done everyone. Dismissed,' said Greaves. He took Rosalyn to one side.

'You're not billeted with us, for obvious reasons. The men are in the house, except for Farrell, because he has a cottage on the estate. I have assumed you would join us for meals but if you prefer to do for yourself, I can ask cook to issue you with provisions.'

'I'll join the group.'

She thought, I don't want to miss anything that's going on under the table.

Farrell joined them. 'I'm going past your cottage. If you like you can walk with me. No lights. Get used to the dark.'

'Yes please.'

They left the smoke and banter and went out into the still cool air. The only sounds were owls and their feet on the gravel.

'Have you been at Pitdown long?' Rosalyn said.

'I came here as a child, no parents. Lived with the gamekeeper and his family. When his lordship took the Hall, the shoots were the only things he kept up, that and the supply of food for the house from the local farm. He let everything else go. Most of the estate is woodland or coverts surrounded by pasture.'

'I used to steal a ride on his land when I was at school.'

'So it was you disturbing the birds,' Farrell said.

'Sorry if it was a problem. I didn't think about that.'

Farrell said, 'It increased my workload dogging in the young birds when they'd been disturbed.' He relented. 'Not as much as the poachers though, or the foxes.'

She turned to look at him and turned her foot on a pinecone. He grabbed her arm and stopped her falling. As she straightened, he took her hand in his and led her forward.

His hand was warm, and Rosalyn was aware of the blood and nerves of their hands together in that clasp. She hoped he would not let go and she dared speak as they walked the rest of the way. Her heart seemed loud, and she struggled with breathing. Did he feel the same? She hoped so and he wasn't speaking so she thought maybe.

Too soon they came to the gate. Still holding her hand, he opened it and they stood together neither apparently wanting to let go. The brevity of life, violence, and the proximity of death overwhelmed Rosalyn. She was facing her mortality, and she found a sob welling in her throat. He squeezed her hand then he left. After two deep breaths she went on wobbly legs up the narrow path and into the cottage. She had difficulty sleeping and felt the sort of homesickness not known since she was a schoolgirl; a sense of utter aloneness in a hostile world.

*

Monday 29 July 1940

The small windows and the proximity of trees threw the cottage into prolonged darkness and Rosalyn woke later than usual. Her watch said she had time to tidy herself before going to breakfast so she did the best she could and at the same time mentally traced the previous evening's exploration of the estate. She wondered if she could find the OB. It had been dark when they came to it. If her inner compass was working, it should be to the west of the house. Also, it took her mind off the anticipation of seeing Farrell again.

She set out early. The tears that had finally led her into sleep had been cathartic she decided. Her feelings for him were exciting but it was a distraction and insignificant in the scale of things. She had to focus on acquiring the skills they were teaching. But why was she brought in so late? She must discover what Osgood meant when he said they had asked for her especially. Who were they? As she travelled around the woodland, she could see how it must have been well laid out originally and was now overgrown and had an air of disorder. Occasionally she stopped to get her bearings and ended up going further away from the main house and the estate tracks. Ancient ditches and coppicing now impeded her progress, and as she walked along the top of a ridge it was clear she was becoming lost.

Then a scent assailed her, it was fox and she had smelled it before as they approached the underground bunker. Just as she thought she could go no further she saw the same earth shape she remembered from the previous night. After a little searching, she found a wooden handle and tentatively pulled up a rope to reveal the entrance to the chamber. Looking around furtively she dropped it and carefully began retracing her steps, not wanting to leave any traces. Fortunately, the ground was so uneven it was impossible to see where she had been.

As she picked her way through undergrowth and ditches, she started to sense that she was being watched. The back of her neck felt vulnerable, a sure sign that someone was behind her and she tingled with the certainty that she was not alone. Every attempt to catch him out proved futile and she had to fight an urge to run. But which way? When she was far enough from the hideout, she stopped to get a sense of the way to go and realised she really didn't know. She stood still, her senses alert for any clue, but the birds had fallen silent and she felt her skin crawl. Rosalyn slowly scanned her surroundings but could see no one. Was it an animal? Without turning her head, she looked as far she could with peripheral vision certain that there was someone looking around a tree at her. She was sure it wasn't one of the group and fought a rising sense of panic. Had she exposed the hiding place to an enemy? To a fifth columnist? Was the game up before it had begun? She quickly turned her head, but it had disappeared behind the bole of the tree.

Rosalyn hurried to the place she thought it had been. It was about twenty feet away and not easy to reach as it meant dropping down into a ditch and climbing up the other side. When she got to the tree there was nothing but a faint smell of mushrooms. Rosalyn began searching the steep bank below the tree, there must be another hiding place.

'Lost something?'

It was Farrell standing at the top of the bank and she felt weak with relief. He smiled down at her and she realised it was the first time she'd seen him smile. There were vertical lines in his cheeks that Rosalyn liked.

'Come on or we'll be late.'

'I thought I saw someone. Can you smell mushrooms?'

'Wrong time of year,' he said, but looked around. The smile vanished and was replaced by a frown. He extended a hand.

'You sure you didn't see anyone a few minutes ago,' she said.

He pulled her up to his level and for a moment she saw concern in his eyes. Then he turned and led her away, still holding her hand, but this time tightly as though fearing to let her go. They entered the densest coppice, it was hard to see a path, the shoots sprang all around like a living cage. He didn't hesitate and gave her no time to rest, almost as though they were being pursued. She followed him through the woodland until they came to a path and were too quickly brought within sight of the house. He turned and looked at her as she caught her breath, then he squeezed her hand, and she felt a rush of desire.

'I have matters to attend. I'll see you later,' he said.

Rosalyn watched him walking away and tried to control her feelings. As she entered the dark Hall, she smelled the cigarettes Brent smoked.

'Holding hands. Don't get too attached.'

'Why not? If we're going to die soon – eat drink and be merry as they say.'

She was more stung by his comment than she would like to admit. She knew nothing about Farrell and this infatuation was stronger than any she had known.

'Get something to eat.'

'I want to see Lieutenant Greaves,' she said.

Brent looked at her coolly then said, 'He's not here. Called away and the other men have gone about their usual business. You're stuck with me. I'm going to bring you up to speed on explosives, unarmed combat, and firearms.'

Rosalyn's heart sank. She was stuck with this odd lanky man and his censorious manner. But the subject of study didn't deter her and at least no one else would witness her failures.

'I'll get something to eat then.'

He accompanied her into the refectory and drank coffee and smoked while she ate. A thought occurred.

'What happens to cook and his assistant if the Germans invade?' Rosalyn said.

'Like Greaves, they're infantry and will rejoin their regiment.'

'In heaven?'

'What?' Brent looked at her.

'They might be taken prisoner and blab about the unit. Greaves said we would need to 'take care' of people who know about the auxiliaries.'

'Sharp of you. But they will be shipped well away from the action and they only know about this unit. The Germans will know we exist soon enough.'

*

They spent the day taking apart and cleaning firearms. Rosalyn was impressed by the weapons provided for them. She had heard that the Home Guard were drilling with pitchforks and replica guns, but the auxiliaries had been given priority as though their placement and preparation was urgent. It was. The Battle of Britain was being fought in the skies to the south of them and lethal and effective bombing raids were taking place on shipping and military targets. Invasion was expected in August.

On the farm Rosalyn had used a twelve-bore shotgun on pigeons, crows, and other vermin. It was not a precise weapon, the shot spread out and easily killed the small creatures. She had seen animals killed for other reasons, out hunting she had seen a badly injured horse shot by the huntsman with a small handgun and that was cleanly done thanks to his skill. Brent now introduced her to the .22 Remington rifle. It was the same as her uncle used to shoot rabbits but this one came with a silencer and telescopic sights. It was clearly a sniper rifle and intended for assassinations. She learnt how to take it apart, clean it and put it back together. Her fingers were nimble, and she picked up the process quickly.

When he was satisfied with her familiarity they went into the woods and he set up paper targets at twenty and seventy yards' distance. Brent had binoculars. Rosalyn had the wit to know that the telescopic sights would be useless unless they had been set so she left them off and used the aperture sight to take her first shot.

She adjusted the sights slightly several times until she had placed a shot in the bullseye. Then she handed it to Brent.

'You've done this before,' he said.

'I've never used telescopic sights like that one.'

He fitted the sights and began making shots at the seventy-five-yard target, checking each one with the binoculars. After half an hour he cursed and muttered something about them being useless. They stood and retrieved the targets and Rosalyn tried not to gloat at the neat line of holes that ended in her bull. When they were at the Hall Brent made an excuse and went to the office. She heard him shouting about the bloody useless sights they'd supplied with the sniper rifle. Someone would be getting a roasting.

After a light lunch he seemed to need to take out his frustration by training in unarmed combat. They started with close wrestling on a mat, learning to fall without hurt. It was like falling off a horse, she decided, tuck your head in and roll. Then it accelerated into full blown body attacks that Rosalyn was expected to ward off with a defensive move. If he got through her defence, as he often did, his fist or hand would lightly touch her but he would say 'you're dead' or 'you're unconscious'. His aim was perfect. He even touched her eyeball.

'Teach me,' she demanded.

'First you must defend yourself automatically without thinking.'

Facing her he threw straight punches at her face and body and Rosalyn learned to use her forearms to sweep off the blow and always follow through with a counter attack to the matching part of Brent. She had quick reflexes, and the adrenaline was such that she didn't feel any pain from the hard knocks to her wrists and arms. It was exciting. He taught her how to gauge out eyes, kick or knee a man in the groin and where to punch most effectively.

'Don't hit him on the chin, the chin is designed to protect the vulnerable area of the throat. Flatten your fist and strike with precision or hit the nose very hard. It makes the eyes water and gives you an advantage.'

The only thing that interrupted their training was Brent stopping for a smoke.

'Where do you get those strong-smelling cigarettes?'

He was lying back on the grass and said, 'I was getting them sent from France but that's stopped now. I've got quite a few packets left and I don't want to leave any for Gerry.'

She sat next to him and examined her forearms. The white skin on the outer side of her wrists were red. 'If they invade, do we deploy straight away or wait to be told?'

'Straight away I should think. It will be chaos, civilians trying to move away from the landing points and troops moving down to defend key targets.'

'The newspapers had photographs of planes shooting at refugee columns. My uncle was trying to decide what to do with his family. He'll stay on the farm.'

They heard shooting close by.

'Hopefully that'll be Farrell shooting rabbits, for the pot.' He looked at her face lazily, but she was confident nothing showed.

'Mmm,' was all she trusted her voice with, and he looked at his watch and announced training for the day was over and that he would let Farrell take her on a night time ramble to get used to the country. No amount of self-control could stop the blush as Rosalyn's heart started to race. She shot Brent a filthy look and stood up.

'See you later,' he said and she marched off to the sound of his laughter.

By the time Rosalyn had rested, washed, and dressed the bruises on her arms were a darkening purple and sensitive to the touch. She was perversely proud of them.

*

The evening was disappointing. The gamekeeper didn't join them for dinner but Osgood did. He smelled of horses and she wondered how much of his business was shoeing and whether that would be affected by the wartime agricultural changes, and mechanisation in particular.

'Is it mostly draught horses that you shoe these days?' she asked him.

He looked surprised at her question then seemed to remember she was a land girl and had experience of the large animals. It took him a few moments of careful chewing and she wondered if he was not going to reply.

'There's a few farmers won't part with their beasts for love nor money and I don't blame them. The new tractors are quick and easy but that'll only last as long as there's petrol, and parts of course. A good horse will work slower but if the animal knows its job it takes less skill overall than a tractor. So you land girls can leave most of the work to the horse.'

'I was wondering about hunters,' said Rosalyn.

Osgood grunted. 'There's a few around. Officers like to charge about on them but more are being broken to harness. Like I say, petrol will be in short supply.'

'What happened to the foxhounds?'

'Oh there's still a few of them. Culled the old ones and kept a few stallion hounds and bitches in case it ever starts up again. If there's a troublesome fox they might go after 'un, informal like.'

Rosalyn wanted to continue the conversation but Osgood clearly did not enjoy speaking to his female comrade.

He said, 'Private Brent, you might like to know I've finished the first of the knuckle dusters you asked for. You can try it out later if you like.'

Brent nodded, 'Excellent. Miss James has been learning unarmed combat today and tomorrow we can try out our more silent weapons, including blades. It looks as though you have escaped a nighttime patrol this evening,' he said to her. 'You can turn in early or stay over here and listen to the wireless or read. There are still a few books in the library.'

The thought of spending an evening with Osgood and Brent made Rosalyn feel exhausted so she opted for a night in her cottage despite the limited light and washing facilities. It was not quite dark when she went back to it, and she could not have been more nervous and alert. It was likely that someone would jump on her as a practice of those skills she had been learning and it was with relief that she closed the cottage door and quietly scanned each room to ensure no one was hiding there. Later she realised how much she would have liked Farrell to be waiting but told herself she must put these thoughts from her mind.

Tuesday 30 July 1940

Despite wandering around the woods before breakfast, there was no sighting of the gamekeeper nor any feeling of being watched. She spent the day solely in the company of Brent and his intensive training with a Colt .038 revolver in the morning and, contrary to expectation, a lesson in the art of climbing trees in the afternoon.

'It may be useful to have a spy point so the tallest trees at the highest points have been rigged with climbing aids. Difficult to spot unless you know where they are.'

The hills to the north of Pitdown Hall had several wooded copses of trees and when they had walked to the highest one, he gave Rosalyn binoculars and showed her a spike, concealed by a branch.

'There's your first. The others are easier to find. Let me know what you see when you get to the top. You don't mind heights, do you?'

There was no way she was going to admit she did not like them but somehow being on a tree made it easier. Rosalyn made sure all her clothing was tight then began the ascent. What she had not expected was the physical exertion of climbing. Although her legs were strong, her upper body was weaker. Her boots were not ideal but her feet being smaller than a man's fitted on the spikes neatly. To take her mind off the height and the danger she counted in her head. Forty steps later she came to an open viewpoint and could see the railway to the south and the Guildford tunnels.

It was exhilarating and empowering. She could see the roads approaching from Hindhead and the Devil's Punchbowl. The view to the west was clear and also the east if she shifted to another position. The tree was a pine and would have leaf cover all the year round. With a grin on her face she began the descent, a few slips and she reminded herself to focus. There was a quick way down and it was not desirable.

'Wonderful,' she said when facing Brent again and they made their way back to the Hall. She was surprised that her legs were shaking and the walk down the hill was at the limit of her endurance. She lagged behind and he noticed.

'You need fitness training. We'll start with runs every morning before breakfast. Up this hill, two minutes rest, then down this hill, five minutes rest. Try and do it three times.'

It was like school all over again. Her face must have shown it because he said, 'Tomorrow, I'll show you how to kill a man in five different ways.'

'Silently?' she said.

'Of course.'

*

Friday 2 August 1940

This regimen lasted all week. Weapons training in the morning, after Rosalyn's fitness training and breakfast, then some form of physical combat training in the afternoon. She was permanently exhausted, so hungry she ate food she would normally not like and enjoyed it. Her sleep was deep and satisfying and she even stopped hankering for Farrell's presence.

Physically she was bruised and aching, but her spirit seemed to be stronger than ever. By Friday she was relaxed in the surroundings of Pitdown Hall, familiar with its layout and that of the estate. So dinner with Greaves, Osgood, Davies and Claff was a shock.

It was clear Osgood and Claff resented her presence and no doubt her newly confident air. At the table she covered up her bruises with long sleeves, kept her head down and listened to the conversation, refusing to be drawn into any discussion of her own activities. The enquiries came mainly from the vicar and he was curious to know what secret skills she had learnt whilst the other members of the group had been carrying on their day jobs.

'Oh just routine familiarity with military matters. The sort of things you've all been through, but quite new to me.'

Brent heard her reply and almost smiled.

'I'm the radio operator,' said Davies. 'I haven't had any military training. My job is to pick up messages from what they call the dead letter drops and pass them on to the next wireless station. I'm assured I won't be required to kill anyone.'

'Won't stop them killing you though,' said Claff and the whole table was looking at them.

Rosalyn did not want this attention so she kept quiet and allowed Davies to continue what appeared to be a justification of his involvement in the unit.

'I, of course, need to travel around my parish and so will be best placed to see what the occupying forces are doing. I'm not so naïve to think they won't suspect me, but I hope that some of them will attend church and take communion. They are not all heathen, I think. Nor are they all Catholic, although the southern Germans and Austrian tend to be.'

It was quiet for a short while and Rosalyn dreaded to think how boring his sermons must be. Then Osgood said, '''Course being a Calvinist you think our fates are predestined, don't you?'

'I'm an Anglican vicar,' Davies seemed inclined to say more but stopped.

Osgood continued. 'You believe we are born in sin and no matter what we do only a few of us are chosen for salvation. So, what's the point?'

It seemed to be Osgood's nature to needle anyone if he had a way to do it. Davies looked at them all with a slight smile on his face and said, 'I'm sure you don't want a lecture in theology from me.'

Rosalyn's knowledge of Calvinism was non-existent, and she was wondering what its implications were when Greaves changed the subject.

'The Luftwaffe are targeting airfields along the south coast; I don't need to tell you this is a step change and means they are determined to destroy Fighter Command in preparation for an attack on our shores.'

'The good weather isn't helping,' said Brent. 'Clear skies mean daylight raids and they have more planes and more pilots.'

'They'll have to be precise to hit smaller targets, planes and hangars, fuel dumps and so on but they can damage the runways with ease,' said Greaves.

'They have those damnable Stukas,' said Brent. The others looked expectantly at him. 'It's a small bomber but dives from about eleven thousand feet so its bombs land exactly where they are supposed to. The noise is infernal.'

'Jericho's Trumpets,' announced Davies proudly.

There was disbelief around the table.

'Air sirens. Designed to instil fear in the targets and effective during Blitzkrieg. I heard them in France, but I understand they've been removed now. They're not needed for the bombing of airfields.' Greaves turned to Brent sitting next to him. 'You heard them in Spain I take it?'

Brent nodded.

Greaves continued, 'The Fascists had air superiority and the Junkers 87 – the Stuka as it's now called – could do what it liked. We have Hurricanes and Spitfires and if they can get into the air in time, they'll pick off the Stukas easily enough. But before that they'll have to tackle large numbers of ME 109s sent to defend them.'

'What about ack-ack guns?' said Claff.

'Not while our boys are in the air.'

They absorbed this then Osgood said, 'Better pray for cloud cover and rain, vicar. They'll need good weather if they have to approach from that height.'

The conversation ended when Farrell walked in carrying his dinner and sat at the end of the table, apologising for his late arrival. Claff and Osgood had finished and left and Rosalyn wanted to stay but could think of no good reason so she went out too. Greaves would no doubt come into the sitting room to brief them on the weekend's training.

Someone had brought in a newspaper and she spread it on a table and studied it, hoping they wouldn't bother her. They began a discussion about a farmer and his reluctance to plough an old meadow and how unattractive his new women's land army recruits were: pasty faced and straight out of London. Rosalyn focussed on all she had learnt that week. Davies soon appeared and looked upset. He had evidently wanted to stay in the inner circle but was not permitted. He sat next to Rosalyn and tried to engage her in small talk.

It was a relief when Greaves, Brent and Farrell came in. The announcement was brief. They would spend the weekend building boltholes and spy points in trees. It was imperative that they were able to attack the railway tunnels and roads and provide information on activities at Pitdown, especially if the Wehrmacht appropriated it for headquarters. They must find a way to disguise the radio aerial, either in the church or the churchyard. Farrell volunteered to help with that.

'What about the Tommy gun?' asked Claff. 'Are we getting one or not?'

Rosalyn could not see the advantage of such a weapon but it was evidently an exciting prospect to some.

'We'll need it if the paratroopers come inland, ahead of the landed infantry and their vehicles,' he persisted.

Greaves said, 'Our instructions are not to engage in battle with the enemy, that's the job of the regular army. They don't know we exist. I only foresee using the machine guns if there is no escape and to make capture as expensive for them as possible. You'll do more damage with your Fairburn-Sykes fighting knife Claff, and possibly with explosives. Secret and silent and familiar with the terrain; those are our weapons.'

'I don't see how they are going to get tanks across the channel with our fleet out there,' Rosalyn could not resist saying.

'If they achieve air superiority the Stukas will pick off our largely undefended battleships and their bombers will destroy any defences we still have left. Even then it won't be easy but they will have requisitioned every suitable vessel from the countries they've conquered and most of our equipment was left on the beaches of Dunkirk. So, you see, this is time critical. We must be ready.'

That ended the conversation and the rest of the weekend was spent in hard work creating a peaceful English landscape that held hidden weapons of war.

*

Monday 5 to Friday 9 August 1940

The following week Rosalyn was put on clerical and administrative duties. A shipment of provisions for the operational base was delivered and she was tasked with recording everything and supervision of its storage in the OB.

Farrell put up more shelves to stow the additional supplies. They worked quietly side by side for a morning and ate lunch with Brent and Greaves. When they returned to the OB in the afternoon, she was in the process of descending the ladder when she asked him if he would inscribe the items on boards so they could be easily identified in the semi darkness of the shelter. Farrell did not reply and when she turned, he had gone. She decided perhaps he hadn't heard her request but thought it surprising he had not said goodbye.

Much of the hardware could be stored now but she did not want to put palliasses, blankets, and pillows underground in case of damp. The cooking utensils were taken down straight away and she could see the orderliness of the OB as it took shape. Each man had a locker for his personal kit and spare clothes. The water cans were to be kept in the crawl tunnel and the Elsan closet with spare fluid in a special recess.

The work took her mind off the closeness of the space but she was relieved not to be sent down there the next day and dreaded spending fourteen or so days in the hole with the men and only getting out at night. Engaging the enemy would be a relief after that. Every night there had to be a mission. Rosalyn was proud to be part of something considered so important but it was still a relief to be told to pick blackberries and help in the Hall's kitchens at the end of the week.

It was a good week, she decided. Eating with Farrell and Brent and occasionally Greaves, they became like family to her. When it was just Brent, she asked why the men had no women in their lives.

'Greaves is married but he's on active service. That's all his family know. He could be anywhere in the world as far as his wife is concerned.'

'What about Claff and Osgood?'

'And Farrell.'

'Sorry?'

'You really want to know about Farrell, I believe.'

There was nothing she could say to that.

'Claff's a widower. Now what about you Miss James? Your father is storing museum treasures and your two brothers are serving, one in the territorials and the other in the senior service.'

'The Navy, yes. I pray to God that the air force can prevent the Germans getting air control. What Greaves said the other day about the ships being sitting ducks for the bombers … it terrifies me.'

'You've been working for your uncle for quite some time, I believe. Before the war started. You gave up the bright lights of London for a sleepy Hampshire village.'

'It's not what you think. I wasn't in trouble in that way. There was a man I met in London and started seeing. Not really courting. But he wasn't for me. He just didn't appreciate that. My brothers took him aside and gave him a 'talking to'. You'd think that would have been enough but he became obsessed and convinced himself they were preventing me from seeing him and that I felt the same as he did. The police were involved and I came to the countryside to let it die down. Then the war started.'

'Do you know what happened to him?'

'No idea. It was two years ago. It's not uncommon you know, some men have difficulty taking no for an answer.'

Brent seemed to think this exchange deserved more information from him and he said, 'Osgood's wife and daughter went to London with the society people who attended parties at Pitdown Hall before the war.'

'I can understand why he's so bitter then. Is he really a warlock?'

'You'll have to ask him.'

'I'd feel more confident of dealing with my unwelcome suitor now,' Rosalyn said.

'Just make sure you use your skills in self-defence. The judiciary might not appreciate the rough justice I'm teaching you,' Brent sounded serious. The playful banter gone.

*

Saturday 10 and Sunday 11 August 1940

The weekend saw another step change in training. They were charged with infiltrating Wanborough Manor on the Hog's Back, the other side of Guildford. It was going to be used to train men for a similar venture. The team had to get in at night, place cards in named positions and leave without triggering any alarm.

Rosalyn's heart was in her mouth at the prospect, but Claff looked at home with the idea of burglary and Osgood volunteered to offer his services as a blacksmith to the people there so he could look at the security arrangements. Greaves told her she was not required for this venture, and she was both relieved and disappointed.

'That's a shame,' Claff said to her. 'I was looking forward to seeing you climbing over the walls.'

'She'd be a darn sight easier to lift than you,' said Osgood.

Rosalyn smiled. The group had come to accept her, it seemed, and they were forming a tight knit band that could carry out tasks without much oral communication. Davies was perhaps the exception. The vicar did not quite fit in but he focussed on his radio duties and studiously learned morse code. He also was to remain behind, and the weekend was the time when he had religious duties in his two parishes. He would come to Pitdown occasionally during the week and had begun to introduce Rosalyn to the wireless equipment he maintained. Everyone needed to be skilled in all aspects of the operation. If they lost a man the unit would carry on operating until there was no one left.

Monday 19 August 1940

It was in the week beginning 19th August that Rosalyn became aware of a change in atmosphere. The men went to their day jobs, and she was left alone with Brent and Greaves. The latter had spent most of the previous week away, and now locked himself in his office for long periods. His usual amicable demeanour had been replaced by something stiffer and more formal and she thought Brent had also noticed something odd about him.

The war was going badly. Stuka dive bombers had attacked the new RDF structures and the early warning system that enabled British fighters to get off the ground in time to defend themselves and the country had been partly shut down. Airfields all along the south coast had been attacked with serious consequences for grounded aircraft and fuel stores. There was a shortage of planes, but more importantly a shortage of experienced pilots. The Luftwaffe's weight of numbers was now Britain's biggest threat. Brent kept Rosalyn informed of the most important developments, and it was clear that despite the numbers of German planes being shot down, more would replace them.

There would be good news, such as when bombers came from Norway to attack the Tyneside shipyards without a fighter escort, believing British fighters were engaged on the south coast. Fortunately Fighter Command had a Group of pilots resting in the middle of the country and they were despatched to defend Tyneside with heavy losses of German bombers for few British planes. At the same time the hard-pressed airfields on the south coast were attacked, as well as the major ports of Southampton and Portsmouth. Dog fights between the two air forces took place for most of the day. Brent explained the disadvantages suffered by both sides in a clinical way, but she could see he was worried.

Saturday 24 August 1940

Rain and dull skies had provided relief on 19th August but the desperate struggle resumed the next day and by the end of that week Rosalyn sensed that some decision had been made about the Pitdown Hall unit. She was eating dinner with Brent when he began asking about her childhood.

'What happened when your mother died?' he asked.

'She died from complications during an attack of influenza.'

'Yes, but how did your father cope with three young children. He didn't remarry, did he?'

'My father said that Hannah, our mother, was the only love in his life and it wouldn't have been fair to bring another woman into the house just to be a carer. There were plenty of candidates, so many women had lost men in the Great War,' Rosalyn said. 'The servants looked after us for a while, then ...'

Brent waited.

'Then we were sent away, to relatives. Father was ill. He'd suffered shell shock in the war. He had a breakdown and he needed time to recover. The boys went to live with a cousin in London. I was sent to live with another cousin in the country.'

'How old were you?'

'About two, I think. I remember nothing in detail about the place or the woman, except sometimes I dream about lots of people coming and taking me away from her.'

'The cousin?'

'They called her auntie, but I only had one aunt and she married a farmer and their farm was where I spent large parts of my childhood, when I wasn't at school,' Rosalyn said. 'But why are you taking an interest now? Surely these things were looked into when I was being selected.'

'This is about the reason for your selection.'

'Osgood implied something strange when I first arrived.'

'He should have kept his mouth shut. Did you know that you were taken while you were at your auntie's?'

'What do you mean?'

'You disappeared for several days. Your relative only reported it after three days when she panicked.'

'Three days? I was two years old, I could have been anywhere.'

'Apparently she thought faeries had borrowed you, but after three days decided you might have fallen into the well.'

'Good grief. Was she bonkers?'

Brent shrugged. 'She lived there for another ten or so years without any problems, but she was considered by her neighbours to be a 'wise woman'.

'You mean a witch?' He didn't reply. 'So, who did have me? Gypsies? Or do you think the faeries might have taken me?'

'All I know is that you were returned by a dark-skinned woman, so you might have been taken by gypsies.'

'Was she punished?'

'Never found, after she brought you back to the cottage. She may not have been the one who took you, of course.'

'My poor father. So that's why I remember lots of people fetching me and auntie crying,' Rosalyn said. 'But why are you telling me this now?'

'You need to be prepared for changes that will take place next week. Lieutenant Greaves asked me to sound you out as we've been working together.'

'Is that why the men have been sent away again?'

Osgood, Claff, Farrell and Davies had not turned up at Pitdown for the weekend.

'They're at Wanborough Manor being briefed separately. Greaves is there too. We are going to continue your training until he returns,' Brent said.

He would say no more on the subject and Rosalyn spent the next few days desperately trying to remember the incident from her early childhood and whether it had ever been mentioned by her father or brothers. The 'auntie' had never again featured in family reunions, not that there had been many. It did occur to her that her mother's family might have stolen her away to be raised in the Jewish faith but she never had contact with them. Who was the mysterious dark-skinned woman?

There was a kind of romantic mysticism attaching to her unknown history and she hoped it would not be a disappointment when Lieutenant Greaves briefed her in full. It even displaced her fantasy about being with Farrell, a dream that had leavened the hard work and boredom of being stuck at Pitdown Hall. She knew he was attracted to her and at some point they would … that was always a little vague.

3 GREYFOLK

Monday 26 August 1940

It was a fine day as Rosalyn walked up to the Hall. She had heard on the BBC that the RAF had bombed Berlin in retaliation for a bombing of London. Herr Hitler was furious and threatened an increase in the intensity of his attacks and the previous day had been awful with more airfields being hit again. Only Davies was at the Hall, working with Farrell on the radio aerial.

Brent was waiting for her, on the steps, smoking. 'Lieutenant Greaves would like to see you when you have breakfasted. In the office. Chin up.'

He walked away down the steps.

This is it then. She would ask lots of questions and insist on answers, but first a hearty breakfast for the condemned woman. In the refectory she chewed the thick porridge with relish, the honey made it palatable, and she took her time over two cups of tea. He could wait.

Of course, if she refused to do anything she considered despicable she might find Brent creeping up behind her to commit some unspeakable method of assassination, and her body would never be found. The imagined terror was interrupted by gunshots, and she almost choked on her tea. She was sitting with her back to the door, and this suddenly seemed foolish. Perhaps she should not keep Greaves waiting any longer.

She went to the office to discover her fate. It was a small plain room next to the remains of an orangery. There was a typewriter and numerous old files, many spotted with mould and the remnants of spiders' webs, the spiders having moved on. Greaves had filled the air with pipe smoke and, when she coughed, partly to announce herself, he stood and opened a window.

'Take a seat Miss James,' he said. 'You've been with us for some time and, it's fair to say, you've settled in well.'

Greaves scanned the room and Rosalyn looked around automatically.

He continued. 'Your inclusion in the team is important.'

'Perhaps you would explain that to me in detail. It's clear I'm not going to be a normal member of the unit, and I know I'm here for some particular purpose. Will you please tell me what it is?'

'You may be aware of a man who was living in this house but has taken refuge in a theatre in London.'

Taking some men's wives and daughter with him, thought Rosalyn.

He continued. 'There is a group of very private individuals that do not engage with most English activities.'

Rosalyn racked her brains for who he might be referring to. 'Conscientious objectors, you mean?'

'No, I don't,' said Greaves.

'I thought I was being asked to fight and I won't be shipped off to a group of conchies who want spend their war dressing up and playing make-believe,' said Rosalyn. She stood up. 'If that's what you have in mind for me then I'd rather go back to the land and do something useful.'

'I told you they are not conchies, now sit down, shut up and listen.'

She sat with as much grace as she could muster.

'Winston wants to prepare for invasion with every possible weapon we can muster.' He swallowed. 'That includes the magical realm if such a thing exists, and most of us are now convinced that it does. They have been asked to assist in the war effort in the event of a German invasion, which is looking increasingly likely.'

Rosalyn raised her eyebrows. 'They?'

'The government, the Prime Minister, has been approached by a man who has lived for many years,' he continued. 'He used to occupy this house and has experience in various types of magic and the occult.'

'Osgood said they'd asked specifically for me. So he must know them. Who are 'they'?'

'That will be made clear to you in good time. For now all you need to know is that you have been brought here because you appear to have a history with the creatures. I don't know what exactly and it seems neither do you.'

So that was what Brent had been doing. Sounding her out for memories of the time she was 'taken'.

Rosalyn said, 'The Prime Minister wants to recruit witches and warlocks to fight Nazis?'

Greaves was red faced.

'Not exactly,' he said with difficulty. 'But we are to leave no avenue unexplored and who better to practice dirty tricks than the secretive creatures who have lived alongside us for millennia.'

Rosalyn thought at once of faeries, elves, leprechauns, and the like. She started giggling and felt the sort of rising hysteria that might lead to tears. Her mind was divided between how ridiculous it was and yet how ridiculous this war was between civilised countries with similar values. She felt displaced in space and time.

'Please try and take this seriously Miss James.'

'What are they going to do with me?' she asked when she had calmed down.

He avoided looking at her.

She was certain Brent and Greaves knew that she was intended for a purpose. Perhaps a sacrifice? She was a virgin, after all, isn't that what they usually need for Satanic rites? Somebody wanted her and had taken her before. She remembered the watcher in the woods.

'Something was stalking me when I first came here, in the woods, near the buried room, the OB.'

He waited. Then he said, 'Did you see it?'

'Not clearly but I felt its presence and it smelled of mushrooms.'

'Greyfolk, we call them. They don't walk in sunlight often. He would have been invisible and you would have seen him only if he meant you to. The Icelandic people call them The Hidden Ones. Every culture has a form of them.'

'Do the men know about them?'

'They've been briefed now, but it was not a surprise. As country folk they have lived with an inherited knowledge.'

'Superstition,' said Rosalyn.

He grimaced. 'Perhaps not.'

'Have they actually seen them?' she asked.

He nodded. Including Farrell, she wanted to ask, but she said, 'What does the vicar think of using the occult?'

'Unfortunately, he came forward when he got wind of the unit and offered to hide the radio under the altar,' replied Greaves. 'We think his vocation would be respected by the Germans, and as a priest he accepts the supernatural must exist, the unquiet spirit, hauntings, and the like. But he believes that any agency that uses pre-Christian means must be acquired as instruments of the devil. So he's not entirely comfortable with our plan. I think he feels a moral duty to look after the souls of his flock in the presence of such unholy creatures.'

'As the Nazis?'

'Funny.' He was not smiling.

'I don't suppose I have any choice,' she said.

'You are aware that auxiliary units such as this are unlikely to survive more than two or three weeks after deployment and yet you agreed to take part.'

'And I am prepared to fight. But the other thing wasn't made clear to me before I came here,' Rosalyn said. 'In fact, none of this was made clear. Are you saying I'm not to be part of a fighting team?'

'Your role is vital,' Greaves hesitated. 'I suspect … my own deduction … I'm afraid it may involve sexual services.' He blushed as he said it.

'With the old man? Or some non-human thing?'

Her first thought was of Farrell, the warmth of his hand, the rare smile. Did he know? Did he feel sorry for her?

Greaves was silent and tapped out his pipe. She felt betrayed and pitied. Farrell had felt sorry for her. She wanted to cry, and she wanted someone to hold her and look after her.

She said, 'I need some time alone.'

Greaves said, 'You can have the office as long as you want. Or you can go back to the cottage. Be careful in the woods. And you can't leave the grounds.'

'Did you find it easy to accept the supernatural?'

'When I was a child I experienced a haunting,' he said, after a pause.

'Please tell me about it.'

'My cousin sat by my grandmother's deathbed for hours, willing her to live. My mother and the rest of the family were downstairs waiting, but Linda wouldn't give up. Mother told me to try and persuade her to let grandma go, but she wouldn't. I sat next to her and watched her focus on keeping the old woman alive. Then I heard a voice speak to my cousin, saying something I couldn't quite hear. Linda started crying. Grandma gave a death rattle and died.'

Rosalyn waited, then said, 'Did you tell anyone?'

'My cousin told me not to. She was older than me and I would have done anything for her. I got the feeling she'd encountered such things before.'

He opened a drawer in the desk and brought out a small bottle. 'Did you notice that the night vision of most of the men is excellent?'

'Yes, I assumed they were used to the grounds,' she said.

'Put this oil on your eyelids. It'll sting a bit, but it will ensure that you can see a lot more than usual.'

Rosalyn took the little bottle and examined it. There was a clear oil inside that moved sluggishly when she tipped it. 'Will it enable me to see the hidden ones?'

He nodded.

'Thank you, Miss James,' said Greaves standing. 'I'll leave you now.'

He left and the implications of his words sunk in. Someone or something had taken her when she was not much more than a baby. A dark-skinned woman had brought her back. Who and why?

She might be sacrificed. She had visions of herself in a white robe lying on an altar as a druid plunged a dagger into her breast. She might be expected to spread her legs for the debauched society with which the old man surrounded himself and this would buy his cooperation. Her dreams of being a modern-day Boudicca or a British Joan of Arc lay crumpled like the pieces of paper he had left in his waste bin.

She put a small amount of the oil on one fingertip and wiped it across her left eye. It stung and the tears so near the surface streamed down her face. When the pain had subsided, she opened that eye and looked around. It was like looking through a glass with a slightly golden and uneven surface. The sunlight shining through the window had motes floating along the beams and her own hand was more detailed, the veins and the occasional freckle more visible.

She needed to blow her nose but her hankie was wet so she delved into the waste bin for paper and opened a partly written draft letter obviously discarded by Greaves. It said *Dee must return to Pitdown we do not wish to bring the girl to London. Can Agremont visit soon.* Dee must be the old man she thought. She was the girl, damn them. Who was Agremont?

Rosalyn stood and looked around the room, relieved to find she was alone. She blew her nose on another piece of wastepaper and tried to decide whether to apply the oil to the other eye. It would be safer to monitor the long-term effects before committing herself. She had been given the morning to absorb what Greaves had told her and it was a chance to recover from her disturbed vision. It was clear she could trust no one at Pitdown Hall. She decided to explore the house and see what else was occupying it apart from the men of this special auxiliary unit.

*

The most direct way into the Hall was through the ruined orangery. Rosalyn looked around suspiciously, but seemed to be alone as she picked her way passed dead pot plants and faded cane furniture. The large dining room was now used as the refectory and the cook's assistant was wiping down and laying tables for luncheon. She nodded to him as he looked up and he did the same. She smiled and was about to engage him in conversation when he abruptly turned and left through the kitchen door. How much did he know about the auxiliary unit at Pitdown Hall, but his panicked exit made her think that he knew something of her involvement and could see the change in her. Even the help knew that unnatural things were going to be done in the fighting of this war, as well as sinister ones.

The walls were dark oak and the few remaining paintings had been badly discoloured by years of smoke, so it was difficult to appreciate much of the artists' skill as she walked along examining them, alternating her normal eye with her enchanted one. There was a mirror. She looked with a mixture of horror and fascination at her own image. Her dark hair was still in its roll and her brows were tidy but her brown eyes were glittering and her mouth was swollen and red as though she'd been eating berries. Was it through both eyes? She closed the one that had received the oil and she looked as she had that morning, a little puffier from tears and slightly flushed. Then she closed her right eye and gasped. She looked just a bit magical. Gold flecks sparkled in her left eye. The effect was so astounding she decided not to use the oil on the other eye until certain it was safe. She would just have to accept lopsided vision.

Rosalyn moved from the refectory and glanced into the sitting room; it was just as shabby as last night but now it was empty and smelled stale. In the gloomy hall the stairs were impressive, heavy oak, and crooked like a dog's leg, a newel post shaped like a pineapple sat on top of the banister. When she was younger, she would have loved to slide down that banister and her brothers would have been obliged to follow suit. She knew how much she had challenged them and now regretted that whilst they were able to fight for their country, she as a woman was just a bribe, part of a deal. Anger was added to the plethora of emotions that had run through her body that morning. Still, the danger was real enough.

She went upstairs and found four large bedrooms overlooking the grounds. The first room was obviously that of Greaves. It smelled fresh and was tidy and his clothes, including his uniform, hung neatly in a wardrobe, boots were polished, ready for inspection. There was a four-poster bed and several pieces of heavy oak furniture. Brushes and combs were laid out on the dressing table. There was expensive looking wallpaper and she thought at one time it might have been the master's room and there was a private washroom and toilet. Pale shadows where paintings had hung revealed how much tobacco had been consumed over the years.

The next room she recognised as Brent's from the smell of stale foreign cigarettes. That too was orderly and there was nothing of a personal nature evident on the furniture surfaces. Curiosity led her to open a few drawers, she guiltily hoped he might have a diary she could pry into, but they were either empty or contained household linen. The sounds of remote explosions and gunfire occasionally made her start, but it meant they were occupied elsewhere, she hoped.

Claff and Osgood were billeted together in the next room, they were locals and must have some accommodation in the area but presumably were required to stay in the Hall for training. Their room was cluttered. Each had carved out an area where he could pile his clothes and personal possessions. Perhaps someone had picked up for them at home, there was a musty smell of clothes long unwashed. She wondered what laundry facilities had been provided for their training.

The Reverend Davies was billeted in the last room and as expected he had carefully laid out some personal items, a bible, a prayerbook and a photograph of a woman, perhaps his wife. What had he told her and his congregation about time spent away? Perhaps he was on retreat or consulting on ecclesiastical matters? Instead, he had been crawling around somewhere on the estate learning to kill with a group of men from a different class. Men who worked with their hands, uneducated and far removed from what she imagined a cleric with a degree in theology would have experienced in anything other than a pastoral capacity.

She was struck with the irony of a man like Davies ministering to a flock of country folk as though they were a different race. It was the tradition of the priesthood and how ridiculous it was, and how old fashioned. And now dealing with an entirely different species, if that's what greyfolk were. She picked up his prayer book and read the inscriptions inside the front cover. He had studied theology in Aberystwyth at the University of Wales. He did not have a Welsh accent but perhaps his family had ties in the area.

Rosalyn carefully replaced it and stared out of the window, closing her right eye so that she could look at the trees and woodland with her left, hoping to see something magical in the grounds that she hadn't noticed before. The scene was more vivid, but she could not see any odd creatures moving about. She turned her gaze back into the room and then she saw it, a concealed door in the dark panelling, something she could not see with her right eye alone.

Fascinated, she moved to it and touched the panel lightly and it swung inwards without a sound. It was dark and she had no torch, but Rosalyn stepped inside and waited for a few seconds for her eyes to adjust. As she hoped, her left eye could see clearly enough to enable her to make her way down a set of stairs, almost tripping over some rags that had been left on the top step. The walls were damp and smelt of mould. It was a long way down and she assumed that she was below ground level when the steps ended. She pushed open a wooden door and walked into a cellar.

There were still a few wine bottles lying in dark corners, probably from the time that theatre people had stayed here. Otherwise, it was a series of empty racks and a single large table; everything was covered with dust. Rosalyn assumed that Greaves knew about the cellar, though he may not have noticed the secret door from the bedroom, but it didn't look as though it had been used and the steps showed no sign of recent footprints.

*

Rosalyn thought about leaving via the cellar stairs and the door that must open into the ground floor of the Hall. But it might be locked, and her footprints would be visible in the dust. Fortunately, the damp floor had not noticeably shown her tramping about. So she would have to return the way she had come in, through the bedroom on the first floor. She confidently mounted the stairs and only when entering the room did she realise that her incursion had been discovered. The vicar was poised with a candlestick raised above his head ready to strike whatever enemy came through the secret door. They were both shocked.

'Miss James. I nearly brained you,' he shuffled backwards and let her through. 'What is this?'

'It seems to be a priest hole or similar,' said Rosalyn quickly. 'Probably from Tudor times.'

'I didn't know there was a hidden passage in my room. I could have been murdered in my bed. All this time I've been barricading the door at night, and I was still vulnerable to anyone with evil intentions.'

'Anyone who knew it was there,' said Rosalyn. She closed the door and it vanished into the general wooden panelling and looked nothing out of the ordinary. Her heart was beating fast, and Davies was white and still clutched the brass candleholder.

'But where did you come from and how did you know it would end here?' he said.

Rosalyn had always thought him an odd addition to the unit, and it was difficult to imagine this conventional middle-aged man being involved with the greyfolk or faerie creatures, whatever they were. The other men had a connection to the earth and to the wild things that lived on and in it; he seemed academic, ascetic even. It would be useful to hear his views on everything at Pitdown Hall. She seated herself at the writing desk as though feeling faint. He handed her a glass of water.

'I must admit I was snooping, looking in any rooms that were open. Just from curiosity you understand, I'm not a thief.'

'I am sure you're not, my dear,' he said.

'And this is the way I went in, through that concealed doorway.' She tried to look earnest. 'Will you help me vicar? I know you've all been in training for weeks, and you've had time to get used to what's going on. If what I was told this morning is correct, about using the supernatural to fight this war, then I have a lot of catching up to do.'

Davies was clearly not happy with the situation. He paced the room avoiding her enquiring gaze. Then he turned, a tortured expression on his face.

'Ah, you've been fully briefed then,'

'That's moot,' she said wryly. 'I get the impression there must be more to come. It would be fair to say a small amount of information has been trickled my way by Lieutenant Greaves. As a man of the cloth, I was hoping you'd be able to put it into perspective for me.'

Davies sat resignedly on the bed and toyed with the candlestick.

'We live in evil times,' he said. 'I was a chaplin in the Great War and despite the horror of modern warfare it always seemed that we were fighting against men and that they were, like us, forced to go to war because their nation required it. But times have changed. The new Germany has a fanaticism that has embraced the culture of the heathen and turned its back on Christian faith and the life of the spirit.'

He paused and picked up the bible from the bedside table.

'And now these hidden creatures have been revealed to us. Creatures that are not in the Bible.'

Rosalyn waited. It was clear he had a lot to say.

'The Nazis have already used the mysticism of older times to recruit men and women in Scandinavian countries.'

'By mysticism do you mean the supernatural?' she said.

'They have reminded them of the glorious days of their Viking past when their ancestors conquered countries and captured people to use as slaves. You know the term slave comes from the Slavs that were taken by Germanic peoples. It was the natural order.'

'When was that?' asked Rosalyn.

'The tenth century.'

'And how do greyfolk fit into the ideas of a racial hierarchy?'

'In an overcrowded world where resources are scarce, yes wars will be fought along racial lines. Competition is part of life. You are familiar with the theory of evolution?'

Rosalyn nodded. She could see the awful inevitability in what he was saying. Darwin's book *On the Origin of Species* had demonstrated that the survival of the fittest was one of the prime laws of nature. But Davies must believe in God and in his creation of all living things. Then she recalled the rest of the book's title - *Preservation of Favoured Races in the Struggle For Life.*

'Do you think God favours some races over others?'

He looked at her intently.

'The Jewish faith believes it is the chosen one and that David was your tribe's great hero. His bloodline was so important in producing the Messiah that the Bible stresses his birth in Bethlehem.'

This was not something Rosalyn had ever considered. She thought conversion to Christianity would be enough to qualify as a non-Jew.

Davies was continuing his discourse.

'Every nation has its great heroes and heroines – Joan of Arc, King Arthur – they are figureheads to which the susceptible are drawn with the promise of something spiritual and transcendent.'

'But they were Christian,' said Rosalyn.

'They were warriors and are now gilded by the passing of time and a dissatisfaction with the present. Take for example the Nazis' search for the Holy Grail,' Davies said.

'But surely if it is Christ's cup from the Last Supper then something like the Grail can only be used for good,' said Rosalyn.

'As you would say, it is moot. But it only needs to be held aloft to gather massed ranks of believers and become a weapon of power. Because if you are in possession of the Grail, you must have been chosen by God for salvation.'

Rosalyn was confused.

She said, 'They haven't found the Grail, have they?'

'Not that I know, but they are looking for it. One of the things we have been taught in the last few days is that Himmler, the head of the SS, is a believer in the occult and his troops are indoctrinated with a belief of their superiority so they think no more of killing 'untermenschen', sub-humans, than of killing animals.'

Rosalyn shuddered.

'Therefore, it is logical for us to fight them using whatever is available, using magic, if necessary,' said Davies.

'A world of subterfuge and deception,' said Rosalyn.

'We are being trained in both, and murder of course. Things we don't understand always frighten us.'

He looked closely at her face.

'Have you used the oil that enables you to see what is otherwise hidden?' he said.

'I have used it; I think that's why I could see your concealed door.'

He glanced over to the wood panelling that looked like any other wall.

'I have declined the use of the oil,' said Davies. 'I prefer to rely on my faith and the grace of God, rather than alchemical magic. I might be tempted to use it if I thought it would enable me to see angels. Angels are holy, I have never doubted their existence.'

'I suppose you're going to tell me that angels are terrifying beings.'

'Of course. They are God's celestial warriors. If you have received any Bible tuition Miss James, then you will know about the Fall of Man and his expulsion from the Garden of Eden, and that this was carried out by an angel with a fiery sword. As a result of the Fall we are all mired in sin and only some of us will be chosen for redemption.'

'They glossed over that aspect in my Sunday school,' she said.

'But you know as well as I that this auxiliary unit will be doing fiendish and bloody work.'

'I happen to believe the alternative is worse,' Rosalyn said.

He held the candlestick in one hand and the Bible in the other and leaned towards her. All he needs is a bell to carry out an exorcism she thought and then shuddered at the realisation that he might easily have struck her with the candlestick as she came through the door. She felt there was an aura of suppressed violence about him as with many men who are out of their depth and trying desperately to hide it.

'Do you believe in God, Miss James?' he said, fixing her with a fanatical stare.

'I think I'm what you might call agnostic,' she replied cautiously. She looked at his pale face above the white collar of his calling and wondered why he had volunteered. He seemed a man uncomfortable in his own skin. He closed his eyes and she thought he might be praying. Rosalyn wondered if she might leave before he began to proselytise, she felt awkward. She started to get up, but he noticed and opened his eyes, so she sat back down.

'Can you tell me anything about my role in this?' she said. 'The land girl thing was a ploy to get me here and it appears none of us is likely to leave this unit alive. But do you know what will happen to me and why they want me in particular?'

Davies sighed. 'I've been vicar here since 1937 and this house was the bane of my life. Local women were seduced by young men with the morals of alley cats. They came here for long weekend parties; they fornicated, drank excessively, and took drugs. Some of the men were actors but quite a lot were sons of wealthy families, foreign diplomats and even a few aristocrats. The women who came with them were actresses from a theatre in London owned by the old man and were no better than prostitutes.'

'Is that what happened to Osgood's wife and daughter?'

She thought many men would have taken a shotgun to him.

'The Osgood women left the village when one of the rowdiest house-parties broke up. We assume they went with members of the party. He never talks about it, but I think that's what turned

Osgood to the ways of black magic. After he hexed him, the old man was carried out raving, in a strait jacket.'

'I suppose it would be useful if we could render the invading army insane.'

But then she thought about the Vikings who were called berserkers and had so little fear, they were terrifying warriors. But warfare had changed, and no doubt Greaves and Brent had some plan to use that magic.

She said, 'What about ghosts? Do you believe in them Vicar? Can they help us? Can we call on the dead of these lands to leave their graves and come to England's aid in our hour of need?'

Davies seemed more relaxed now and after thinking about her question said, 'I'm sure that humans have souls and there is a heaven and a hell, but they are separate from this world. If ghosts exist in the sense that they are lost souls unable to ascend to heaven or descend into hell, then they would have no corporeal form. Their lack of agency would render them of little use in this war. It's a romantic notion. We can't frighten the Germans from our land.'

'Well said Vicar.'

They jumped. The secret door had opened silently, and Brent stood in the room.

'I understand you've been exploring,' he said to Rosalyn. 'And if you have finished interrogating Mr Davies, you'd better come with me.'

He closed the hidden door and moved to the main one, opened it and beckoned to her. Rosalyn thanked the Reverend Davies and followed him out. Lunch was being served but she was not hungry and declined his suggestion that they eat. If she thought she might escape his attention she was disappointed. He must have seen some indication of her intrusion in the cellar and he invited her into the chapel.

*

Brent unlocked the heavy door. As they left the noise of the refectory with its clanging pots and plates the first impression on entering the chapel was of profound silence. The smell was musty, and Rosalyn saw it was stacked with books from floor to ceiling. Some of them were made of parchment and, as she drew closer, she thought, possibly of calf-skin vellum.

'May I touch?' she said. He nodded.

It was soft and pliable, the skin of a young animal, and the colours of the inks still brilliant. The handwritten letters were from a western alphabet, but she couldn't understand the language. It was unlike any she had encountered at school.

'What language is this?'

'I think he would call it Enochian,' said Brent drily.

'Agremont?'

'Is that the name Davies told you?' Brent seemed surprised. 'These are not his books, they belonged to the owner of the house. Agremont was a visitor to the property.'

'What's the name of the man who owns them?'

'Doctor Dee,' Brent replied.

Rosalyn wandered around the chapel, looking at the carvings and paved floors for features of interest. The stained-glass windows were high and gaunt and the setting neo-gothic and elaborate. At the end of the nave where the altar would have been there was a carefully arranged storage area for luxurious cloth. Unusual fabrics that she had never come across in the compulsory needlework lessons her school had insisted she study. Perhaps the chapel had been used for theatrical purposes. It was obviously a warehouse and a library, so it didn't seem strange to find fabrics.

Brent said, 'Greaves has been speaking with Dee. He's our chief connection to the greyfolk, and they've agreed your transfer to London will take place soon.'

My father's there thought Rosalyn, perhaps I can escape and go home before this nightmare gets any worse?

As though reading her mind Brent said, 'Your father is in Wales with the most precious books belonging to the Library. Don't think about trying to escape. I wouldn't like to have to kill you.'

She stared at him and stuck her jaw out, determined to face him down at least.

'Greaves wouldn't tell me why they've asked for me. Do you know?' she said and walked towards him.

'I don't. Apparently one of your ancestors did some harm to him and he's borne a grudge for a long time.'

Rosalyn felt sick, she didn't feel brave anymore. There were so many questions. What ancestor? If it was one of her grandfathers, then why call him an ancestor. How long ago was it? How old is he? She wished she'd declined the invitation to serve her country.

'What sort of harm? And which of my ancestors? How old is this man – so his name is Dee. Is he a man?'

'I did try to warn you,' Brent said.

'Did I really have any choice in this?' she said.

'They hoped you would agree. I didn't. But quite possibly it wouldn't have been negotiable. If you'd refused, you might have found yourself involved anyway. You were the only specific thing he asked for.'

'What's he going to do to me – this man.'

'It's unlikely he will do anything to you, but as they asked for a human woman as part of the deal he saw his chance to nominate you.'

'The creatures wanted a woman? So I am a sacrifice.'

'Fortunately you are acceptable. Lord Agremont confirmed it this morning.'

'I haven't met him. I suppose he's the thing that was spying on me. How despicable.'

In her head Rosalyn swore as many bad words as she knew, but it was a frustratingly small number. Her fear was replaced by anger and frustration.

'Can I have a cigarette? I'd like to smoke in the chapel and stub it out in the font – if there is one. Oh, and I want a very large whisky. That's fair, isn't it? The sacrificial victim lives the life of Riley before they go to slaughter.'

'I don't know what they have in mind for you,' he said.

'You're a very bad liar Private Brent. It could be a fate worse than death, whatever that means.'

He gave her a cigarette and lit it, then fetched out a hip flask.

'This'll have to do,' he said. 'Are you enjoying the smoke?'

She shook her head, and regretted it because it was spinning. Inhaling the strong smoke deeply as she had seen other people do was a mistake and there was no pleasure from it, she just felt sick. She sat down and swigged the rum quickly; at least the flavour of tar hid the taste of the cigarette. It was a relief to put the hot stinky thing out on the floor and stamp on it.

More of the rum helped and the raw spirit was bracing and relaxed her, though the smell was off-putting. How disappointing they both were. She wondered if sex would be just as disappointing and thought, oh bugger, I haven't even been with anyone. Perhaps Farrell would sleep with me. I might be able to seduce Greaves or at a pinch even Brent. I wonder if those scars go all the way down his body. She was a little tipsy but no longer feeling sick.

They sat in silence for a while.

Rosalyn, seeking a distraction asked, 'You have the gold flecks in both eyes, you've used the oil. What happened to your face? And don't fob me off with the pheasant thing.'

He looked at her fully and fingered the puckered tissue and misshapen eye.

'It was shrapnel, and I can assure you this was a minor injury. My friends were blown to pieces. The enemy assumed I was dead from the amount of blood. The torn flesh that covered my body had belonged to my comrades.'

'Was it in Spain?'

He nodded.

'How horrible people are. Have you read War and Peace?' asked Rosalyn. He shook his head. 'The dilettante civilians view war as an entertainment. I seem to remember them and Pierre Bazuhov observing the encroaching French forces as they secretly admired Napoleon Bonaparte. The young officers are keen for battle. After they taste its horror they understand that chivalry and codes of conduct are irrelevant. War is an all or nothing nightmare.'

'Chivalry,' Brent said. 'In medieval times, when so much was written about it and the romance of war, the common soldier was always slaughtered because he had no value as a prisoner. War was different for aristocrats and wealthy men; they could be ransomed. No distinctions are made today, everyone can fall victim to the bomb, women and children will not be spared. We saw that in Spain.'

Rosalyn voiced her suspicion. 'You're a communist. That's why you refused a commission.'

'This is an all or nothing war Miss James and you will be part of the battle whether you like it or no.'

They sat in the smoky haze of the quiet chapel, surrounded by beauty and transience.

'How long have I got before it happens?' she said.

'It'll be quite soon.'

He led her out of the chapel and back to the refectory. Davies, Greaves, and Farrell were there with the cook's assistant. Greaves nodded to her as they entered and she was almost tempted to curtsy or stick up two fingers in the manner of Churchill, but she did not. How much do they know? Rosalyn looked at Farrell and their eyes met briefly. They both looked away and she wondered what he was thinking. She took a portion of vegetable and cheese pie and sat opposite him. There always seemed to be space around him. The others resumed their conversation, and she could hear mutters of 'rum' and knew she appeared tipsy, and was tipsy. She ignored them. Eventually they cleared up and left with Brent who seemed to live on cigarettes and coffee.

'Aren't you going with them this afternoon?' she asked Farrell.

'They're learning about codes and things like that.'

'And you don't need to know about it, or already do.'

He didn't meet her eyes. 'I'm not one for book learning.'

With a shock she realised he was illiterate; it was the reason he hadn't helped by labelling the OB shelves. It must have showed in her expression because she saw in his face the humiliation of a wretched child. There was no one else in the room so on impulse she reached across the table and took his hand. For a moment she thought he might pull away, but she drew it towards herself and opened his palm. She used her fingers to smooth it out and made as if to read his fortune.

At home her father had a book on cheiromancy, palm reading, written by a famous practitioner of the occult. Rosalyn had absorbed it as a teenager, seeking to answer all the many uncertainties in her young life. She ran a finger down his lifeline first and was pleased to see it was long and well formed. She looked up and was about to tell him when she realised, they were all destined to die an early death in the war. He read her mind and a smile appeared deepening the lines in his cheeks.

'Perhaps the Germans won't invade,' he whispered, and she smiled back conspiratorially.

'You have a good headline too. See how it dips down. That shows an artistic nature, and this indicates a tendency to keep your thoughts secret. And this is your heartline. There's a break in it.' She looked up at him and he nodded. 'That's a very strong fate line, it means –'

'I know what it means,' he said and catching her own hand drew it to himself in both of his, like a captured bird. He spread her fingers gently.

'From your lifeline it looks as though the Germans won't invade. Don't tell the others, they're having so much fun.' He caressed her palm with his fingertips. 'You are practical and outspoken. You will marry once and have two children, a girl and a boy.' She laughed. 'You will die when you are very old surrounded by your family.'

She could hardly breathe. They sat holding hands across the table and not daring to look at each other. The tension was so great that she had to break it.

'What, no mention of being served up like a sacrificial lamb for the foul purposes of a pagan monster, or whatever he is.' She held onto his hands and indulged in a moment of self-pity; tears flooded her eyes.

When she looked at him again, she noticed that his blue eyes didn't sparkle with gold flecks but she was sure he could see in the dark.

'What are you doing this afternoon?' she said. 'Can I come with you? If they are in a classroom there's no chance of being blown-up or shot.'

'You can come if you don't talk too much.'

'Am I annoying?'

'No, you'll scare the game. I want to hunt.'

*

She followed him from the great hall to his cottage where his dog greeted them both and Rosalyn made much of the old hound. They set off along an ancient drover's road, then turned off through coppiced woods, passed charcoal kilns. In the very darkest part of the pine forest he shot a buck, killed it cleanly and gutted the beast there and then. They carried it to a stone building set in a small clearing and circled by drying frames and the remains of fires. A large pot had cooled to one side and when she peered in, she saw the skull of a deer cleaned of its flesh.

He hung the fresh carcase on a hook inside the building and went around the site checking that all was as it should be. She sat on a tree stump and soaked up the few rays of sun that penetrated the canopy. She felt exhausted from the day's revelations and hoped they might stay there and rest for a while. It was warm and smelled of the fresh pine wood, a relief after the smells of the deer's blood and hide. The dog sat by her, and she fondled his silky ears. Farrell returned and looked at her closely, tilting her chin upwards like that of a child. She was tired and bloody, and it was a hot August day. Taking her hand in his, he led her through the dense undergrowth.

After a few hundred yards they came to a quiet pool with a small island in its centre. It was completely enclosed by thick shrubs and tall trees. Dog went straight into the water and drank happily. Then he found a soft bank of grass and went to sleep. The man put down his gun and game bag and took off the waistcoat he always wore. Rosalyn washed her hands and face in the cool water and found some blackberries. They didn't speak, and she was glad he gave her space to come to terms with her strange predicament. Lying back, she gazed at the blue sky so far above, her thoughts drained away, and she fell into a dreamless sleep.

Something woke her and Rosalyn struggled to remember where she was and at what time of day. The ground was cool, and she moved, then sat up. Farrell was nowhere to be seen but his clothes lay in a pile where he had been sitting. His sleek head appeared in the pond about fifteen feet out and he grinned at her, diving again like an otter.

She loved to swim. As a child her father had called her a water baby and she longed to get into the water now. The question was - did she have to strip off or could she retain her underwear. She didn't want to seem prudish, but despite having brothers, she had never seen a naked man except in art books, and she had never shown herself naked to any man.

She took off her blouse and her shapeless trousers. Socks came next, but he had resurfaced and was watching her. She wore a silk camisole edged with lace and she decided that would do as a bathing costume, so she wriggled out of her bra and dropped it on to the other items. Her hair was in a ridiculously neat victory roll. She unpinned it and let it fall onto her shoulders. Barefoot, she walked into the water and when it reached her knees she dived in fully, swimming underwater as far as her lungs would allow. It was dark, and only when she broke the surface did she see how close she was to him. They trod water smiling at each other.

To break the tension Rosalyn floated on her back and again gazed at the cloudless sky. She felt his hand clasp hers and when she looked over he was doing the same. She regained her weightless position, her ears underwater so that only bubbles and clicks could be heard. They floated hand in hand, passively, in a still, calm piece of England, in an uncaring universe, while terrible things were happening and were going to happen. Something broke the surface near them, then flashed away.

'Did I tell you there are pike in here?' he said.

'Oh no,' said Rosalyn and she swam and staggered from the pond.

'Don't you like fish?'

'Not the sort with nasty sharp teeth that eat ducklings,' she said.

He laughed.

She found a patch of sunlight, sat down, and squeezed the water from her hair trying to comb it with cold fingers. She didn't realise how much more seductive she looked in her wet camisole than if she had been naked. He stayed in the water until she had turned the other way.

'I'm coming out so I should stay looking that way if you want to maintain your modesty.'

'You're laughing at me.'

She was tempted to turn round, but perhaps it was his modesty in question. She heard him leave the pond and waited demurely.

'Is it safe now?'

As though to answer her she felt him gathering her hair from her shoulders and running his fingers through it.

'My wife used to like me doing this.'

Rosalyn felt an immediate sense of loss and was glad he couldn't see her face. Of course he was married. How could he not be?

'Don't you do it now?' she said when her voice was almost under control.

'No I don't,' he said.

'Has she cut her hair?'

'She's in London with the theatre company.'

'Oh, not that man Agremont.'

He didn't reply and she was embarrassed but pleased that his wife had run off with the people from the big house. Like the Osgood women, she realised. She resisted the temptation to ask more questions.

He continued to sort out the tangles and drew his fingers across her scalp so that she fell into a trance like an animal being stroked. Then she felt him firmly and surely start braiding her hair.

He said, 'I'm surprised your hair is so long. As a modern girl weren't you tempted by the film stars, the glamorous pictures in the magazines, plucked eyebrows, lipstick. You're natural.'

Having finished the plait, he twisted it round her neck, quite tight she thought, then used it to pull her head down onto his lap. And there he looked at her upside down and bending, kissed her. She closed her eyes and waited for more, but he placed her head gently on the ground and moved away to finish getting dressed.

Rosalyn wondered why he did not try and make love to her. Other young men had made advances and she had let them have a kiss and a cuddle only stopping them when their hands wandered too privately. It occurred to her that she had to remain a virgin for the sacrifice. It was infuriating, but she was determined not to speak of it. She watched him for a few minutes as he dressed. Then observing the law of silence, she quickly pulled her clothes over her wet camisole, stuffed her bra into a pocket and was ready for him when they left the pond. Dog sat beside her wagging his tail. They marched back through the quiet woods, disturbing a few birds and small animals, and all too quickly they were at her cottage door.

He turned and she knew he was going to kiss her but what then? Would he walk away? Should she turn from his kiss and leave him as he had left her at the pond? Or should she hold him and show her passion? She did neither, and he did kiss her, but this time it was different. He held her close, and she opened her mouth for him and closed her eyes. He finished by kissing her neck and then her closed eyes. Then he left and dog went with him.

4 BIRTH

Tuesday 27 August 1940

Dinner that evening was a mixture of torture and pleasure for Rosalyn, and she thought it must be the same for Farrell too. The mutual attraction was undeniable, and they worked hard to hide it from the others. She was sure that everyone except Brent was unaware, and she imposed on herself all the primness and propriety taught her by the various girls' schools she had attended. Farrell was untalkative by nature it seemed, and the other men did not include him in their banter.

She sat between Greaves and Davies again and this time engaged them in a discussion of the use of greyfolk in the guerrilla attacks they were planning to make. Rosalyn did not reveal her concern about her own fate and tried to behave as though she would be a genuine member of the unit.

'Do greyfolk usually kill humans?' she asked Greaves.

'That's an interesting question and the short answer is no.'

'So how do you plan to use them?'

Greaves appeared uncomfortable but after a short pause he answered.

'They're masters of illusion. For example they can conceal our traps and explosives so that the enemy will drive or march right into them. They can conceal our presence as we lay the mines.'

Osgood added. 'They don't like iron so they'll be no damn good in a fight with guns and tanks.'

'And they can be killed,' said Claff.

'But they're quick, invisible, and some of them can fly,' said Osgood. 'That's good for gathering intelligence.'

Rosalyn smiled and thought of the delightful drawings of faeries in her childhood picture books. She stole a brief look at Farrell simply for the pleasure of seeing his face.

'Are they faeries? What do they look like?'

'Not what you'd expect,' said Osgood.

He was the resident expert she decided. Despite her fear of what was to come Rosalyn was curious at the thought of another world existing in parallel to her own, populated by a people she had only seen hinted at and never acknowledged.

'Short, ugly, untrustworthy,' said Claff.

'Except when they want to appear tall, beautiful, charming,' said Osgood.

'And are they all over the world?' asked Rosalyn. 'Or just here in Britain?'

'They're everywhere,' said Osgood.

'Don't the Germans have their own greyfolk working for them?'

'There's more space for them in most other countries so they just move into forests and mountains. The spread of our industry has caused problems here.'

'They want something from us,' said Claff.

'That's enough talk about them,' said Greaves. 'Tonight we will focus on approaches to the railway. That will be one of our main targets and I need to be sure that we are familiar with the best routes and weakest points.'

'Am I invited?' said Rosalyn to Greaves quietly.

'It might be better if you stayed here with Davies and he'll show you how to operate the radio with the new aerial.'

She glanced at Brent. He was lighting another cigarette as the men finished their meal and went into the sitting room for coffee. She looked at all of them equally in turn and Farrell's look lingered longer than it needed to and said so much and yet when he left, nothing at all. A hollowness took her, and she went with Davies to a small room set aside for the paraphernalia of the radio.

They spent the evening studying the thing and sending a practice message to Greaves at an unknown location. When they had explored its functions, they stopped for coffee and Rosalyn tried to make conversation with him by discussing ways the information might be supplied.

'Just imagine having flying creatures, invisible ones, to look at the enemy's position and perhaps eavesdrop at important meetings.'

'You asked a good question earlier,' Davies looked at her steadily. 'Are there fae anywhere else and will the greyfolk of Germany be called upon to assist their nations in the same way. Don't forget the warning that they're not entirely trustworthy. My personal suspicion is that they want humans to destroy each other, the better to allow their own kind to flourish.'

Rosalyn saw an opportunity.

'They must want something very much to be prepared to cooperate with us,' she said. 'Do you know what that might be?'

Davies was sitting in a large armchair and his body language was evasive. Before he could reply there was the sound of a car pulling up in front of the Hall. They looked at each other.

'Are you expecting someone this evening?' she said

It was nine forty-five and Greaves had said the men would be out most of the night. Davies shook his head. Car doors slammed and they heard voices.

'I'd better see who it is. Do you think I need to be armed?' asked Davies. He went to a drawer and took out a pistol. 'Just in case.'

Rosalyn followed him into the hall where they stood hesitating. A woman cried out and Rosalyn immediately opened the door. A soldier in uniform helped a heavily pregnant woman through it.

'She needs help. The pains got worse as we drove up here. I wasn't sure where the nearest hospital was, and she was very insistent that we come here.' The young man was a corporal. 'I can't stay or I'll get into trouble.'

'Who is she?' asked Rosalyn.

'No idea. She was walking along the main road and I nearly knocked her over. I couldn't leave her in that state.'

'She must go to a hospital,' said Rosalyn.

The woman wailed. 'No, no hospital.'

Davies said, 'Take her into the sitting room.'

He said quietly to Rosalyn, 'I know who she is. We'd better get rid of him. I mean send him away.'

Rosalyn took charge of the woman while Davies escorted the soldier off the premises.

When he returned, he took her to one side and said, 'I told him she was a servant here before the war and obviously found herself in the family way and had nowhere else to go.'

She was lying on the chaise, panting from exertion, but obviously not in pain at that moment. Rosalyn saw a red-haired woman of about thirty years. She was wearing a strange combination of a soiled satin dress and fur stole, silk stockings and bedroom slippers. She was clutching an old canvas bag.

'Poor thing,' she said. 'Shouldn't we get a doctor at least?'

Davies's reaction amazed her. He laughed, almost hysterically.

'Dear God no. What happens tonight will be His retribution and ordained. She must give birth here.'

He began to drag the woman from the chaise. 'Help me get her to one of the bedrooms. Come on.'

Rosalyn was expecting them to go to one of the larger bedrooms on the first floor, but Davies insisted they carry on upstairs to the attic rooms that used to house servants. They settled her onto a bed and fetched what linen they could find. Towels and hot water thought Rosalyn. She had birthed a lot of lambs in her time but never a human baby.

As she busied herself in the kitchen Davies stayed and talked to the woman. When she returned, he was white-faced and praying urgently. The woman was experiencing contractions and Rosalyn felt a rush of irritation at his piety.

She realised he would be of no practical use and when she raised the woman's wet skirts to examine her, he fled the room. She held her hand and talked quietly to her. Was it her first? No she had others, but they had been taken away. Stillborn. Poor creature, she thought.

Rosalyn timed the contractions and waited, checking every now again for signs of a head.

'Tell me about your husband?' Rosalyn said. 'Is he serving?'

The woman seemed confused.

'My husband's Farrell the gamekeeper. He's here somewhere. I've come back so he can look after us. I don't want them to have my baby.'

The blood drained from Rosalyn's face and her body went cold. It could not be more dreadful. Farrell's wife and his child in her hands. She wanted to run away and join Davies downstairs. She felt sick. The woman screamed again, and Rosalyn came to her senses and was able to do her duty as best she could.

During the gruelling hours of labour the woman cried out and cursed. Davies must be able to hear it, perhaps that was why he had installed her at the top of the house. At around midnight the baby's head appeared, and she was relieved that it turned and was quickly followed by shoulders and a long grey body. It made no sound and did not move. She knew that babies were born covered with a white waxy substance and was not surprised that it was colourless under its mother's blood. She looked at the face. It was screwed up tightly and with horror Rosalyn realised it must be deformed. Should she hold it up by the feet and smack it to try and induce breathing as she would with a lamb? She did it. There was no sound or movement.

Born dead, she thought. How awful. She wrapped the child in a towel and placed it on the woman's belly then turned her attention to the mother. Rosalyn knew there would be a placenta appearing soon but lambs' umbilical cords fell away on their own and humans didn't. She would have to do something with this one and perhaps keep the placenta attached to the baby, even if it was dead. Once it was out the mother would be safe, provided she stopped bleeding.

'Mrs Farrell,' she said. 'I've wrapped baby in a towel, here.'

She placed the woman's hands over the small bundle on her chest.

She was relaxed after her labour. Rosalyn hated her and yet felt compassion. She must try to help her.

'Can you feel if the afterbirth is coming?'

She put a hand on the still swollen abdomen, and it moved sluggishly causing her to quickly pull away. There might be another baby. Was it going to be born now as well? This one was definitely alive but its mother was still unconscious. How would she push it out?

Rosalyn squatted on the floor next to the bed. She could just let them all die and he would be free. But the baby was innocent, and it might be his baby. Or it might not. She stood at the basin and washed her hands and arms thoroughly. Then she heard a thin wail. She would do whatever she could to bring it into the world and help it to live.

Rosalyn was filthy with blood and other body fluids and was not facing the woman on the bed. Perhaps the infant was not dead after all. She turned and saw mother with the dead child on her breast exactly as she had left them. Her eyes were staring, unseeing, her jaw slack and the mouth open. The woman was dead, and the bundle was not moving.

Something else moved on the bed between the woman's splayed legs. Clutching a towel Rosalyn moved to get a better look. The lights she had set up shone on a creature with short legs and arms waving about; it was alive. It was smaller than the first and although vulnerable there was a strength to it. She looked at the woman's genitals for signs of an afterbirth, but they were unrecognisable. In a wave of nausea Rosalyn realised that the creature had forced its own way out of its mother, tearing her flesh in the process and releasing a vast amount of blood that flooded the bed and dripped through the mattress onto the floor.

*

When she finished vomiting and had wiped her mouth, Rosalyn edged to the door and was about to leave when the creature wailed again. It sounded like a kitten, and she could not ignore it. She took another towel and approached it. Trying to ignore the carnage she picked it up and took it to the wash bowl. The umbilical cord had broken like a lamb's, and it cried plaintively and reminded her of a little animal so when she reached the water, she couldn't drown it as she had intended. She was never able to drown kittens on the farm. It felt just the same in her hands, it was really quite sweet, its eyes were closed and its ears were pressed against the round head. She saw a snub nose and tiny pointed tongue peeking out of a small mouth. After washing it Rosalyn placed it on a towel away from the cadaver of the woman and its twin.

It was time to confront Davies. He must know more than he had told her. Rosalyn started down the stairs but then stopped. What if he killed it? She felt bonded to the vulnerable little thing, she couldn't blame it for fighting its way out of the dead woman. It had no choice. She would not let Davies or the other men destroy it.

Rosalyn went back to the top floor and looked for another room to hide the living baby. She would find a way to feed it and take it back to her cottage. It was like any other little animal after all. There was another room with a single bed and some linen. There was a large jug and a basin and in the hope of preventing more trouble she put it in the basin on a bed of cloths and loosely covered by a pillowslip. It peeked out at her with dark blue eyes and she made the sign for silence and hoped it would understand.

She slowly went downstairs holding the banister to steady her legs. She found Davies in the sitting room. He was doing something with the radio and covered it as she walked in. He seemed shifty and she had the feeling he'd already told someone what had happened, either on the radio or by telephone. Rosalyn helped herself to a whisky.

'Have you called the doctor?'

He shook his head. 'Couldn't get through.'

'Too late anyway. The woman and baby are dead,' she said.

'Both?' She nodded and he seemed relieved and suddenly interested in the phenomena of childbirth. 'Can I see?'

They went upstairs to the room in which the bodies lay. Rosalyn realised too late that she had not covered the woman's nether regions and they lay in full view of Davies as he walked in. They looked like a red fruit that had burst in its ripeness. She was glad that he almost collapsed. When she thought he had been punished enough for his cowardice she calmly covered the splayed legs and showed him the dead baby.

It was horribly deformed with a non-existent face and elongated limbs. It seemed barely human. Rosalyn dreaded hearing the other if it started to cry and she was relieved when Davies said he had seen enough and left.

She made the woman look as respectable as she could, closing her legs and covering her with a sheet, then cast around for a way to smuggle the other creature out of the house before the men returned. She saw the woman's bag and looked into it. It would do. She tipped out the lipstick and the face powder, the little hankie with *SF* amateurishly embroidered in its corner. It reeked of scent and, combined with the stench of blood and death in the room it made her retch again. She hid the personal items in a cupboard and looked at the woman's face, trying to imagine her with Farrell. Her hair was short and curled. She must have changed it either before she left him or when she was in London, this couldn't have been the woman he fell in love with. Rosalyn pulled the sheet over her face.

She opened the door to the other room and, holding her breath, looked into the basin. It opened its eyes and mewed at her, just like a kitten. She made gentle sounds and lifted it out and held it close to her body for reassurance.

'Let's get you something to eat, little one.'

Saying that out loud she felt foolish but was compelled to nurture and care for it. An animal would have started to produce colostrum and the newborn needed it. She pulled back the sheet and looked at the nipples of the dead woman. The white breasts were full and although it seemed a desecration, she squeezed one gently and was rewarded by the production of a golden liquid. Rosalyn put the mouth of the infant to the breast and it latched on, greedily sucking the swollen teat. An odd feeling of jealousy touched her. She looked for something to milk the other breast into. The whisky glass was there, and she drank it and rinsed the glass. She had milked ewes and applied the same technique on this poor dead woman. She and the creature, robbing the dead.

When they had finished, she quickly packed up the woman's things. It would be better to leave before the men returned and there must be milk in the kitchen. She placed the little one, now sleeping, into the bag and walked quietly down to the kitchen. There was a bottle of milk, that would do, and some biscuits and she was about to tell Davies that she had to go back to the cottage when voices outside the door alerted her, and she just had time to hide everything under the stairs.

The door opened and Greaves walked in shortly followed by Brent; Farrell was not with them.

'Where's Farrell?' said Davies.

'Gone directly to his cottage. Why?'

Greaves could see from their faces that something had happened. Rosalyn was desperate that they move out of the hall in case the other made a noise and alerted them to its presence.

'It would be easier if we went upstairs and you saw for yourselves,' she said.

They started up the stairs with Davies hurriedly explaining that a woman had arrived and died in childbirth.

'It's Farrell's wife,' blurted Davies.

Brent pushed him on, followed by Greaves and Rosalyn. What was the matter with him? He had nothing to do with it and she wondered if he had really been unable to contact someone. They entered the room and she hung back as they examined the body.

'You're sure this is Farrell's wife?' asked Greaves.

'Yes. I recognise her. Claff and Osgood would know her too, but it might signify something terrible for Osgood. Look at the state of her.'

They looked at her pale face, calm in death, then examined the deformed baby and shook their heads.

'A soldier found her walking here and gave her a lift,' said Davies. 'Then he left and we brought her up here, she was in labour.'

There was a pause.

'What happened then?' said Greaves.

Davies said nothing and looked at Rosalyn.

'The Reverend left us. Women's work obviously,' she said.

'There was nothing you could have done for that baby,' Greaves said.

'It was born dead.'

Brent made to look at the body further, but Greaves stopped him.

'It's obvious she bled to death. The bed and floor are soaked. You left the cord in place. We'll put them into a coffin together. I don't want speculation on the nature of the deformity. Farrell can see her in the coffin. It's not his baby.'

'Not his baby?' Rosalyn couldn't stop herself.

'Apparently, she left him more than a year ago. But he may still have feelings for her, and it would be cruel.'

And draw attention to our little group thought Rosalyn and noticed Brent looking at her curiously.

'I'm tired. May I return to my cottage?' she said.

When Greaves consented, she left and hoped that Brent wouldn't follow her but he was immediately engaged by the Lieutenant in the practicalities of disposing of the body and Davies dared not leave them, given his desertion during the event itself. Rosalyn quickly collected her bags from the understairs cupboard and skipped out of the Hall.

She made it to her cottage in record time, never quite breaking into a run. Deeming downstairs too open to prying eyes she took the precious bundle upstairs and opened it on the bed. The creature clung to her and plaintively cried. It was hungry again. Rosalyn poured some milk into a saucer and added the colostrum but it obviously didn't know how to lap, so she introduced drops on her little finger into its mouth. When these were found acceptable, she soaked a cloth and squeezed more drops in until it refused to take the milky mixture and yawned, evidently satisfied.

Unwilling to part from it Rosalyn placed it next to her on the bed, opened a window as it was a warm night, and settled down to sleep. She lay awake for a while; her eyes became used to the darkness and she listened to the hunting owls and foxes in the woods. She heard her own little creature snuffling as it slept, and she felt a protective maternal instinct that kept her awake until tiredness overcame it.

*

Wednesday 28 August 1940

The dawn crept into the room slowly and late, the light was green from the surrounding trees. She woke slowly, feeling sluggish and it took a few minutes of drowsiness before remembering the events of the previous night and her new responsibility. She could not hear it breathing and it must be hungry again. She felt the bundle of cloths it was wrapped in but it was cold and bony. In a panic Rosalyn sat up and looked down at the place where she had put the creature. In dread she opened the cloths. Instead of the sweet face and little arms there was a large pinecone and a pile of twigs.

'No, no, no. I can't have imagined it.'

Rosalyn searched the room thoroughly. In the morning light she found the bag she had taken from the dead woman, and she smelled it for a trace of the creature. She could smell its body, like warm biscuits. But she had brought biscuits with her. Was she losing her mind? It had been a nightmarish ordeal and perhaps she had imagined the second animal-like baby and its sweet face and sounds, and the bloody mess it had made of its mother. There was nothing now. She must have picked up the cone and the twigs as she walked back from the hall and made it into the baby she had wanted it to be. That was the only thing that made sense. She was losing her mind or had hallucinated or dreamed the whole incident. She wanted to cry but could not.

There would be a reckoning today and she must tell her side of the story. She washed and dressed and prepared to face the men at the house. She was sure Davies had called someone and they would be sniffing around but Greaves would deal with them. It would be impossible to explain the second one, the creature she had abducted, the 'other' as she had to think of it, obviously a figment of her imagination. She washed her clothes in the butler sink struggling to clean the blood out. Then she hung them over the bushes in the back garden. When she felt composed, she walked up to the Hall, looking forward to tea and perhaps toast, her appetite returned, so that when she arrived, she looked pale but normal as she checked her reflection in the mirror.

Then she saw Farrell, his face stricken, leaving the chapel. They must have put the bodies in there, of course. He saw her.

'It was my wife. They say you tended to her. Thank you.'

Rosalyn started to cry. All the pathos of the previous night and the loss of the one good thing to come out of it overwhelmed her. She clung to him, weeping into his waistcoat, her nose running and great sobs accompanying copious tears. He held her and the noise brought Brent who seemed never to be far away. They took her into the chapel and eventually she was prised away from him and settled with tea and handkerchiefs. Davies and Greaves peered in but soon left. At last she regained self-control and was persuaded to look at the bodies, one peaceful in death, the other hidden in swaddling clothes.

She looked at Farrell.

'It wasn't my child,' he said.

With the clinical composure of a surgeon, or a butcher he opened the clothes of the swaddled child exposing the body, and turned it over revealing the terrible defects. They looked at it and the unspoken question lay between them. Was it human? Farrell wrapped it again when Greaves called them out to a meeting in the sitting room. Osgood and Claff had been summoned so everyone was present as he addressed them formally.

'Mrs Farrell travelled from London in her gravid state, no doubt suffering from an infection caused by the dead foetus and under the delusion that she would find her old home exactly as it was. Miss James, I am sure did her best, but childbirth is a dangerous experience and the poor woman died after delivering a stillborn.'

'Is it true that the kiddie was – abnormal?' asked Claff.

'There were a number of birth defects, yes.'

There was an awkward silence. Then Osgood spoke.

'Sir, I have to ask this. What I want to know is, was it monstrous, not human?'

Greaves looked at them one by one. Rosalyn looked away.

He said, 'You mean was it the product of a union between one of the greyfolk and a human woman?'

Claff and Osgood nodded vigorously, Davies had closed his eyes and might have been praying and Brent lit yet another cigarette. She looked at Farrell and he gazed back sorrowfully.

'It's possible.'

Osgood swore and began muttering angrily. Claff put a hand on his arm and Greaves continued.

'But not conclusive. The baby looked human but had deformities and that might be simply bad luck.' He quickly moved on. 'The relevant authorities have been informed and her body will be collected later today.'

'Will she be buried here?' asked Farrell.

'Ah, well we don't know just yet but I'm sure her remains can be brought back for interment in due course.'

'So they're gonna cut her up,' said Claff.

'A post-mortem will be performed as is usual in such matters.'

That seemed to settle things for the time being and after expressing their commiseration to Farrell the men went about their duties. Rosalyn said nothing, she was still unsure whether she had experienced some sort of hallucination. She couldn't tell Greaves that she had stolen the other baby, nor even why she'd done it. She was exhausted and tried to fortify herself with tea and avoided looking at or thinking about Farrell. Perhaps they suspected her of murder, Brent certainly had suspicions and he knew there was an attraction between Rosalyn and the gamekeeper. It made her feel uncomfortable that her innocence was in question in some way. She had only had a fleeting idea to let the woman die and she had done everything she could to help her. These thoughts were circling when Greaves came into the room.

'I've received instructions that we're to travel to London today. Collect your things. Brent will accompany us. We leave in half an hour.'

They want to interrogate me, she thought. They suspect something. But she nodded and went to the cottage to prepare for the journey. As she left the house a van went past her, no doubt to collect the remains of Mrs Farrell. She had been looking out for Farrell in the hope of saying goodbye, but now she hurried on with a dread of seeing him. At the cottage she couldn't help hoping for a sign that the little creature had been there but found only the sticks and the pinecone. Rosalyn put the pinecone into her bag.

5 HERMITAGE THEATRE

The sky was not quite so blue for the journey to London, high clouds obscured the sun, and shortly after they left there was a dog fight above them. The noise of the planes alerted the driver and he stopped so they could watch it. Rosalyn's stomach clenched as a Messerschmidt soared high and fell backwards to take position behind a Hurricane. It struggled to come out of the dive and this gave the British plane the chance to turn towards it and strafe it as it passed before him.

A dark stream of smoke came from the German, but they were too close and clipped wings. Brent and Greaves swore as both planes were disabled, and they prayed for the tell-tale parachutes to open. The tree cover was in the way, but they heard an explosion and saw a plume of black smoke.

'Which one?' asked Rosalyn.

'The Hun hopefully,' said Greaves. In the silence they could hear the sound of multiple large aircraft from some way to the southeast.

'The airfields again,' said Greaves.

'Dorniers,' said Brent and spat. 'Messerschmidts too obviously. They must have airfields close to the Channel to get this far inland.' He looked at Greaves. 'It's getting bad.' He paused then said, 'Did you hear Churchill on Sunday – 'Should the invader come to Britain there will be no placid lying down of the people in submission before him, as blah blah in other countries. We shall defend every village, every town, and every city'.'

'And so we will,' said Greaves.

'That's what I'm afraid of,' said Brent.

'Then we need to give them a bloody nose right now, so they think twice about invading. You're a damned defeatist,' said Greaves.

'I've been defeated once, so I know what it's like. I've no intention of surviving this war unless we win.'

They got back in the car and were driven to the railway station in Guildford. As always, the train was full, and they were obliged to stand most of the way. To take her mind off the hellish night Rosalyn squatted on the floor with many of the young men in uniform. They were playing cards and she quickly insinuated herself into the game by helping one young man who had not much of a clue. The others objected and they dealt her a hand. She ignored her companions until Greaves indicated his rank, pulled her from the game, and dragged her down the train. They were almost at Waterloo.

A taxi took them to Soho, to a small theatre frontage with red paint and coloured lights. The windows were criss-crossed with anti-blast tape and heavy blackout curtains hung behind. Greaves rattled the doors.

'They're locked. We'll have to use the stage door.'

He led them through an alley to a single door and a sharp rap brought an older man to peer out at them. He opened it when he saw Greaves's uniform and saluted.

'Come in Sir and you other two. I'm to get you some tea and put you in a dressing room. It's a long walk to the dressing room you've been allocated so I'll get that tea now sirs and miss.'

He obviously had a pot of hot strong tea in his little office because he almost immediately appeared with three mugs of the steaming brew, each one had been sweetened.

Greaves, Rosalyn, and Brent followed him through badly lit corridors until they were deep inside the theatre. For every set of stairs there seemed to be a door and a turn and a few more stairs so she could not understand how the old man found his way about. Her sense of direction was unable to adjust to the complexity of the building.

'I wish I'd brought a ball of string into this labyrinth,' muttered Brent.

'Let's hope there isn't a minotaur at the centre,' said Greaves.

'Funny you should mention minotaurs,' said the old man. 'A few years ago we did a play about the creature, written by Mr Loveday, he's usually stage manager, but he can turn his hand to just about anything. It was based on Greek stories, he said. We have such wonderful special effects in this theatre and somewhere in this building will be the minotaur. Well parts of him at least. I hope he doesn't come back to life, it was one of the scariest creatures I've ever seen and we've had lots of frighteners in this theatre. Vampires, Frankenstein's monster, the witches from the Scottish play, you know the one I mean. We do a lot of Shakespeare.'

How can he talk and walk so fast thought Rosalyn, trying not to spill her tea. When they were thoroughly lost, he opened a door and switched on a light.

'Here you are, your very own dressing room. There's a lav just down the corridor. Somebody will come and get you when they're ready for you.'

With that he ducked out, seeming not to expect a tip, such things were not forthcoming from actors it appeared. They stood in the windowless square room and took in the accommodation. There was a bed, two chairs and a long table in front of a mirror which had a row of bulbs above it. Greaves turned them on, and as it was too bright, he removed a couple of the bulbs.

'That'll do, I think. Anyone need to lie down? I'll have a chair but I'll recce the toilet first, make sure it's not too hard to find, don't want anyone getting lost.' He said with a pointed look at Rosalyn.

When they were alone Brent said, 'Are you alright? You're pale, and it must have been a terrible night.'

'I didn't kill her,' she said.

'Of course. It doesn't matter,' he took out his cigarettes. 'But that baby was monstrous.'

'Poor thing,' she said.

'Don't start crying again. Take the bed. There's a blanket. I'll put it over you and you can ignore Greaves when he returns. Pretend to be asleep.'

His consideration touched her, and she nodded, unable to speak and fearing tears. When Greaves returned, she was facing the wall and covered in a blanket. They both lit cigarettes, despite the lack of ventilation, and spoke in hushed tones about the plan for the evening once they had handed her over. She was like a package, like a hostage, she thought.

Sleep would not come and to soothe herself she thought of her day with Farrell in the idyllic woodland and the pool, the sunshine, wild blackberries, his touch on her hair, his kiss, and the smell of his warm skin. Then she wanted to cry so she thought about today's journey by train and taxi and the people they'd encountered.

In London there were men and women carrying gas masks, not to do so would mean a fine. Brightly coloured clothes seemed to have virtually disappeared overnight and been replaced by hardwearing wools and tweeds. She saw several queues for food shops, presumably they'd taken delivery of off-ration goods, possibly luxuries.

There were men in uniform everywhere, not just the armed services but fire wardens and policemen. All windows were taped to reduce glass fragments, slit trenches had been dug in parks, and sandbags were ready in streets for use against blasts. Sirens and barrage balloons loomed over the city streets.

Her breathing slowed and, with the panic of self-pity quelled, Rosalyn thought about her father. Was he still living in London or away in Wales as they'd said? She wondered if she would ever see him, or her brothers, again. She wished she had been able to visit and say goodbye but that would have been impossible given the restrictions imposed on them all. She sat up.

'I take it we're not locked in. I'd like to visit the lavatory.'

Greaves stood. 'I'll show you the way.'

He accompanied her and waited outside. When they returned to the dressing room a man was in the doorway speaking to Brent. Greaves was obviously acquainted with the newcomer and introduced him as Dee's assistant and stage manager, Mr Loveday.

His voice was high and slightly metallic.

'You can't see him or Lord Agremont today.'

'You promised me we'd be able to negotiate with him this time,' said Greaves quietly as they crowded into the small room.

'The seolfor still operate a feudal system and he must pass everything to Lord Faerie,' said Loveday. 'And Faerie behaves as though he's a king,'

The man shrugged and turned his back, Greaves grabbed him and spun him round.

'Don't turn your back on me, Loveday. I have instructions from Churchill, and I will not accept any further delays.'

Rosalyn was surprised at his anger.

Loveday raised his arms.

'I surrender Lieutenant. Don't take it out on me. He wasn't always like that. He changed when that man Osgood hexed him.'

'I don't blame Osgood. Your nasty little parties took liberties with the local women.'

Loveday seemed to notice Rosalyn for the first time.

'Not in front of the lady.'

He tried to move towards her, but Greaves stood in his way, and he stopped, but drank in her presence with his gaze.

She was fascinated. She found him repulsive but interesting, and for the first time it occurred to her that he might not be human.

'It was the others.' Loveday did not take his eyes from her.

'You were the facilitator,' Greaves said. 'A procurer, a pimp. You deserved the curse as much as Dee.'

'I just do as I'm told. He was the one who enjoyed holding court with members of the company – you know what they're like: actors, writers, painters, and other artistic types.'

His voice was wheedling, and his bland, golden eyed face appeared hurt by Greaves's comment on his role in the affairs at Pitdown, but it was a mask. Rosalyn judged him deceitful and cynical. She felt sure that inwardly he was calm and in control. Greaves on the other hand had overstepped the mark and needed to backtrack quickly.

His flash of righteous anger had betrayed him, and she knew he had to find a way to restart the negotiations ordered by the Prime Minister. There seemed to be no option except through Loveday.

As though sensing this he smiled, all the time looking at Rosalyn and she knew he had specifically asked for her.

He said, 'Nobody forced those women, they loved the glamour and excitement. They chose to be seduced and to come to London with us.'

Greaves's ears turned red, but he forced himself to apologise.

'Sorry, I can see that you were following orders. But now we have ascertained that greyfolk exist we cannot go back without trying to find a way to bring them into this war on our side.' His tone was measured and he tried to hide his disgust.

Brent spoke for the first time.

'Have they chosen a side? I'm certain the Nazis have their own mission to persuade the fae to join them.'

Loveday took his predatory eyes off Rosalyn.

'The seolfor are slippery in all their dealings and very secretive. I have not been appraised of their current position. Initially they wanted humankind to destroy itself and could see only benefits from another world war.'

'He was persuaded to actively deal with humans by Lord Agremont and Doctor Dee.'

Brent said, 'The greyfolk of Spain had no love for the kings of Madrid yet they would not assist the republicans to oppose the fascists. It wouldn't surprise me if the fae were already hand in glove with Hitler.'

Greaves shot him a warning look.

Loveday shrugged. 'There are greyfolk all over the world except in the arctic regions. They each have their own customs and relationships with local people. Many have not changed for millennia. I can't speak for the fae of Europe but the ones of these islands will make their decision independently and they now wish to be called seolfor.'

'I don't care what they call themselves. I need to speak with them now,' said Greaves. 'Can you arrange it?'

'Because I am a facilitator? A procurer?' said Loveday and enjoyed the look of discomfort on

Greaves's face. 'I will do my best. In the meantime, you will stay here.'

'How long?'

'Time means little to them, it could be an hour, a day or a week.'

Greaves said, 'Miss James should be accommodated separately for form's sake.'

Loveday smiled lasciviously, or so it seemed to Rosalyn.

'That can be arranged. Remain here and someone will come for her.' He left.

Rosalyn suddenly panicked at the thought of being separated from her human companions. They had not treated her well, but they were flesh and blood. Goodness knew what sort of monsters roamed the corridors of this theatre and where she would be taken.

In the windowless dressing room they sat morosely waiting for Rosalyn to be removed. When no one came, Greaves and Brent ignored her and discussed Dee and his mental state.

'What the hell is Dee playing at? He offered to broker the deal. How can he exercise influence over the bloody creatures? What does this new name 'seolfor' mean anyway?'

'I suspect it means silver,' said Brent. 'The metal is sacred to them, unlike iron which they hate.'

'We'll have to rely on Loveday then. Is he even human? Did you see the colour of his eyes? And his skin is almost reptilian, made my flesh crawl.'

'He was human once, probably, but he's spent too long with greyfolk and away from his kind. I wonder what the rest of the theatre company's like?'

They jumped when there was a gentle tap on the door. It opened and an elderly dark-skinned woman looked in and pointed at Rosalyn. She said nothing but when Rosalyn picked up her bag and made to follow Greaves grabbed her roughly.

'You know the rules. You've signed the official secrets act, if you talk it will be treason and punishable by death.'

'Let me go. Don't take your frustration out on me.'

She knew he was angry, but she was desperate and at that moment made the decision to escape.

They glared at each other. She tried to prise his fingers from her arm, and Brent stood to intervene. The small woman managed to get between them and was pushed aside in the tussle. The distraction enabled Rosalyn to pull his hand away and flee. She shut the door, noticed a key on the outside and turned it. They were locked in, and she ran.

*

The corridor was dimly lit and gave no indication of an exit. Knowing they would soon break out she turned a corner as soon as possible and kept turning, hoping she would not be faced with a dead end. Then the grimy linoleum floors and painted brick walls ended, and she could hear Greaves calling her name. The only exit was an unpainted wooden door and she prayed it wouldn't be locked. She gently turned the latch as quietly as she could, looking back for fear the pursuers would appear. It was dark but she slipped through and in silence she closed it behind her and waited.

Rosalyn could hear nothing in the embracing darkness. All the sounds of the theatre had gone. She was aware that the floor sloped away from her but had no idea what would be under each step. Even the sound of her breathing, laboured from the chase seemed muted. She squatted and waited until her heart rate had slowed. No one burst through the door. She couldn't hear them.

She was free, but where? On trembling legs she stood, orienting herself by feeling the wall on her right. Even with her partially enhanced vision she would have to rely on touch to make any progress and she gingerly reached one foot in front of the other, anticipating at any time the floor might become stairs or a precipice.

After a dozen or so steps she noticed a faint glow ahead and felt a lurch of relief that was quickly followed by a sick recollection of the caretaker's story of a minotaur. Surely that was just a play, and the real worry was that she might find herself in the realm of the greyfolk. The attraction of light was too much to resist, and she slowly progressed down to a small chamber stacked with boxes, some of which were covered with cloths. The source of the light was a single electric bulb. No magic, she thought with relief.

The boxes were wooden and painted in a Victorian circus style with rope handles but were now dirty and broken. Rosalyn walked round them to another larger double door and listened for voices. It seemed safe so she opened one of them and looked into a much larger vaulted chamber, again lit by electric light. It was lined with cages.

She sniffed but could smell no animals and the cages contained cots and small chairs and tables as though they were designed to hold humans. Rosalyn shuddered. What unnatural experiments were being carried out here? She moved through the vast space and then heard a murmur of voices and found the entrance to a corridor that lay in darkness.

With all her courage she entered the space and the sounds became more clear. There were women talking. Perhaps they were human, or perhaps fae but she was encouraged by the thought that they might help her. There was laughter and a few snatches of music as someone tuned a radio. They must be human she thought and then heard a well-known jazz orchestra and decided to find a way into them. That is if she could locate a door. The dark wall was clean and firm to her touch but there was no sign of a handle. She was just about to call out to them when a soft hand covered her mouth. There was a floral fragrance.

'Don't say anything Rosalyn. I will tell you everything, but you must come with me.'

She knew that the small woman had found her and the gentleness of her voice and touch convinced Rosalyn to nod and allow herself to be led away.

As they hurried up numerous stairs and corridors, she wanted to ask questions but clearly it was necessary to make no sound. They made several stops as they climbed, to get their breath and to pick up supplies from the bar and a sort of tearoom. They had arrived in a light and airy office decorated in pink and gold and were, she reckoned, right at the top of the building.

The woman beckoned her to come over to the window and Rosalyn looked through the taped panes over rooftops to the west where the sun was blazing in a sky of heavy clouds that could have been painted by Michelangelo. The glow in the room lifted her spirits and she sat in one of the chairs, also gilt and pink fabric, got her breath back and looked carefully at the other woman. She was perhaps middle eastern, and her hair was completely white in a thick plait down her back. She wore a tabard over a long skirt and had sandals on her feet. She made tea for them.

Rosalyn said, 'You helped me escape, didn't you?'

The woman nodded, smiling. 'They shouldn't have dragged you into this. If you take my advice, we will get you well away and you need not be part of this experiment.'

'I want to know who was in that room. Where you found me.' Rosalyn said. A terrible idea had entered her mind. 'Are they the women who were taken from Pitdown?'

Rosalyn wondered if they had really gone willingly. The chatter had seemed light-hearted. Then she remembered the room she had shared with a woman screaming in pain and pumping out blood as she gave birth to something monstrous. And what was the other chamber and the cages? What were they for if not to imprison the babies and their mothers? She faced what she had always suspected. It must be a terrible crossbreeding experiment of human and greyfolk.

'What are the cages for?' She persisted.

The woman placed a cup of tea in front of Rosalyn and sat down.

'The women came to London when the master and his entourage moved here in November. They weren't forced to leave their homes but no doubt there was a certain amount of non-human glamour that influenced them. They are content for the moment.'

'And the cages. What are they for?'

She looked shrewdly at Rosalyn. 'Loveday told me that Mrs Farrell died in childbirth.'

'But it wasn't a child, was it? I saw it. I was there. It was monstrous, and it was dead.'

Rosalyn debated whether to tell this strange woman about the other baby, the small, kittenish thing and its appealing eyes and mewling and snuffling mouth. How she had longed to keep it and to love it. Then how it had changed into sticks overnight. She remembered the pinecone in her bag and had to stop herself from looking in its direction. This woman would miss nothing.

'Mrs Farrell was the first woman to fall pregnant. She became very ill and they brought a doctor to the theatre to see her, fearing it was pre-eclampsia. She was afraid and managed to escape. We should have guessed she would try and go home.'

'She wanted her husband to look after her.'

'Of course, it's only natural. How did she die?'

'She bled to death.'

The woman frowned and Rosalyn took the opportunity to ask about the other women.

'Are they all pregnant from intercourse with greyfolk?'

She nodded.

'Can I meet them?'

'It would be better if you didn't,' the woman said with concern. 'Their fate is set now, it cannot be avoided, and they came here willing.'

'But I'm not willing. So why am I here?'

'I will explain it all to you but please, take some food.'

Rosalyn realised she had eaten nothing since breakfast. She took a piece of bread and butter; it tasted so good and stimulated her appetite, so she listened.

'I know you are Rosalyn James,' the woman said. 'And I am so very pleased to meet you. My name is Mariel McKinley, and we have a connection, you and I.'

She told Rosalyn how she had joined a travelling theatre group as a seamstress when she was fourteen. How it was run by Doctor John Dee, a man who had lived many hundreds of years and whose actors and actresses also had the gift of unnaturally long life.

The company used puppets in their Shakespeare plays, but they were not made of wood and cloth but were living faeries. They had been sold into servitude by their lord in exchange for a human soul to be provided every seven years by Dee. The soul was then paid to an older power by Lord Faerie as a tithe. The tithe enabled the fae to maintain their realm of bucolic peace and tranquillity.

Rosalyn said, 'I keep hearing about this man, Dee, but no one has explained how he could have lived so long.'

'He was an alchemist at the time of Queen Elizabeth and he discovered a stone that enables a man to live beyond a normal span.'

As the afternoon passed Mariel described the time she spent with the 'boskies', as she used to call the greyfolk, and how they were old and yet quite childlike in many ways. They were very different from their lord and master whom they called Lord Faerie. The boskies were freed from their slavery to John Dee by the efforts of three men and she had married one of them. His name was Robert McKinley.

For his part in returning the old fae to their home he had made Doctor Dee his enemy but during their marriage they had not encountered Dee again. Robert and Mariel had three children and were happy until his death from typhoid in 1897. Life had not been easy, they lived on his earnings as a portrait painter and at his death the savings soon ran out.

She was tired of the struggles of life in those times and the prejudice they had faced after their marriage against her race and class. The world of the fae seemed to be a world of colour and beauty and the simplicity of a bygone age.

'But you left your children behind when you went to the fae.'

'They were grown up, Rosalyn. My eldest son had died, and his wife had remarried. They were kind to my granddaughter Alice, and I knew she would be well provided for, but the colour of my skin was a reminder to everyone of my lowly birth. I told them I was going to India to seek my 'other' family. Sometimes I visited her in secret and watched from a distance and did the same with your father. I have seen you and your brothers on several occasions.'

Rosalyn put aside her plate.

'But the years go by so very quickly with the greyfolk and I realised that it is a life of pretence and glamour,' Mariel said.

'What do you mean by 'glamour?'

'It is deception by magic.'

Rosalyn said, 'My father's mother was called Alice and I seem to remember her maiden name was McKinley. Are you --?'

'I am your grandmother's grandmother.'

Rosalyn felt her face drain of blood as she struggled to come to terms with the idea that one of her great great grandmothers was sitting in front of her. They stood up at the same time and Mariel held out her arms. But Rosalyn was wary.

'How do I know what you tell me is true?'

Mariel said, 'I thought you might be sceptical, so I've brought photographs.' She removed an envelope from her pocket and laid three photographs on the table. One of them was an old sepia daguerreotype and showed Mariel with a stocky middle-aged man. 'This is my Robert. And this is your grandmother Alice with your father as a little boy. Here is my son John with his wife Ruth.'

The people in the photographs were familiar to Rosalyn and she could see the resemblance. They sat side by side on the sofa looking at the images.

'What about your other children?'

Mariel sighed.

'My daughter died in childbirth and the baby soon afterwards and my little boy became a soldier and died abroad.'

'I'm sorry,' Rosalyn said. She had a jarring memory of the pain and death of the woman at Pitdown the previous day. It seemed so long ago. And she had to remember that this happened fifty or sixty years ago. 'How have you lived so long? You are alive, aren't you? I mean, you're warm and solid.' She touched her shoulder.

'A night spent in the glamour of the seolfor's world is equivalent to seven years in the human world. I looked like this when I went in. It was so different that coming back was a shock. London was dirty and grey in 1899 but there were horses and carts. Now it is machine ridden, so full of iron and smoke,' said Mariel.

'I wish I'd known you. Mother died when I was two, from the Spanish flu. Father never remarried, she was the love of his life,' said Rosalyn.

'And your mother was a Jewess who 'married out' so her own family were not supportive. You were all sent away to your aunt's house with her farmer husband, or to boarding school. Where you misbehaved,' said Mariel.

'Just a minute. If you know so much about me then you must be aware before that I was taken from a cousin's house when I was only two years old. And returned by a brown skinned woman. Was that you?'

'You remember that? I thought you were too young to be fully aware of it.'

'Someone found out and told me,' Rosalyn said. 'Did you take me? It caused grief and I do remember lots of people and auntie crying. That was cruel.'

'I did not take you, my dear. There is something you must understand. The female seolfor of all types are not fertile. It is a source of great distress and is one of the reasons they spend so much time in the hidden realm.'

'Is this the reason for the cross-breeding experiment?'

'Yes. The proliferation of iron in your world makes them sick. Some fae hope that they can breed a resilience into the race.'

It took Rosalyn a few minutes to absorb this and she felt sympathy with a species that was in danger of extinction, especially if it was because of human industrial proliferation.

Mariel continued. 'A seolfor female wanted a baby. Your cousin lived in a country populated by all types of fae and one saw an opportunity.'

'But you got me back?'

'I have contacts with the lower kind of seolfor, the artisans I suppose you might call them. They're physically different from the lords and warrior class. Much more practical and sympathetic. They've lived alongside country folk for millennia with tolerance and affection.'

'What would have happened to me?'

'From what I have seen you would have been a sort of pet, spending time either in the real world of fae or the dream-time world.'

Rosalyn said, 'There are two worlds?'

'Sadly, the dream-time world is becoming more popular as the modern human world becomes uncomfortable. Dream-time is bliss, euphoria, like an opiate, but it comes at a price, and one night costs seven human years.'

'You have partaken of this, haven't you?'

'I have had six nights in the dream-time and it cost me forty-two years in your world.'

'It was lucky you were awake to rescue me,' said Rosalyn.

'Luck had nothing to do with it. I was woken by a fae I have known a long time. His name is Gilgoreth and he still lives among farming folk. Though for how long I cannot say. Horses being replaced by tractors.' Mariel shook her head.

'What else can you tell me about the seolfor,' said Rosalyn.

'They've inhabited the earth for millions of years and have coexisted with primitive man, at first on equal terms and then by hiding and exploiting men's greed when it suited them. Only in the last three hundred years have they begun to fear for their very existence. They're in decline, Rosalyn. Their powers wane and many live in small illusions of their own history, rural and bucolic.

Nostalgic. I call it a dreamtime. Lord Faerie encourages it.'

'Is he prepared to help us fight the Nazis?'

There was silence.

'I very much doubt it,' said Mariel, eventually.

'Brent says the Spanish fae supported the fascists and didn't like the idea of a republic. He says they're a feudal people,' said Rosalyn.

'Fortunately Britain has a royal family and if they stay here and lead their people then it might be enough --' Mariel looked down at her brown wrinkled hands.

'You don't believe that,' said Rosalyn. 'Why are you here?'

'I have lived a hundred and ten years in human terms. I once worked for an old man who said that to live a long life can have the effect of etiolating your soul, stretching it thin. I don't want that to happen to me, and you, my kin, are in mortal danger.'

'Danger from interbreeding with something not human?'

'I'm sorry you had to see that woman's death. It doesn't always end like that.'

'I've been told that Dee wants revenge,' said Rosalyn.

'Your brothers are out of his reach in the forces and your father is in Wales.'

'What are they going to do to me?'

'There are many different factions existing within the fae world, not to mention the humans that have been corrupted by their involvement with greyfolk. Some want to help Britain and others only see it as a way to gain an advantage. The proposal to breed mixed race beings has divided the seolfor community. The lower folk are opposed to it and the higher races, more human-like themselves, are in favour as a way of achieving power over humans. The fertility of all the seolfor has suffered. They spend much time remembering and dreaming of past glory and delights.'

'Are there such things as surviving hybrids already in existence?' said Rosalyn, thinking of Farrell and what she had been told about his origins.

'They do exist, not changelings, that was only ever a rumour to cover the unfortunate death of an infant, but real love matches, or sometimes rapes, have occurred. The progeny usually have an unhappy time not fitting into either the human or the fae world.'

'Changing their name to seolfor,' said Rosalyn. 'What prompted that?'

'If they are to live side by side with humans they must be taken seriously and they want more recognition than that given to the creatures of fairy stories only children believe in,' said Mariel.

They looked at each other for a long while. Rosalyn wondered how it must be to live two lifetimes in two separate worlds. Then it occurred to her that Mariel was already from two worlds, she was mixed race.

'And was Dee happy to see you again after all these years?'

Mariel laughed. 'He doesn't recognise me. I'm an elderly servant, with white hair. Loveday would be a different matter, he's as sharp as a razor, but he didn't know me in 1848. That was the year he volunteered to surrender his soul as Lord Faerie's sacrifice, which was fortunate or it would have been either Robert or me.'

'So he is human?'

'He was, but subtle changes have been worked on him. He has ingratiated himself with the seolfor and Doctor Dee in equal measure. We cannot trust him.'

'What will happen now?'

'The Pitdown women you found in the basement will give birth soon,' said Mariel.

Rosalyn shook her head in disgust. 'The cages. They are for…'

'The offspring and possibly their mothers. As a precaution.'

*

Rosalyn imagined the women in their gilded cage, expecting – what – to be cherished when they gave birth? They were the subjects of experiments like so many animals. Perhaps that's how the seolfor saw them.

Her mind flashed back to the discussion about the minotaur in the labyrinth. The minotaur was a punishment by the gods and the product of unnatural love by a woman for a bull. Those women had been bewitched to think themselves in love with creatures that were not human.

'I won't submit to that,' she said. 'I'd rather die.'

Perhaps they expect to have human babies. That would be the glamour of their seduction. Surely Mrs Farrell's death would wake people to the hideous reality of their likely fate.

'What do they think will happen when they give birth? Has it been explained to them?' She knew it was unlikely. 'Do they have any idea what sort of creatures are growing inside them?'

Mariel stared at Rosalyn. Had she stupidly revealed that there were two babies? She kept cool and stared back. It could be taken as referring to the multiple women.

'I have been told they all willingly slept with their suitors, some of whom were seolfor of a human type and all handsome and well-made. If they even thought about pregnancy they had no reason to think the progeny would not be tall, beautiful, and intelligent. They are not aware of the true nature of their lovers.'

'Even Mrs Farrell?'

Mariel replied with a dark anger. 'I understand that if they didn't show signs of being with child then other forms of fae were allowed to enter their beds. It was at night under cover of darkness and with the aid of glamour. Their dreams would have been filled with erotic pleasure; eventually all the women conceived.'

'How can you bear to be part of this?' Rosalyn stood up. 'You're as bad as they are.'

'I wasn't here then. I only entered the service of Dee when I heard from Gilgoreth that you were to be brought here and forcibly impregnated by Lord Agremont. I could not allow that to happen. That was when I found out about the other poor souls.'

'So Agremont is one of them.'

'Of course. You have one anointed eye, I think, so you'll be able to see them if they are near.'

They sat glumly contemplating the deception and the trap awaiting Rosalyn.

Mariel said, 'Do you have anywhere safe to go if I can get you out of the theatre?'

Rosalyn thought about the home where her father might be, but Greaves had told her he was now in Wales. She shook her head, then remembered her best friend from school who was working as a forestry girl near Winchester. She had been a rebel too and they had bunked off as much as possible and ridden their ponies bareback to escape the strict school regime they both hated.

'Perhaps, if I can get to Winchester.'

'I have money,' said Mariel. 'You take a taxi to Waterloo Station and then the train to Winchester and call your friend or get a bus to her residence. You'll be safe in London and on the train, there are so many troops moving about. But then you must hide.'

'She works in a forest and there are bound to be hiding places nearby.' She paused. 'But won't that put her in danger?'

'Possibly, but I'll find out where your father is and write to you. Then you'll have to make your way to him.'

She wrote down her friend's address. Then Rosalyn and Mariel hugged each other.

Looking steadily into her eyes, the older woman said, 'If I can arrange it would you consider going to ground with the fae?'

'Seven years out of this world?'

'It may not be possible. Don't get your hopes up.'

'I can't think about that. It's all too soon.'

'A route to join your father then?'

Rosalyn nodded. 'Will you get into trouble for letting me go?'

'They won't suspect me, and I have a plan to occupy them that will take their minds off you,' said Mariel. She looked at the low afternoon sun. 'We haven't long. Here is about twenty pounds.' She gave Rosalyn a leather bag with a few notes and a lot of smaller change. From a larger bag she took out a light duster coat and a hat that would shade most of Rosalyn's face. She put them on and they left the pretty little room at the top of the theatre. She followed Mariel down a different set of stairs and they emerged into a plush but shabby foyer. It was empty and she opened the side door.

'Will I see you again?' said Rosalyn.

'I hope not,' said the older woman and held her face for a long look.

'What will you do?'

'I'm going to take the pregnant ladies out for the evening. We'll go dancing. They'll like that.'

'Be careful,' said Rosalyn.

'Always. And you.'

She closed the door behind her.

6 ST JUDE'S

Rosalyn's journey across London on such a beautiful Summer evening was sweet and sorrowful in her memory. People bustled about carrying parcels and gas masks, and everywhere there were sandbags and men in uniform organising the city for the night ahead. She looked through the taxi window trying to see and remember it all. Her home was so familiar and yet so changed, and for the first time she felt different too. The Victorian and Georgian architecture above the shops and places of business seemed so vulnerable. Between them were older and occasionally medieval houses that had survived the great fire of London. For the first time she noticed a few people who did not fit, who did not move like the others, and she wondered if they were seolfor going about their business.

Waterloo Station was filled with hurrying passengers, and she caught a commuter train. There were bowler hatted men who bustled into first class carriages, and elegant ladies who carried their shopping like trophies. She stayed in third class and hid amongst the cigarette smoke in the dirty seats. It was late when she disembarked in Winchester and, looking around the station, was reminded of the first time she saw Brent, just a few weeks ago.

It was a beautiful city, with its Norman Cathedral, and Rosalyn remembered it had once been the capital of King Alfred's Wessex. Under his reign the Vikings had been halted in their invasion of Britain. Davies's comments about the Nazis' affinity with the Nordic

Aryan culture made her wonder if it would always be a struggle between tribes.

At the station there was an empty Ladies' Waiting Room, quiet and solemn in its nicotine-stained walls and wooden benches. It was stuffy but reassuringly familiar and she gratefully sat down. Being alone she lay on a bench and rested her head on the bag, hoping for some sleep.

She woke when a couple of ATS girls came in chatting excitedly and smoking. They exchanged polite hellos and Rosalyn closed her eyes again. At last they could not resist including her in their conversation. Resistance was futile and she sat up.

'Have a ciggie. No?'

'She's a land girl, aren't you?' said a bright blonde with heavily teased hair. 'Recognised the trousers. I do really like your coat though. It's a lovely colour and suits you.'

'Thank you,' said Rosalyn, smiling and engaging fully with them because she had no choice. 'Where are you stationed?'

They laughed.

'We could tell you, but then we'd have to kill you.'

Rosalyn thought about the ways of killing she had learnt at Pitdown and mentally weighed them up. A savage blow, delivered without mercy, to each face would stop them, she decided. Little noses are so fragile when the attack is not anticipated. She felt sick. She thought about the pregnant women and what horror awaited them, and to her embarrassment started to cry.

Their response was immediate and sisterly. They put their arms around and comforted her with 'there, there,' and 'would you like a cup of tea'. The café was still open so the mousey girl went to fetch the all-sustaining beverage and Rosalyn knew what they were both thinking. She'd got herself into trouble.

'Is it a man, dear?' the blonde said.

Rosalyn shook her head.

'They're not worth it. Has he taken advantage of you?' she continued.

Rosalyn wished he had. She longed for Farrell's touch, she wished he had taken her to bed and that she would not be a virgin for Agremont to have for himself. She blew her nose.

'It is a man, but no I'm not in trouble, just hurt and lost at the moment.'

'Have you got somewhere to go? We'll be travelling on tomorrow. They told us to get off here and stay the night so we can keep you company. Are you running away?' she asked after a short pause.

'Yes, I suppose I am,' said Rosalyn.

The other girl returned with a pot of tea and three cups.

'You haven't told her about Dorchester? Have you?' she said.

'Well, I don't need to now do I? Anyway she's in the services just like us.'

'We'll serve in the NAAFI,' said the mousy girl. 'If we're lucky we might find ourselves in the officers' mess.'

They laughed conspiratorially.

'Are you running away from a man or to a man?'

Rosalyn thought about it and wasn't sure. She felt the intoxication of love for Farrell. What she knew of him she liked, and she did not want to be part of a breeding experiment with the fae.

'Both,' she said. 'And I really can't tell you any more than that.'

'Or you'll have to kill us,' they chorused.

She didn't laugh and thought that if she didn't kill them then someone else might. They calmed down and drank their tea quietly and smoked until by mutual agreement they took a bench each and slept as well as they could.

Rosalyn woke in the night and thought she saw a grey face peering through the door glass. Ladies' Waiting Rooms were sacrosanct and usually no man would enter but she did not think it was a man. Was it friend or foe? If Mariel had informed her 'boskies' about the seolfor's intentions regarding Rosalyn then perhaps they were looking out for her. But if it was an agent of Agremont then the ATS girls also might be in danger. She decided to leave as soon as there was light to see her way. At dawn she gathered her bag and crept out of the waiting room without waking the other women.

Thursday 29 August 1940

She left the station and walked quickly down through the empty city streets to the branch line that ran under St Giles Hill. It came out on the east side of Winchester in the direction of the forest where her friend was working. Rosalyn's uncle's farm was on the opposite side of the city, closer to the River Test. With Mariel's coat and slouch hat she didn't expect to be recognised but farm folk were up and about very early especially where dairy work was involved. By knocking on the back door of a bakery she managed to buy a loaf.

Rosalyn boarded a train at the little station, travelled through the St Giles Hill tunnel and left at the next stop. She intended to walk the rest of the way to Stansham, a village she had visited only once when a child. Before petrol was rationed a 'drive' into the countryside on a Sunday was a treat. Father had taken Rosalyn and her brothers to see the standing stone and the old church of St Jude on its lonely hill.

She hadn't liked it much, the surrounding yew trees made it dark and oppressive. She and her brothers were fascinated by the story of a murdered child found in the churchyard well in the middle ages. Her father explained the authorities had blamed the killing on local Jews and that this was known as the 'blood libel'. They were too young to appreciate the significance of this but relished the idea that Passover bread might be made with the blood of little Christian children. It was just one of the many injustices meted out on minorities in those cruel times.

Rosalyn thought about the injustices meted out on the other side of the channel right now and that not much had changed, despite the passing years. The railway didn't go as far as Stansham but, hazy in the far distance, she could see the ring of yew trees that surrounded the church. She would walk along the green roads between protecting hedges and then along the ridgeway of the downs.

She nibbled on the crust of her bread as she walked but felt desperately thirsty. Did she dare ask for water from one of the cottages along her way? She decided there was no choice, and an old woman obligingly provided a cup and finding a friendly soul soon began telling her all the gossip especially that concerning the Women's Land Army and Forestry workers.

The local farms were mainly sheep on downland, though Rosalyn expected as much as possible was now down to wheat and the land girls were hard at work harvesting. It made her feel useless and guilty. Was it wrong of her to avoid the allotted duty to serve her country? After all, she had signed up for it.

She trudged on, having willingly paid for cold meat and salad onions from the cottager and regretfully declined the chance of taking a rabbit with her. The old woman's son kept her provided with game it appeared. How different this country life was from the smoke and iron of London and other manufacturing cities. It was as though there were two different countries; but they were fighting one war and needed to be one people, united in that struggle to stand any chance of survival.

As a member of a special auxiliary unit Rosalyn knew her presence was a danger to everyone she met. Her secret knowledge, so potentially lethal now, might be unimportant in seven years' time. If there was a chance to enter the dream-time world of the fae perhaps it would be better to take it rather than endanger her friend and her father.

The South Downs were gentle slopes, but the chalky ground was baked hard, and the open aspect provided little respite from the sun. At least towards the top of a hill there was a breeze from the north. Rosalyn realised she was on the highest point of the western edge of the downs and could see many miles in both directions. She allowed herself another rest and marvelled at the natural amphitheatre created by the escarpment. It was exhilarating to be free, and she ate her lunch listening to a skylark singing high above. She lay back and tried to spot it against the blue dome and might have dozed if the sound of planes hadn't woken her.

From the south a formation of five bombers and seven fighters were approaching at a great height. Then, from the southeast Spitfires and Hurricanes appeared. At first it seemed they would be going further; then the noise increased, and the bombers began to dive. Her first sight of the enemy in all-out war. The noise was awful.

The planes, she was certain now they were Stukas, flipped sideways and plunged vertically with screaming sirens. Surely, they would crash into the ground, or into the intended target? Almost at the last minute they released their bombs and pulled up.

It was on a small station to the north of Winchester. She thought it might be Micheldever. It must be a target of importance or why would they take the risk of a daylight raid? If it was arms or a fuel dump, she expected the explosions to be followed by a much bigger blast. The attack appeared to have been futile and her attention was transferred to the aerial battle between the fighters.

The Spitfires had broken away from the formation and were attacking the Messerschmidt ME 109s that had accompanied the bombers. The Hurricanes focussed their attack on the bombers as they pulled out of the dive and began climbing again. One of the slower German planes was struck. As the Hurricane pulled out a German fighter strafed it and a burst of smoke indicated that it too had taken a hit. Rosalyn cried out and watched as a parachute opened, showing the pilot had escaped. She didn't see what happened to the German crew but there were two more parachutes and an explosion as it crashed.

Having dropped their bombs the other Stukas were heading home, but not without more attacks by the British planes. Rosalyn's attention was torn between them the aerial dogfight between the ME 109s and Spitfires in the sky overhead. Her heart was beating hard and anxiety flooded every turn and burst of gunfire.

As the bombers roared away south, they were harried by the Hurricanes. But they returned fire and one of the British fighters produced smoke then broke off and flew away to land somewhere. A Messerschmidt fighter was caught by a short burst from a Spitfire and burst into flames. There was no parachute. Rosalyn felt both exultation and grief.

The whole group went southeast with occasional bursts of gunfire, and she watched them from her vantage point as they flew out over the Channel.

The target of the raid in Micheldever seemed to have suffered little harm, the few fires, evidenced by smoke were soon extinguished and the quiet of the English countryside returned. But the sky was peppered with drifts of aerial vapour, like dirty grey clouds, and smell was now of modern warfare. To the south the burning wreck of the German fighter threw up a filthy column of smoke. At least the pilot of the Hurricane had survived and managed to land his plane. To the north the wreck of the Stuka burned and local troops from the Winchester barracks would be on their way to round up survivors.

*

The sky was so big, the battle so swift and savage, that she was again worried about this course of action. Fleeing from the task her country had asked of her, might not be the right one. Those young pilots, her age, had been called upon to defend Britain against an enemy she knew was the embodiment of evil. Her feelings towards the Germans were more confusing. Were they all Nazis? Did they believe in the ideology that says their race is superior to all others? Or were they young men who had been called to serve their country and did so out of duty. It didn't matter, she decided, they were here and that made them the enemy. Rosalyn returned to her journey and left the ridge of the downs for a wooded path to the east and to the church Mariel had suggested as a place of safety.

In that state of emotional conflict Rosalyn entered a dense woodland in a valley and the path became narrow and the air quiet during the midday resting time for birds. Her feet were sore, and she was hot and had bundled the coat and hat into her bag. The woods looked so uniform and overgrown that she might be walking in circles. The sun was not visible and she hoped she was heading in the right direction.

The beauty of this land, she decided, lay in its contrasts. Lush green woodland was less than half a mile from the exposed bare downland. It was gentle and sweet smelling, and she began to relax, enjoying the fresh fragrance of leaf and growing things in the humid air.

So it was a shock when a building appeared before her, as though in camouflage, and she approached with caution. It was made of wood, painted green, and Rosalyn briefly wondered if this might be an auxiliary unit's hideout. But surely, they were below ground? It was not some organic thing, yet it blended into the surroundings. As she studied it, she noticed the cross on the top and realised it was a tiny church hidden in the woods. From the path recently trodden, it was clearly still in use.

Perhaps it had belonged to a persecuted religious minority in earlier years. Then she thought back to a time when attendance at church on a Sunday was expected and it would be convenient to have a local chapel. Also, if you worked on the land, it might be essential in a rural community as a way of meeting your neighbours. A country life could be very isolated and, at a time when there were no wirelesses, how would you know what was happening in the world? I'd like that life, she thought. Ignore the world and its chaos. That's what the fae do.

She opened the door and entered the cool building. There was an odour of old wood and polish, an oddly reassuring sensation, like home or school, and there were flowers that had been there a few days their petals crinkled and the scent old and decaying. She sat gratefully in a pew and looked about. The simplicity of the place of worship was beguiling and honest. Homely touches, the hymn books were tied together with a cloth and the little windows were clean, convincing her that women had prepared it. There was nothing pompous about the chapel.

The pinecone that had been left in the place of the baby was in her bag and she took it out, turning it in her hands and wondering what she had held in her arms on that bloody night of trouble.

There was an urgency about the air battle she'd witnessed and a feeling of her own unimportance that prompted Rosalyn to say a prayer for all the people she knew who were in danger. Although not religious, she closed her eyes and put her palms together in the conventional way. Even this simple act provoked a question. Why do we pray like this? Recent military training suggested that it would be impossible to do it while holding a weapon. Perhaps it was symbolic of surrender.

The prayers included her father and brothers and now this strange great, great something grandmother. She would just think of her as a grandmother since she had never known her more recent ones. Rosalyn also included Farrell but wondered if he ever thought of her in this way. Having listed them in her mind it was a struggle to think of appropriate words; keep them safe was the overall gist. It seemed quite selfish, so she added - and help our brave pilots and servicemen and the government in its fight against the injustices of Nazism. Amen.

When Rosalyn opened her eyes, it was a shock to see that she wasn't alone.

A small person sat to her left.

'Hello,' she turned to look at it, tensed for flight or fight.

In the gloom of the church she could not guess its age but it seemed like an old man and there was an aroma of wheat and straw. The creature winked at Rosalyn. She winked back, closing her left eye and in that instant the figure disappeared. Greyfolk of some sort, she realised, but it seemed friendly enough.

'You're not human, are you?'

The creature sighed.

'Always questions from the people of iron,' it said in a deep voice.

Rosalyn shrugged, she lifted the pinecone and made to place it in her bag. The little person would speak to her if he wanted. A brown slightly hairy hand touched her own that held the pinecone.

'You keep it with you,' he said.

Rosalyn felt a rush of feeling. This creature knew of the pinecone's significance.

'You know what it is. You know what it represents. Was it real?'

The creature chuckled.

'Of course. We had to take her back to her own people.'

'You stole her from me and put twigs in her place.'

'It was a message, so you would know her own people had removed her and that it hadn't been a dream. Have more confidence, Rosalyn James.'

'How do you know my name,' asked Rosalyn. Suspicion that this might not be a friend intruded on the warmth of their conversation.

He produced a small, folded paper and offered it to her.

'Mariel sent me. I am to make sure you find the place to hide and I can take a message to your friend if you decide to stay in the human world for the duration of this conflict.'

She read it.

Dearest Rosalyn, the plan worked better than I could have hoped. Misrule drove all the humans and their seolfor allies to search for the missing women in the pubs and dance halls around Soho. Once caught they were not keen to return to their imprisonment. Take shelter in the church at Stansham, I'm assured the bell tower is hardly ever used. Write on this paper and Gilgoreth will make sure it gets to your friend. He is utterly trustworthy. Love M

Rosalyn wondered how she would write another letter on that tiny paper and what anyone would make of the message about seolfor. She glanced at Gilgoreth and then back at the paper. The message had gone. The faerie chuckled and handed her a small quill. She slowly wrote and words appeared in her own handwriting.

'I'll assume you will have no problem recognising my friend.'

Gilgoreth smiled and stood. He tilted his head and took the letter.

Rosalyn walked to the door.

'Wait,' he said, and joined her. He looked carefully around before they left. A slight breeze was moving the tops of the trees and birds were starting to sing again. Rosalyn felt strangely comfortable holding the hand of this creature; it was cool but pleasant. Then she looked down at him and gasped. She was holding the hand of a golden-haired boy.

'Glamour,' he said. 'Don't believe everything you see around us. Now come with me.'

They walked away from the chapel in the wood along a well-trodden path then turned off suddenly into a deceptively hidden green lane.

Rosalyn said, 'I'm surprised you took that woman's baby, though it was barely human. I was told you didn't want hybrids.'

'Truly, there is deep division among the higher fae, they who now want to be called seolfor. Many would disapprove of the mixed blood child, claiming iron bloods cannot blend in harmony with silver bloods. They want to keep the fae bloodlines pure. But others, seeing our numbers dwindle from infertility or want of ambition, are keen to experiment by breeding with humans. You know all this Rosalyn James. You are being saved from it and I am happy to help.'

'Why are you helping?'

'Robert McKinley saved some of us from a type of slavery. Not me,' he insisted. 'I had already escaped, but he was useful to us.'

Rosalyn stopped walking and looked down at him.

'I saw the stillbirth of a monster. What would have become of that child if it had lived? Can you tell me?'

Gilgoreth avoided her gaze.

She continued. 'The second baby, sweet though it appeared, ripped its way out of its mother. Is it also a monster?'

'I can help you forget what you saw.'

She stopped and shouted. 'I don't want to forget, I want answers. And I don't want a bloody pinecone.' She took it from her bag and threw it into the woods.

'That might have had magical properties,' he said.

'Did it?'

'No, but you didn't know that.'

Exasperated and confused Rosalyn said, 'It seems to me you fae can't be trusted. That pinecone could have been a weapon of some sort or cast a spell on me.'

'Or been useful,' he muttered.

'Shut up.'

He led her through the deep woods and between tall hedgerows that were spotted with late Summer flowers and fruits. A truce settled over them, and he allowed Rosalyn to pick berries and drink from a clear stream. Finally they stopped at a grove of trees on top of a small hill and Gilgoreth told her to hide while he scouted.

He returned.

'Only friends in there.'

'What sort of friends?' asked Rosalyn warily.

'Come and see.'

They climbed the slope and found a way through a thick tangle of brambles that was obviously used by foxes and other small animals. There was a clearing at the centre and with her left eye Rosalyn could see the shapes of more creatures similar to her guide. Feeling large and cumbersome she sat down and they slowly approached. It seemed natural to close her eyes as a sign of trust and she was overwhelmed with a scent like green things and soil and animals. It was pleasant. She could not hear them and was surprised when she opened her eyes and they were very close.

'This is Mariel's kin,' said Gilgoreth now in his usual form, that of a small man about four feet nine inches with clothes of some sort and an old face like a gargoyle.

The others were similar. They too seemed old, and cooed, stroked, and sniffed her and Rosalyn thought they might sit in her lap, but they held her hands and put theirs into the crook of her arms like family. She was overwhelmed with happiness. She turned to Gilgoreth.

'They know Mariel?' she said.

'Some of them were with me when your forefather challenged the authority of Lord Faerie and his arrangement with Doctor Dee.'

Rosalyn recalled Mariel's incredible story.

Gilgoreth continued. 'Robert McKinley is a hero to us. We are the ones he freed from slavery. Except for me, of course. We are the lowest rank of the seolfor kingdom. We give service to the ruling greyfolk, Agremont and Faerie. They are not your friends and some of them will betray you for favour. It's the same in all races.'

'Do you all know about the plans to breed with humans?'

A look of fear ran around the group and some nodded gravely. They knew.

'There have always been encounters of that kind,' a female said. 'Love between humans and faerie folk is not unknown and is the reason why there is so much variety in the world of men. Some unions work and others do not.'

'I suppose it's been the stuff of romance for centuries,' said Rosalyn thinking of her fairy-tale books and the work of Romantic poets like Keats.

'Usually human offspring cannot pass in the kingdom of the fae so they remain with you.'

'The taint of human blood would make them unclean to us,' a thin creature said.

He was taller than the others but his statement brought forth a chatter of recrimination in a language she could not understand. There appeared to be as much dissension in the kingdom of the fae as in the human world when bloodlines were under consideration.

'What will happen to that baby?' Rosalyn asked.

The chatter increased and at last Gilgoreth nodded and one of the old folk left then returned holding the strange creature she had looked after and held it up for her to hold. It was not moving and for a second she feared it might be dead.

'Just give her a few minutes. The journey is less traumatic if she is asleep,' said Gil.

The face was as she remembered, kitten-like with large eyes and small but pointed ears, a snub nose and small mouth. But the colour was different and the pale skin now flushed pink and yet her hair was reddish. Mrs Farrell's hair was red, and Rosalyn knew it was natural and not dyed.

The little mouth opened and yawned. The fae seemed fascinated.

'It's called a yawn,' said Gilgoreth. Then by way of explanation, 'Fae do not have such a habit. This is a human quality and will mark her out as mixed race.'

'Does that mean she may not be tolerated? Will she come to harm?'

'Possibly. It depends how she turns out. We'll try to ensure she's safe,' Gilgoreth said hopefully. 'We will care for her until we know if she is equipped with enough charm and glamour to pass as fae.'

Rosalyn thought about the drowning of kittens and the rejection that humans often have shown for children with birth defects. She remembered the cages in the underground room. They want something from us and we need something from them.

'What about the ones who don't fit in?'

'In the past they haven't survived,' Gilgoreth said.

As she held the mixed-race child Rosalyn thought about it. This more recent experiment is part of a programme that has the backing of powerful seolfor like Agremont. He intends to judge the surviving offspring, grade them, and use some as servants or slaves. In that way they can increase their numbers and compensate for the infertility. Perhaps the more accomplished will be selected for further breeding, assuming they were fertile.

How will men like Churchill respond to the eugenic aspects of the proposals. Her own Jewish race was singled out for particular hatred in almost every society and had traditionally kept itself pure by marriage within its own tribe and by following the female line. Presumably they traced lineage through women because there was less certainty of paternity. It was the world in which she had been brought up, where mixed race marriages were discouraged, and white nations considered themselves superior to peoples of colour. And yet Mariel's Indian parentage was evident, and Rosalyn was herself of mixed race.

She reflected on Brent's words. He was right that the Empire was crumbling. As a communist he should not heed race and he was evidently an atheist so religion was irrelevant. Yet religion had been a major reason for war in the past, despite Christianity and Islam claiming to be multiracial, indeed evangelising to all peoples.

As Rosalyn held and made faces at the blue-eyed baby her mind ran on, stopping when she touched on the theory of evolution. Was there an order of superiority? Where did the fae fit into it? What will the world look like when people claim their right to self-determination and cast off the mastery of the older nations?

There was evidently a rigid class hierarchy among the seolfor that would reinforce the inequality in the world. Brent must surely hate the proposal to acknowledge and breed with this oldest and most mysterious of races.

The creature that had brought the child now took her from Rosalyn.

'Times have changed,' Rosalyn said. 'You need us or you may become extinct.'

'There are too many of you and our numbers are dwindling, for whatever the reason,' Gilgoreth said. 'We think your iron has polluted our world and is polluting your own.'

The other creatures nodded.

The taller one looked around then whispered, 'Some fae would take more drastic and violent measures.'

There was general disagreement at this, and he said no more.

'Then the breeding experiment might be prevented,' Rosalyn said. 'If Mr Churchill does not agree to it ...'

'Then the seolfor will not help you defeat your enemies,' said Gilgoreth. 'When they invade.'

Rosalyn wondered how much the government knew about the creatures they were dealing with. Very little, she suspected, and it might bring trouble. At present, death and destruction across the channel and the battle for aerial superiority was at the forefront of everyone's minds.

Gilgoreth continued, 'Whatever they do, we want you to be safe, for Mariel and Robert McKinley's sake so we have a plan and when all is ready, we will tell you. But now you must hide from human and seolfor alike.'

He stood and the others let go of Rosalyn so she could follow the faerie to the other side of the grove. He pointed to a hill in the distance.

'That is the hill on which stands the church of St Jude. Hide in the bell tower, I will find you and we will help you, if we can.'

Rosalyn could see a dark mass of trees in the haze of the afternoon, solid and almost blue on a single round hill with the remaining henge of a hill fort running its girth. The way was clear across a sheep cropped expanse of downland. She turned to ask a question, but her companion had gone. She went back into the grove, and it was empty and quiet, the air heavy and still. There had been so many of them and they had gone so quietly, as though a curtain had fallen between their world and this. Rosalyn felt lonely and knew she was getting a headache. The sun had disappeared behind the hazy sky and purple clouds were on the western horizon. She had to move fast to get to the church before the coming storm.

*

The yew trees were massive, and the shade they cast was cool and silent. Rosalyn walked cautiously around the graveyard wall to see if there were any other visitors. When satisfied it was empty, she entered the old church and allowed herself to marvel at the colourful windows and imposing brasses. A three-part stained-glass window portrayed St Jude, the patron saint of hopeless causes, Christ in the centre and Judas the traitor hanging in the third.

It was a disturbing image of a man in despair as life was squeezed from him and his pieces of silver lay among flowers on the ground, below his kicking feet. How depressing for the worshippers. Most of the brasses were shiny but beneath the window there was a blackened brass, and she wondered why they did not clean it. Too close to the image of the hanged man perhaps?

Rosalyn could not find an entry to the bell tower inside the church, so she left through the porch just as heavy rain drops began to patter on the grass and the gravestones. She ran around the building until she found a wooden door, partially hidden by a yew tree growing against the wall. It opened inwards easily and she slipped through and mounted the spiral stairs. The view was over the western side of the churchyard, and she could see the entrance by road. She would know if a vehicle approached and might slip down the steps unseen and into the trees, perhaps.

A violet light thrilled and then shocked her when the first clap of the thunder resonated through the tower. She crouched on the dirty floor as the storm began passing overhead and hoped she would be safe from a lightning strike, then laughed and cried at the futility of her situation in the face of nature's power and the world's indifference. Rosalyn was overcome by a sense of hopelessness and a niggling feeling that she was a coward and a funk. The image of the Judas figure stayed in her mind, and she wondered if she also could be described as a traitor. Sleep was impossible, the storm seemed to fade and then another one appeared, or perhaps it was the same storm returning.

Her father would have called it a 'Gethsemane' moment, referring to Jesus in the garden before he was taken up by soldiers and his fate sealed. He reminded them of the biblical reference whenever a difficult decision had to be made and one of his children needed to search his or her conscience. Owning up to a misdemeanour was one thing but Rosalyn was able to serve her country, albeit in a bizarre and obscene manner, and was thinking of avoiding that service. By the time of first light Rosalyn was exhausted but had managed to decide.

Friday 30 August 1940

The storm had gone, the air was cool and clear, and Rosalyn's mind was the same. If the deal with the seolfor was one that might save England, then she had a duty to do whatever was required. Running away seemed tawdry and unpatriotic. She would be a deserter and forever hiding and pretending. The people who helped her would be placed in grave danger.

What would her brothers say when they found out? She was overcome with tears of shame. Mariel had acted with good intentions but perhaps the elderly lady had spent too long away from the world of man. In a state of penitence Rosalyn looked out of the Norman windows high above the Hampshire countryside. She could see little beyond the ring of yew trees.

There was a slight breeze to her left. Rosalyn turned and saw Gilgoreth perched like a gargoyle on the other window ledge some thirty feet above the ground. He was eyeing her quizzically. A pigeon landed next to him and strutted about, cooing for attention until he picked it up and stroked it.

Rosalyn said, 'I didn't expect to see you again so soon.'

He looked at the bird and seemed to speak reluctantly. 'We are afraid for you if you stay in this world. Your friend, who cuts down trees, is part of a small company of workers and your presence will be noticeable. We don't think she can hide you; but we have found members of our community who are prepared to take you until the threat is past.'

'What do you mean: take me? Take me where?'

'Into our own kingdom where a night can be as seven years in this world,' Gilgoreth said. When she shook her head he added, 'You can care for the baby and spend time in this world too so you don't lose touch with humans. It is what Mariel has done for many years.'

Rosalyn thought of all the people who had died in Mariel's extended life and it seemed so sad. She might never see her father, her brothers and Farrell again. All the people she had prayed for in the little green chapel might be gone when she could return. Despite the attraction of looking after the baby she knew from her nighttime dilemma that she would not take his offer.

'I'm going back to do whatever has been decided as my duty.'

'So I've had a wasted journey,' he said.

'At least you didn't wear out shoe leather.' She studied him but could see no wings. 'How do you fly?'

There was no response to her question. But then he said, 'You've been offered shelter in the realm of the fae. You should consider it, you know, a beautiful place where time passes quickly and when you return to the world of men this nonsense will be over.'

The ultimate betrayal, Rosalyn thought. A hiding place while death rained down upon her people, and Nazi tanks destroyed her homeland. She would never abandon her duty and yet it was so tempting. Then she thought of her friend, working hard in a dangerous job, and the two ATS girls headed for Dorchester and cheerfully willing to do their bit. Then, of course, her own dear brothers. How could she leave them behind to fight the enemy if she had run away? Her father, isolated in Wales, would mourn her as dead. What would she return to? She'd seen photographs in newspapers of towns and villages devastated by the Nazis in their quest for world domination.

She beckoned to him.

'Come with me, tell me what you think of this.'

She descended the stairs and he appeared at her side as they entered the church together. She took him to the Judas window. They stared at the horror and Rosalyn was about to explain how she would feel like a traitor if she hid from the war. The old faerie cried out and clutched her arm. Surprised she looked down at him and he pointed at the blackened brass that was fixed to the wall below the window.

'Evil. There is evil in this place.'

Rosalyn could see no features on the brass but the air was cold, and the silence was broken by dripping water so she began to feel uneasy. He pulled her backwards out of the church, never taking his eyes off the brass that lay behind the altar under the window of despair and death.

Outside in the clean air, amongst the soaked grass and weeds of the graveyard he took both her hands.

'There is an evil thing in that church.'

'What sort of thing?' said Rosalyn looking into his pale grey eyes.

'The snake eating its young.'

'What does that mean?' She asked patiently.

'Or eating its tail. Continuing the cycle, using its young to perpetuate its life.'

'That sounds like nature,' she said.

'Not when the original thing never dies, and eating its children is how it renews itself.'

She shuddered. 'Does it threaten the local people?'

He looked back at the church.

'The power of the new religion will keep it in place. For now.'

'You think of Christianity as the new religion?'

Rosalyn walked back to the tower door.

'Will you make sure that my friend doesn't come looking for me, please?'

Gilgoreth nodded gravely. 'She will never find the letter that waits her at her lodging. So you are decided on your course?'

'Thank you for the invitation, but I will return to my assignment.'

If she expected him to try to change her mind, she was startled when he hopped onto a tall gravestone and bowed elaborately. Then he sprang into the air and flew away.

Rosalyn gathered her things and began the walk to the village and the awkward phone call to Greaves or Brent at Pitdown Hall. She just hoped that her grandmother's grandmother would not get into trouble, but then again, she had the sort of friends who could help her.

7 THE FALL

Saturday 31 August 1940

Rosalyn sat alone in the gloom of the dining room and tried to swallow her sandwich. She had walked the walk of shame through the sitting room where there were not even any snide remarks. When a young corporal from a local regiment had delivered her to Pitdown she had suffered being shouted at like a naughty schoolgirl by Greaves. She had said nothing, even when Greaves revealed that he knew of Mariel's involvement and threatened to have her arraigned as a traitor. It was clear he thought her just a wardrobe mistress and Rosalyn knew she was resourceful enough to slip through his fingers.

Eventually he simply asked why she had returned.

She said, 'My night in the church of St Jude's was my 'Gethsemane'. When I thought about my brothers and why we're fighting, I realised that I could never desert. I will stay with the auxiliary unit and do whatever is asked of me, and any sacrifice, even if it's a hopeless cause.'

Poor St Jude, she thought, constantly espousing hopeless causes.

He looked at her tired and dirty figure, lit another cigarette, and then turned to Brent who had been silent.

'Well, you were wrong. She knows what her duty is, and I don't see any need to lock her up.'

Brent shrugged then stood.

'I'll take her to get something to eat. Cook might rustle up a sandwich and I could do with coffee.'

He turned his damaged face towards Rosalyn as they walked through the hall.

'And there was I thinking you'd come to your senses.'

She recalled his sarcastic comments when they first met. It seemed like years ago and yet it must have only been a month.

She kept quiet except for minding her manners and sat at the long table alone. Brent left with the other men for some sort of training in how to kill people quickly and quietly.

As it turns out I don't need that sort of training after all, she thought, more's the pity.

Farrell was not with them. He must be out on the estate about his gamekeeping duties. Brent had told her to spend the day at the cottage and get some rest. Perhaps the shadows under her eyes would not please her seolfor suitors. Less a blushing bride, more a bought and paid for brood mare. Before going to the cottage she would find an interesting book and went into the library to find something to take her mind off the past few weeks.

She secretly hoped for a modern novel to suit her new fallen status, perhaps one by D H Lawrence, but she was disappointed and left with a copy of *Eminent Victorians* by Lytton Strachey. As she walked back to her quarters she reflected on the pleasures of reading and that Farrell could never enjoy it. Had he ever had a poem read to him or heard the words of Shakespeare?

The cottage was cool and dark as ever and she found a patch of sunlight where she could sit, legs tucked under her, reading about the life of General Gordon. When sleep became imperative, she slept on the settee, occasionally waking but unable to move until again surrendering to the sweet oblivion.

Rosalyn woke hot and sticky, aware that she stank and longing for clean clothes, but first she decided to find that pool and, pike or no, swim around the island in the middle and claim it as hers.

*

In the wood, as the late summer sun beat down on her, she stripped off her dirty breeches and socks. The surface of the pool was smooth, just brushed by the occasional dragonfly and she longed for its cool depths. Rosalyn straightened and looked about her at the still shrubs and thick undergrowth that surrounded the pool. She could see no watchers, either human or fae and she removed all her clothing, looking down at her body exposed in the open as it had never been before. Perhaps as a tiny child, but she did not remember. The habits of home and school, the sense of shame at nudity, crowded her mind and it was with a courage she did not feel that she stood naked on the grass.

Waiting for some shout of disapproval from the universe, she resisted the urge to hide herself in the water. Feeling Eve-like, Rosalyn walked along the edge of the pond until she felt more comfortable. What if Brent or Greaves were looking at her? Then, with more reluctance, Claff or Osgood? Why should she care? Davies would be disapproving. Wasn't it his religion that censured women and their bodies as the source of evil, the reason for the Fall? She realised it was the prurience of men that was the shaming of women and recalled being shown depictions of Suzannah and the Elders from the Bible. The reason for the painting was obvious. It was a chance to depict a naked woman and call it art.

Laughing out loud at the ridiculousness of it all Rosalyn slipped into the warm silky water and swam out to her island. The fear of nakedness was gone, replaced by the fear of pike and other invisible things. She hauled herself onto the island and sat like a mermaid combing her hair with her fingers. As her skin dried in the sun she closed her eyes. When she opened them, it was with a shock so physical that she put a hand to her heart. She recognised the short bark of a dog, and Farrell stood at the water's edge.

He gazed at her for what seemed an age, then turned, and she thought he would leave. When he took a few steps away it caused a pain that Rosalyn found perplexing and unbearable. Instead without looking at her, he stripped and dived into the pool. He swam a long lazy crawl with his head down, but when he surfaced, he didn't take his eyes off her. She did not look away. He stepped up onto the island, scattering birds that were sheltering in the reeds.

Like a snake basking in the sun she was warm and naked and he, an otter, wet and cool as he touched her, drops falling from his hair onto her skin as his mouth explored her. For a long time they lay side by side talking and kissing. Birds and insects went about their business, and they forgot the war and the future and lived in the fullness of their time and the closeness of their bodies.

When the biting insects emerged, they swam back to the shore, always in contact with each other, collected their clothes and walked to her cottage, followed by his patient old dog. This time he lifted her over the threshold like a bride and carried her upstairs to the quiet dark bedroom.

*

Sunday 1 September 1940

A long time later, she lay in bed naked, curled like a foetus, her eyes tightly shut as her mind recalled the events of the previous day.

He was not with her now. She was in a small bedroom at the top of the main house, an attic room in Pitdown Hall with only one door and it was locked. There was no chance of escape. The bed was comfortable and clean, unlike the damp blankets of the cottage. And the smell was different.

She remembered the smell of his skin, warm and musky, and the taste of it. The caress of his hands as they touched every part of her and how she had wanted to touch all of him. The act itself was uncomfortable, even a little painful, but her desire outweighed the physical intrusion, and he was gentle.

You must piss now, he'd said, when they were finished. Otherwise you will be sore. She obliged, using the chamber pot conveniently placed under the bed. It was bloody and she searched her things for the rags she normally used.

She slid back into bed with him and realised he was asleep, but he turned and embraced her in his dream. Eventually she too slept and when she woke, he was still sleeping. After listening to his breathing for a while she became aware of the smell of urine and decided she must empty the chamber pot.

She pulled on a clean camisole and trousers, and a loose shirt, and took the offending vessel downstairs and out to the earth closet. The night was dark but still warm. She wished she could make a cup of tea, but would have to drink water and went to the kitchen to fill the jug. Immediately she knew it was different, the door to the stairs was closed and Brent stepped from behind the outer door and put a finger to his lips. Greaves walked in behind her and she was trapped.

Upstairs there was a single cry and then the sound of heavy boots on the stairs as they took him out of the cottage. His dog whimpered and Rosalyn started to cry. She cried when they took him away and again in the comfortable bed in the attic of the house. They had taken her clothes and she lay unmoving and remembering everything he'd said and done. The memory of him was all over her body.

He must be dead, there'd been no sounds of a fight. She could imagine the scene, the knife and the blood or the garrotte and – she tried not to imagine it. Was it her fault? She'd wanted to lose her virginity before she was handed over to the seolfor. She had wanted him. The reason for his initial reluctance became clear; he must have known where it would lead. Eventually, in a turmoil of horror and pity, she fell asleep.

In the morning Greaves unlocked the door and came in carrying a parcel. He looked stern and was in uniform.

'Get dressed. Apparently, you are still acceptable despite being 'used goods'. I hope you realise you would be dead if they didn't want you, and we've lost a good man because of your recklessness.'

'What did you do to him?'

He turned and began to leave the room.

'And make sure you wash thoroughly. You stink.'

In a fit of anger Rosalyn picked up a glass from the bedside table and threw it at him. It smashed against the door.

'You filthy bastards,' she shouted. There was someone else outside the door and she heard Greaves speaking angrily. The door reopened and Brent came in. He was laughing.

'Pax,' he said. She clutched the bed clothes to herself, and he sat lazily in a chair and lit two cigarettes, offering her one. She waved it away, but he said, 'It's traditional to have a post coital cigarette.'

He seemed as unfazed by the development as Greaves had been shocked by it.

She said, 'You knew it was going to happen, didn't you? And you let it, and now he's dead.'

'It's unfortunate, but he knew the rules and obviously thought you'd be worth it. Quite flattering really. You, of course, will never see him again but you have what you wanted, to be relieved of your virginity by a human.'

Rosalyn was stunned by his callousness. 'We love each other.'

He didn't look at her.

'How did you know?' she said.

'It was obvious. And Farrell is human, sort of.'

'What do you mean 'sort of'?'

Brent leaned forward and spoke quietly. 'Farrell has some odd blood. He can move around the forest like a spirit. His parents were Romany people, and they threw him out as a child because even to them he had strange, unnatural abilities.'

'So he's Romany and I'm Jewish and the Nazis will treat us both as subhuman,' Rosalyn said.

'Not just Romany, something more. Possibly not human. And I am not thinking in terms of the eugenic philosophies of our enemies.'

'Not human?'

'Or not human enough.'

Rosalyn remembered that there were already people in the human world who were the result of interbreeding with seolfor. She thought about his wife and the trauma of her death and the strange twins. But they were not his babies. She was reminded of the pregnant women in the basement of the London theatre.

'That wasn't his baby.'

'You seem certain,' Brent looked smug. 'Claff says he cared more for his dog than for her. Claff will take over gamekeeping now.' He looked at her stricken face. 'Farrell was expendable Rosalyn. You are not.'

'Please tell me where he is,' she pleaded, and immediately regretted it. Brent became cold.

'Greaves is right, you do stink. Of sex and blood. So be a good girl and wash thoroughly and I'll send up some breakfast.' He looked around the room. 'Pity it's not the honeymoon suite.' Then he left quickly, before she found something to throw.

*

Rosalyn stayed in her room for the whole of that day. She had no choice, the door was locked. Occasional visits to the lavatory were accompanied, and after much begging and pleading she was permitted to take a bath. Although it would be good to wash off the pond water from the previous day, she was reluctant to wash off Farrell's scent. She often thought about the day and what they had done together. Her feelings of sensual longing were tempered by the uncertainty of what had happened to him. If they killed him where was his body? Could she look for it?

The attic room contained no books and she searched for a concealed door; but there was none. No escape and nothing to do except think about Farrell and his warm muscular body and searching mouth. She slept and dreamed of him but, when she woke, raged at what had been done to them. Carefully picking up pieces of the glass thrown at Greaves, she concealed one in case she should need to cut anything, like rope, or someone's throat. Alternating with mourning for his loss were thoughts of murderous revenge. She would be like Judith smiting Holofernes and take her enemy's life after he had done whatever he was going to do. With frustration she realised that the enemy was not the seolfor but the invading Nazi army, and her tiny part would be as a passive sacrifice.

Monday 2 September 1940
The attic window looked out onto the back of the building and in the morning she watched the men going to their day jobs, leaving only Greaves, Brent, and the catering staff on site. Davies was probably hanging around somewhere too. He always seemed to be where he wasn't wanted and if he were not a vicar, and therefore beyond reproach, Rosalyn would have been suspicious of him.

They disappeared in the afternoon, and she wondered if that meant an all-night exercise. There had been talk of visiting local farms and creeping around unseen by the farmer and his people. Claff claimed that he had got so close in the dark that a farmer had stood on his hand without knowing. It was all he could do not to pull it away and alert the man to their presence.

In the sleepy quiet of the warm afternoon, she heard talking through the open window and peered down. She saw two people walking from the woods towards the back door, but it was a hazy picture and only by closing her right eye did she get a clear image. She could see one of them only through her left eye. It must be seolfor.

The other was Loveday, the assistant to Doctor Dee that she had met in London. He was human and she could see him with both eyes. He was slim and walked with a lightness similar to that of the creature he accompanied. As they came closer she could see the creature was female and her hair was long and plaited, running down her back to her waist. She wore a surtout of silver grey and riding boots. The human wore tweed breeks with brogues and could have been out for a day's shooting. Greaves came out from the house and met them and after a short conversation they all went into the tree cover.

Rosalyn waited, hiding behind a curtain. She was about to give up when the shrubs under the trees moved and a group of strange folk came into view. They looked like the woman and were not visible through her right eye so they too must be seolfor. They were carrying a large box between six of them and it was draped in a grey cloth. That too was not visible with her right eye, so only someone who had been anointed with the oil would see it moving through the countryside. Greaves walked in front of the procession and led them into the orangery. She could not go downstairs to see where it was being taken but by listening at her door she knew it had not been brought upstairs. It would be either in the chapel or in the cellar.

Rosalyn paced the room, her thoughts in turmoil. Was it for Farrell's body? Was he already in there? She caught sight of the six bearers as they left the Hall and went back into the woods. Greaves, the female seolfor and Loveday were not with them. From the back of the house, there were the sounds of tea being prepared and that might mean a tray being brought up to her. If she could overpower the person who brought it then it might be possible to escape and find out what was in the box.

Rosalyn bundled her bag and some spare clothes into the bed so it looked as though she was sleeping, then waited behind the door. She heard the rattle of tray and crockery. Then the tray was set down and the door unlocked. As she hoped, he picked up the tray again and carefully entered the room. He approached the table, treading quietly so as not to disturb her. She went through the door and locked it.

'Sorry,' she said. Relieved that she hadn't had to knock him out. It was the cook's assistant, and he would doubtless call from the window for help but unless someone chanced to be at the back of the house, his calls would go unanswered. The cook had taken tea into the refectory ready for the men who were in the house. The boy would be missed eventually but she reckoned she had about fifteen minutes to get into the cellar by the secret stairs.

She crept down to Davies's room. If he was there, she would persuade him to come to the cellar with her and find out whatever had been brought in. Fortunately, he was not. Rosalyn opened the concealed door and could hear voices in the distance. The cries of the cook's assistant had died away as she got further from the attic, the many doors between below and above stairs, between servants and gentry, had deadened the sounds. But now she could hear something from the bottom of the hidden stairs. She crept forward then stopped to look more carefully at the rag on the top step. Someone, probably Brent, had kicked it to one side, and there seemed to be hair on it.

Tentatively she picked it up and went towards the window for a better look, then quickly dropped it. There was hair and underneath it but separate from it was a long braid, similar to the plait that Farrell had made in her hair. It had belonged to a woman like herself. And the rag - was skin. The revulsion felt was lessened by the obvious fact that it had been there a long time, but what horrors had taken place in this house she dared not contemplate. What sort of person would skin a woman? A memory came unbidden. Farrell had shown his skill with the knife when he killed the deer.

She made herself look at it more closely. There was a split along the length of what would have been the spine, but the limbs were intact. The arms and hands were empty, but the fingers could be easily distinguished. The legs with the gently tapering feet lay like an empty pair of silk stockings. She steeled herself to look at the face and that was the worst thing. It had been a woman, once, with full lips and dark arched eyebrows but now empty and collapsed. The eyes vacant and the nostrils like slits in a flat mask. It looked like the face of a snake.

Rosalyn was drawn to the braid, so like her own, and picked it up. It was warm and silky. With a gentle, almost caressing movement, it wound itself around her arm. Was it a reaction to the warmth of her skin, the passing of electromagnetic energy. The suspicion that entered her mind and lingered was the thrill of magic. Instead of horror she felt affection, as though it were a pet. She let it stay there but hid the skin in an empty drawer in one of the heavy oak tallboys. If someone finds it let them make of it what they will. Then she descended the secret staircase. It was clear where the ground floor was from the noise of returned men smoking and drinking tea. At the bottom of the stairs she listened at the door to the cellar. There were three people in conversation.

Greaves was speaking urgently. 'This is not what was agreed. Dee was going to negotiate for their support, if and only if, the Germans invade and begin pushing through the country. The Prime Minister does not have the authority to grant such a large area of land exclusively for their use unless there is an invasion and we are fighting for every acre of it.'

'It's not so much, given the vast empire this country has under its control,' a female voice said.

Greaves said, 'You asked for Wales. You must realise that is out of the question.'

'I think that was said only in jest,' said Loveday. 'And given Mr Churchill's history with the Welsh.' He tried to laugh it off.

'We'd be happy with Cornwall,' said the female. 'I believe that is being considered by your Winston Churchill.'

'But only if there is an invasion and then only if we win with your help.' Greaves was already angry, and Rosalyn could hear him struggling to control himself. 'These demands for land were not part of the original negotiations. Agremont wanted a breeding programme to assist the fertility of greyfolk.'

'We are called seolfor now,' she said. 'But that would take a long time and may not even be successful as the recent human female's death has shown. In any event we shall need a land of our own, free from your industrial madness. We will need 'lebensraum' I think it is called.'

Greaves was silent and Rosalyn could sense his fury through the door.

'We can always open negotiations with Herr Hitler,' the female continued, her voice becoming brittle.

'That would be an act of bad faith and betrayal,' said Greaves. 'Remember, he has a habit of breaking his word.'

'A binding spell would ensure that he did not.'

'I'm sure it won't come to that,' said Loveday, his voice placatory.

There was another long period of silence and Rosalyn wondered if they had left or had detected her presence.

Eventually Loveday spoke. 'Perhaps you should look at it this way. English women breed with the fae and their offspring are offered a piece of English land where they can live the life that is approved by the seolfor, without the foul taint of iron and with the benefit of fae customs and magics.'

'Well it's done now. Agremont has met with the Prime Minister. God knows what he made of it and it is all conditional upon the assistance you will provide in the event of an invasion,' Greaves said.

'Yes, quite,' said Loveday hastily.

'Then we find a room of pregnant women under the theatre and no one will explain what they are doing there. They should have been evacuated from London.'

'But why? There is hardly any bombing. Your evacuees are returning to their slums, tired of the privations of the countryside,' the female said.

There was another silence. Rosalyn could sense the hostility.

'And now this – abomination,' Greaves's voice was strained.

There was a longer pause and the sound of fabric being moved. She imagined that Greaves was examining the box they'd brought into the cellar and heard someone prise open the wooden lid. He gasped.

'Good God. Nobody must know about this, do you hear? If this gets out there will be mayhem. I hope for all our sakes it doesn't work.'

The female voice said, 'And yet in the deepest part of your heart you pray that it will.'

There was a silence then Greaves spoke again.

'I hold you responsible Loveday. You knew what Dee was planning and you made these preparations without discussing it with us. Our Prime Minister would not sanction what you propose. It's a desecration.' Greaves was furious. 'I will have to inform him.' He seemed to turn away from them.

Loveday's placatory voice stopped him. 'Before you tell Mr Churchill, you should consider whether he would really want to know about something that, as you say, is a desecration. And it may not succeed. Doctor Dee has not delved into this particular branch of alchemy for many years and would do it only as a last resort.'

The seolfor spoke again. 'I believe your Mr Aleister Crowley tried and failed.'

Rosalyn thought she could hear Greaves him pacing. After a few minutes he said, 'I suppose it may fail. Perhaps we should let him try and only report it to the Prime Minister if it succeeds and then decide what to do with it - him.' He was evidently considering his options. 'He could be a powerful uniting force.'

'The Nazis are exploring every aspect of sorcery to enhance their own weaponry,' said Loveday. 'And I imagine the Prime Minister would prefer to have plausible deniability.'

'I am not happy with this.' Greaves moved to the staircase and she heard him mount the stairs. 'Loveday, will you come with me?'

'I will go with Eoldrith,' he replied.

The key turned and Greaves left. Rosalyn heard the door being locked.

'You shun the company of your fellow man,' said Eoldrith.

'I have met them, they are not fit company. Though, I should like to see the girl again, but she is locked in a room, they think she might escape if given a chance.'

Rosalyn realised she had run out of time and if she was to keep her eavesdropping a secret, she should return to the first-floor bedroom and then hide somewhere so they could find her. She ran as quietly as possible up the stairs, dreading the sound of the lower door opening, and entered Davies's room, relieved not to find him there. At that moment planes flew low overhead, and everyone ran out to look at it, in the hope of seeing a dogfight. As the main door closed Rosalyn went onto the landing, threw a leg over the banister, and slid down it. She had very little time but noticed a cupboard under the stairs and hid herself inside.

She just missed being seen by the cook who was shouting for his assistant. The planes had gone, and Brent was first back in and asked what the matter was. As soon as he heard where the boy had been sent, he ran upstairs to Rosalyn's room. There was no chance to change her hiding place because cook remained outside the cupboard door. She heard Brent go into the vicar's room and search the secret stairs. How gratifying that he would not find her but she had been a fool to move the skin. Then she remembered the hair braid. It was still on her arm and was evidence of her venture through the concealed door. She undid her shirt and wound it around her waist. The shirt was baggy enough that they shouldn't notice. Did it tighten slightly? It might have been her imagination.

Brent returned, and Greaves and the others joined them. After a respectable time she opened the door and came out shamefaced. In her best schoolgirl manner she weathered the telling off she got from Greaves and apologised to the cook's assistant. She did not look at Brent in case her eyes gave her away, but knew his expression would have been cynical and dared not tempt further questioning. When had she ever been so contrite?

*

Her punishment was to spend the rest of the day doing laundry and basic kitchen work. She didn't need to pretend to be broken-hearted and kept as far away from Brent as possible, he at least refrained from commenting on her fallen state, having said all he wanted that morning. She listened at every opportunity for any whispers concerning Farrell, hoping to hear what had been done to him but they were tight-lipped about his fate.

Greaves was absent most of the time and she got the impression he was engaged in weighty telephone calls with someone at the War Office. As evening drew on, Rosalyn began to feel the burden of her new knowledge and was desperate to speak to someone about it. The cook's assistant stared at her resentfully; she had made a fool of him, and no amount of apologising would make up for it. Eventually she would be escorted back to her room and locked in. The Reverend Davies was reading a book in the sitting room and in a quiet moment before her incarceration she passed a note to him asking to speak, and implying there would be a confession. He nodded his tacit acceptance.

Back in her room Rosalyn waited impatiently for his knock at the door. She had unwound the hair braid and was surprised to see that it was more lustrous, dark, and thick. It was the same type of hair as her own but must have been floor length on the woman to whom it had belonged. She rewound it and placed it under her pillow. There was a quiet tap on the door.

Davies was unwilling to let her out, but she promised to behave if he would unlock it and spend some time with her. He came in and bade her sit, his disapproval at her behaviour was obvious from his expression. She meekly sat on the bed, allowing him the chair.

'What have they done to Farrell? I know you disapprove of the sin of fornication, but you know what they intend for me. I love him and I believe he loves me.'

'Your night of sinful lust has cost him dear.' The vicar looked embarrassed and yet severe. He folded his arms and pinched them in a manner she thought must be painful, perhaps it was a sort of penance for his own sensual thoughts. He suddenly crossed one ankle over a knee, and she suspected he had an erection. Rosalyn was shocked by this, feeling somehow violated by his thoughts. She turned away from him and wiped her eyes as though weeping.

'I don't know what happened to Farrell,' he said. 'He didn't deserve to die, and for all I know, they may have simply shipped him off somewhere else.'

She thought he sounded sorry for her.

'These are terrible times and the stakes are high.' He continued.

'So he might not be dead?' Rosalyn said, in real tears from relief.

'They may have given him to the greyfolk.'

What did that mean? Was Farrell related to them and what would they do with him?

Davies continued. 'You will have seen the creatures by now, having used the oil. I too have availed myself. A painful unction, but necessary given what we must do,' he said. 'To think they have been among us all this time, greyfolk, the fae, faeries.

Rosalyn looked at his eyes and saw the tell-tale golden flecks.

'I never gave faeries much thought.' He seemed pleased by the revelation. 'Arthur Conan Doyle believed in them and also in the ability of some people to contact the spirits of the dead. But I considered them to be mainly legend and not relevant to my life or my training in the Church, unlike human souls.'

'You've seen the fae?'

'One of them, Lord Agremont in fact. He demonstrated some of his power to us all last week at Wanborough, and convinced even the most sceptical. Some people used to think they were fallen angels, but I don't think we can attribute the virtues of angels to them.'

'Do you think they're dangerous?' asked Rosalyn.

'Very. I take it you haven't been introduced?' She shook her head. 'No, well they are almost colourless and sometimes silvery but also able to absorb light and disappear into natural places.'

'How did the other members of the unit take it?' Rosalyn asked.

'Osgood was not surprised. Claff's eyes lit up at the thought of ways to make money. Farrell also seemed to accept them as a natural phenomenon, but I got the impression that Greaves dislikes and distrusts them.'

'What about Brent?'

'I think he'd come across their type in Spain in difficult circumstances, but you'll have to ask him for more detail.'

Rosalyn wondered if she was really to be given to Agremont and if she did go to the fae perhaps see Farrell again, if he was alive. A glimmer of hope sparked in her breast and she tried not to show it. Davies was looking at her kindly and he had told her more than any of the others.

'Will I be given to the old man or just the fae?' she asked.

'They haven't told us. The fae have their demands in consideration for their help, but few people know about the negotiations. Belief in the existence of the fae has diminished despite the prevalence of other superstitions in human society. Only three people not in this group are aware of them, and one is Winston Churchill. No politician in his right mind would ever dare to profess a belief in faeries. Three humans, that is, there are a few of the fae of course, and several creatures I might call hybrid.'

'Hybrid?' She pretended to be ignorant. 'You mean part human and part fae? Have they already been breeding with humans? That is what they want me for.'

They sat in silence and Rosalyn recalled what the female had said in the cellar. As an alternative to the breeding with humans they now wanted Cornwall. Then she remembered Greaves's reaction to the thing in the box. She had to tell someone else about the box now in the cellar.

'When I escaped earlier, I was trying to find out what had been brought into the Hall by people dressed in grey. I saw them from my window. And now I know what they were and why I could only see them with my left eye. I went to the cellar using the stairs that lead from your room. I really thought you might have put a heavy piece of furniture over that panel,' she said. 'Anything could come through.'

'Yes, I suppose I should,' Davies replied flustered at the reminder that the fae were able to get into his room so easily.

'And right now, there is a big box in the cellar that could contain anything, and from the way they were speaking it must be very dangerous and –' she searched for a word. 'Ungodly.'

'What makes you say that?' His eyes widened.

'They said that someone called Aleister Crowley had tried to do whatever it is and failed.'

'Crowley? That beast. It must be dark magic. Did they indicate what they planned?'

'They said a Doctor Dee would be doing it and that even he was out of practice.'

'Surely not. He can't be alive still?'

She nodded cautiously. 'I think he was the old man who lived here.'

'But he was an alchemist who lived at the time of Queen Elizabeth. She died in 1603 so he can't possibly still be alive.' He put his head in his hands. 'Unless he found what he claimed - the Philosopher's Stone, the secret of immortality.'

Rosalyn felt a thrill of triumph in the way she had manipulated him.

She said, 'But what could be in the box? And why was Greaves so horrified by their proposed actions? He is pretty gung-ho about most things, wouldn't you say?'

He stood up and said, 'We have to find out Miss James, if Greaves is horrified then 'ungodly' may be exactly the right word and I must know what is down in the cellar.'

'I'm coming too,' said Rosalyn.

'I'm not sure you should. It's probably a dead man and they intend to resurrect him.'

All Rosalyn's triumph vanished with a chill of horror as she realised the dead man could be Farrell and he was to be the subject of a terrible experiment.

'I'm coming with you,' she said firmly.

They crept down to his room, went in, and locked the door. Davies collected a lamp; they opened the panel and entered the staircase.

'I'll go first,' whispered Rosalyn. 'But we mustn't speak until we know the cellar has no creatures in it. And don't make any noise, they may have sharp hearing.'

She was determined to see what was in that box. The enjoyment she would have found leading a middle-aged vicar down secret steps had become a grim resolution. It might not be Farrell's body in the box. What if it was alive?

They listened at the cellar door and heard nothing; the rats are quiet, she thought. Then she cautiously looked and declared the room was empty, so they went in and she was able to look around with the benefit of the lantern. She turned to find Davies examining the cloth covering the box that had been placed on the table. She could see the box was about eight feet long and three and a half feet wide.

'It's a strange material. I don't believe I've ever encountered anything like it before,' said Davies.

'I think the cloth makes it invisible when they carry it in daylight.' She remembered the little procession and was certain she had only seen them through her left eye.

He was still dithering, so she pulled it off and they stood back and looked at a plain wooden box.

'We have to open it,' said Rosalyn, feeling along the edges. She looked around the room and found a corkscrew, inserted the point under the wooden edge and prised it open. A few more and they were able to lift off the lid. Davies shone the lamp on the contents: it was another box.

'It's a coffin,' he said as Rosalyn stepped back in horror.

'It's Farrell,' she cried. 'They've killed him and now they're going to bring him back to life like those Voodoo things.'

'Necromancy,' said Davies. 'They raise the dead and make them do their bidding. An army of the dead with no fear and no souls.' He was clearly horrified and was just in time to stop Rosalyn from throwing herself at the box and trying to open the coffin.

'No, you mustn't, you don't know what's in there. It might be Farrell but it might be someone or something else. Let me look at it.'

She stood back. The spark that had ignited at the thought of him being alive expired in a surge of pain. Davies held the lamp above the coffin, examined the aged wood for marks, and gasped as he found a language he recognised.

'It's Welsh. There are Welsh words here, I'm sure. Difficult to make out but *ein brenin* something *a'r dyfodol*. What could it be?'

He muttered something in Welsh under his breath then quickly straightened up.

'Oh yes. But surely not.' He rubbed his head, shoulders jerking involuntarily.

'What does it say?' Rosalyn pressed close to him, but she could just see a few letters and some pictures, and they made no sense.

He turned to her with a disturbing smile.

'Come on Miss James help me put this back together. We don't want them to know we've found it, and I can assure you it isn't Farrell in that casket.'

'How do you know it's not him?'

'I know who it is,' he said. 'It's a miracle.'

He refused to discuss it further but convinced her that they should leave the cellar before they were discovered. Back in his room she tried and failed to make him tell her who it was, but it was enough to know that they were going to make a revenant from whatever was there. Davies's eyes glittered. Rosalyn had not seen him so animated and excited.

'Let me assure you it is not an evil thing in that coffin, it is a blessed soul. I am sorry but you are going to have to return to your attic room and I must lock the door. Perhaps you will help me move this tallboy in front of the panel, I'm not sure I would get any sleep tonight otherwise.'

Rosalyn tried to wheedle a name from him but without success, and she did as she was bid and went back to her room to be imprisoned again. It was growing dark and she looked wistfully out of the window hoping to see some activity in the limited light. She did see something. With her enhanced vision she recognised the vicar as he left the Hall by the back door and disappeared into the woods.

She cursed her inability to follow him and was sure his journey had been prompted by whatever secret thing they had found in the cellar. All she could do was try and remember everything she'd heard about dead bodies being brought back to life. She found herself thinking about Mary Shelley's novel 'Frankenstein', one of the few books she'd enjoyed at school. That night she dreamed about Farrell and the time they spent together, so brief and intense. She woke at 7am in a state of bliss. It took a few moments to remember he was probably dead.

*

Tuesday 3 September 1940

When she realised what the date was, Rosalyn remembered it had been exactly one year since war was declared. The anxiety returned quickly and sped up her preparations for the day. Although she had not dreamt about corpses and body parts or superhuman creatures that may not be controlled by their makers, there was a sense of urgency related to the thing that lay under the building. The identity of the corpse had astonished Davies and it was enough to impel him from the Hall in the dead of night.

Cook invited her down to the refectory for breakfast and wearing her customary baggy trousers and checked shirt she wrapped her hair in a net and a scarf and looked every inch the land girl. Unfortunately, some instruction had brought Osgood and Claff to the Hall that morning. They leered at her then settled to their conversation and she had no choice but to listen.

Claff said, 'I went out this morning to see to his dog and he went for me, see, bit my hand he did. So I despatched him there and then. He was an old dog anyway, wouldn't have wanted to live without his master.'

This was too much. Rosalyn was overcome with tears of sorrow, anger, and frustration. She knew he was an old dog and would have missed Farrell. He was lucky to be alive anyway, so many pets had been euthanised at the start of the war when food shortages were expected. But he was a working dog and knew his job. What a filthy waste.

She lowered her head to her porridge and muttered under her breath, 'I hope you get gangrene.'

On the cusp of bursting into tears she tried to think like a farmer, no point being sentimental, but that was not the real reason she wanted to cry. She was so close to breaking down and couldn't bear to listen to them talking about him. She had to create a diversion.

'What did you say?' asked Claff.

Struggling to control her voice she said, 'What do you think of the Welsh corpse they've got downstairs in the wine cellar. Going to bring it back to life I heard. That's a rum do wouldn't you agree?'

They stared at her open mouthed. Brent put down his coffee and glanced at the door. Greaves and Davies were not in the refectory and Rosalyn glanced at each of the men present and was convinced that none of them had known of the delivery to the cellar.

'What are you talking about?' said Claff.

'The box, containing the coffin, that the greyfolk brought here two days ago. It's in the cellar. Doctor Dee is going to raise the dead.'

'Necromancy. The devil,' said Osgood, his voice thick with excitement. 'He's still alive is he? Surely not.'

'Never heard of him,' said Claff.

'He must be hundreds of years old. An alchemist, astrologer, and sorcerer,' said Osgood.

'You should know,' said Rosalyn. 'You hexed him.'

Osgood's jaw dropped. He stared at her.

'What? You mean he was the old bastard that …' he stopped, speechless, as he realised the significance of his actions.

'Blimey,' said Claff. 'Did you know about this Brent?'

Brent stood up and took Rosalyn by the arm.

'Come on, leave your tea.' When they were in the hall he said, 'I never had you for a blabbermouth. You should have kept that information to yourself.'

'You didn't have any idea, did you?' she said boldly but secretly regretting her foolishness and knowing it was because she was upset over the dog. They went to the office where Greaves was poring over a book that he closed when they entered.

'There's something you need to hear from Miss James.'

She repeated what she had said in the refectory. He was angry but seemed weary and resigned. It was odd given his objections in the cellar two days before.

'How do you know this?' He asked her.

'I saw the Welsh writing and I know about Doctor Dee's plan to raise the dead. An army of zombies that will have no fear and no souls.'

She did not mention that Davies knew, nor that he had left the estate in the night. She hoped he had appealed to a higher authority in the Church, and they would have the blasphemy stopped.

'So that's what you were doing when you were out of your room, eavesdropping,' Greaves said. 'You are a nuisance James,'

He put a hand on the book he had been reading.

'But you've only brought forward what was going to happen anyway. Do you speak Welsh?'

'No. It just looked like Welsh,' Rosalyn had given too much away; Davies could read it. She still hoped he would soon appear and prevent the ceremony. But the country was at war, what power did the Church have? And how long would it take them to appear at Pitdown Hall? Poor Davies, sent on a foolish mission by her impetuousness.

'Get the men into the sitting room for a briefing,' said Greaves. 'You may as well all hear about this new development.'

Brent and Rosalyn left. On the way he whispered, 'You must be more careful what you do and say, this is a dangerous situation. Not all the greyfolk are happy with Agremont's proposals, in fact there is a strong faction who believe the race of the fae should remain pure.'

'You seem to know a lot about it.'

'When you saw me on the railway platform I had come from London where I met Doctor Dee and Agremont. They were discussing how to structure a breeding programme, as an incentive for help if the Germans invade.'

'What's all this about Cornwall?'

'Those opposed to the breeding programme want a land for their kind instead. You don't need any more information.'

Rosalyn knew a great deal more. They assembled with the men in the sitting room and she was pleased to see that Davies had reappeared, although she dared not meet his eye. Claff and Osgood stared at her, and she stayed away from them. The farrier's excitement was palpable and intimidating.

Greaves entered, carrying the old book he had been reading in the office and a few notes. He stood at the fireplace and the men lounged in easy chairs. He ignored Rosalyn but addressed Osgood specifically.

'Osgood, we know you have experience of witchcraft so if you feel inspired to add or correct anything I say then please do so.' He turned to the others. 'You're all aware that we have been in negotiations with Lord Agremont of the fae – I should inform you that they have decided they want to be known by a new name – the seolfor. Apparently, they're tired of being connected with faeries as illustrated by Arthur Rackham.' Claff and Osgood had no idea what he meant, and Brent was impassive. Davies nodded vigorously.

He continued. 'In exchange for their help in defeating the Nazis they have asked for a homeland. The size and location of this is under discussion but it would be remote, Cornwall has been suggested. Apparently, they already have a strong presence in the area. Our introduction to these creatures was through a man with a lot of experience in the field of magic, his name is Doctor John Dee, and he was born in 1527.'

There was silence from most of the men. If they knew about the breeding programme, they would not speak of it.

'That's what Osgood said, but I don't believe he could be human,' said Claff.

Greaves ignored him. 'I believe that he is a loyal British subject and wishes to help in the defence of the realm.'

Osgood quietly said, 'Are you telling me that the old man that caused us so much grief was John Dee.'

'That's exactly what I am telling you,' said Greaves.

'And I hexed him,' Osgood said with satisfaction.

Claff laughed, slightly hysterically Rosalyn decided. They watched for any further reaction, but Osgood just smiled. Greaves continued.

'When he had recovered from whatever you did to him, his seolfor associates saw an opportunity to engage with humans for mutual benefit. You are all aware of our attempts to enlist them in the fight against Hitler should his armies invade.

'There has been another development,' he looked sharply at Rosalyn who kept a neutral face and avoided looking at Davies, though she was sorely tempted.

'Doctor Dee or his associates found something else when they went searching for secrets in the ruins of Glastonbury Abbey. In 1191 a group of monks alleged they had found two skeletons in a hollowed out oak trunk surmounted by a lead cross that said –' he opened the book where it was marked and read '*Hic jacet sepultus inclitus rex Arturius in insula Avalonia.* This was translated as *Here lies interred the famous King Arthur on the Isle of Avalon.*'

There were gasps and a chuckle from someone. Rosalyn looked at Davies and realised he had known it was Arthur and that was why he'd said it was not Farrell.

'You said it was a Welsh body.' Claff looked at her.

'No Latin inscription, no lead cross. How do we know it is Arthur and not some chieftain of the greyfolk?' Osgood growled.

Greaves replied, 'Arthur was a Briton and a Christian. When the Saxons invaded Britain about 1500 years ago, the Romano British fled to Wales and Cornwall and probably spoke what is now Welsh. I have seen the oak coffin; it has Arthur's standard of three crowns on it and an inscription in Welsh translated as *our once and future king.*'

Again, an air of expectation silenced everyone, until eventually Claff spoke. 'What are you going to do with a skeleton? Wasn't he a king who fought with a sword and rode a horse? He can't help us fight tanks and bombs.'

Greaves did not reply. He looked embarrassed and Rosalyn felt sorry for him. Perhaps he hoped that reanimating the dead will fail and the original plan to use the seolfor can continue, difficult though that will be.

Osgood said, 'Doctor Dee is going to practice necromancy, isn't he?'

'That is the intention, unfortunately,' said Greaves.

Rosalyn looked at Davies expecting him to denounce the practice as blasphemous, but he sat absorbed in his own thoughts. She must be patient; it would take time to contact people in power and influence the Prime Minister away from this strange turn of events.

'But we have a king,' she muttered. The men ignored her.

'Bones,' said Claff. 'He'll be dust and bones, that's what the monks found, you said. What good is that?'

'Faerie glamour,' said Greaves. 'The monks saw what they were supposed to see. The legend says that Arthur sleeps until his country needs him again. And now that day has come.' He seemed resigned. 'And we will be the first Britons to welcome him back.'

'As long as the dark magic works,' said Brent.

'Well we'll find out tomorrow. Doctor Dee and his entourage will be travelling down by train. Claff, can you collect them from the station? He'll be bringing a man and a woman.'

Claff grunted reluctantly.

'Do you have any questions that I might be able to answer?'

Osgood said, 'There is always a price to pay for dark magic. Do you have any idea what that might be?'

Greaves shook his head, 'I have been able to find some information on John Dee but according to my research he only used necromancy to converse with the dead when he was seeking information or trying to predict the future.'

'It is likely to be a sacrifice, either human or animal,' said Osgood.

'I should have left that old dog alive,' said Claff.

Rosalyn wanted to hit him.

She said, 'It could be any of us, couldn't it? We have all committed to sacrificing ourselves for our country. Perhaps we should draw lots.'

There was a growl of disapproval and Greaves broke up the meeting. Rosalyn wanted to speak more to Brent so she asked him for a cigarette, and he indicated they should go outside to smoke.

*

It was another beautiful day and reminded Rosalyn of the time she'd spent with Farrell in the pond and on the island. She breathed deeply the slight autumnal fragrance and a drift of harvest and wood smoke.

'If Farrell is dead – I know you won't tell me - do you think Doctor Dee could bring him back to life?' She asked when they were alone.

Brent looked at her with something that might have been pity.

'You must forget him. He's gone. There are more important matters at hand. 'Whose idea was this and why did Dee and Agremont not mention it when I met them in London?' He stopped, pulled her towards him and looked into her face. 'I assume you eavesdropped from the secret staircase when they brought the casket into the cellar. What else did you hear? Anything might be relevant.'

Rosalyn was shaken. 'I didn't hear much; Greaves was shocked and it was a surprise to him, I'm sure. The seolfor female was called Eoldrith and the man was Loveday. Does that help?'

'Loveday again. Always in the middle of everything. He's Doctor Dee's amanuensis.'

'What's that?' said Rosalyn.

'His right-hand man.'

'Also the creature said that they could do a deal with Hitler and, if necessary, put him in a binding spell so that he couldn't break his word. Now that's something I'd like to see.'

'No it isn't,' Brent began walking again, fast, and making he stride out to catch up. He swore. 'Don't you see, this is worse than I thought. If the other faction is pushing for the return of the 'once and future king' there is a strong possibility that he will replace our own King George.

'Surely not.' Rosalyn was incredulous.

'A lot of people believe we cannot win this war. Germany, Italy, and Russia are allies. Japan is consolidating its position in the Pacific and America is steadfastly neutral. Our Empire is far away and geared up chiefly to supply us as trading partners, not with armies and weapons.

'Our only strength is the Navy and the enemy has U-Boats and God help us if we lose the air to the Luftwaffe. There are those who would favour a settlement with our enemy rather than face invasion.'

The possibility of peace made relief flood Rosalyn's mind. No more death and destruction. Life returning to normal. Her family back together.

Brent could see the hope in her face.

He said, 'There are fascists in this country who hold the same right-wing beliefs as their Nazi counterparts. It's only a matter of time before the ruthless eugenics of Europe will be applied here.'

'But we're British. The right settlement would guarantee our independence.'

'Under a puppet government. Why else would they bring him back? A long dead king will be malleable, will know nothing of the complexities of the modern world.'

'But Frankenstein couldn't control his monster.'

He looked at her with derision and continued.

'Appeasers would see an opportunity to save the fiction of Great Britain and its Empire. They would kill Churchill immediately and the best of our leaders and soldiers. There would be a cull of any future threats so there could be no opposition. That's how dictators operate. The war cabinet would be ousted and someone like Oswald Moseley made Prime Minister. I dread to think what would happen to the royal family.'

By now Rosalyn's hope had become nausea.

Brent continued. 'Factor in the seolfor behind the scenes pulling the strings and this country will regress to the time of the Norman Conquest with a hierarchical society based on bloodlines. Freedom will be non-existent.'

They had walked several hundred yards from the house and turned to look back at it. Birds were singing as they prepared for a midday rest, and it seemed peaceful. Rosalyn tried to imagine what this country was like when Arthur had lived. She had believed him to be a mythical figure. Since 1066 Britain had been a fortress and most fighting had taken place on foreign shores.

'Who do you think is really in that coffin?' she asked. 'I thought King Arthur was just a character from a story written hundreds of years after he was supposed to have lived.'

'The Bible was written a long time after Jesus died. Did you know there were originally more than the four gospels that have come down to us. They told different stories. The Roman Empire selected the ones that suited their purpose. Plenty of people believe in that story,' said Brent.

It came as a shock to Rosalyn to realise that believing in God was similar an act of faith as believing in the existence of Arthur or indeed, that of the fae.

Brent continued. 'The Arthurian legends appear in early medieval histories but are likely to have a seed of truth in them. Greaves just explained there was a time when the Roman legions left and Germanic tribes, Angles and Saxons, invaded and settled. They eventually controlled what is now England, but Cornwall, Wales and Scotland remained separate. Arthur may have been a Romano British warrior.'

'But if he failed to repel the Germanic tribes in the past then I really don't see how he could help us now.'

'I suspect the sudden appearance of his body is a deliberate distraction from the breeding programme by those seolfor who oppose it. But you have a good point,' Brent said.'

'This is worse than the breeding programme, isn't it? That only happens if we need to use the seolfor after the Germans invade, and there's still a chance they might not. We might win the air war.' She looked at Brent hopefully.

He shook his head. 'It doesn't look good. The attacks on the airfields and the shortage of pilots puts us in a weak position. From what I hear they are readying themselves for an invasion very soon. Our climate is not so severe that a winter war on land would be impossible. With the loss of leaf cover and our shortage of heavy weapons it might be a walk in the park for seasoned Panzer divisions.'

The thought of her brother in the navy, and the dive-bombing Stukas she had seen near Winchester made Rosalyn shiver. 'They have parachutists too, don't they?'

'Yes, fallschirmjager. Experienced fighters with a year of warfare under their belts against raw conscripts and a small, recently beaten professional army. The odds are atrocious.'

It was hateful to feel weak and small, like a woman in a man's world. She remembered the poor women held in the basement of a London theatre.

She said, 'Farrell's wife was not the only Pitdown woman impregnated by seolfor, and all those women that escaped at the theatre carry fae-human hybrids and may not survive the birthing?'

He did not reply and starting walking back to the Hall.

'You don't care,' Rosalyn shouted after him.

He stopped and turned to her.

'If the fascists invade, I will do anything to defeat them. Our lives, those of the women, are worth sacrificing to achieve this. Did you know that Stalin, with his country's vast resources, is trying to breed a human-ape hybrid? You look disgusted. They use artificial insemination. It's not so different to what's being done here. The only difference is the apes don't have a choice and have nothing to gain.'

He spoke quietly.

'If the Spanish seolfor had chosen to help the republic, they would have made a difference. They exist in the countryside there, as here. But the suffering of humans meant nothing to them. If British seolfor want Arthur alive then they must have an ulterior motive. They can't be trusted.'

'There is something I haven't told you,' said Rosalyn. 'Davies was with me when I looked at the casket. He recognised the writing.'

'So that was how you knew it was in Welsh.'

'I think he identified the inscription. I thought as a man of the cloth he would be appalled at the idea of bringing a dead man back to life, but he seems almost happy.'

'I suppose Arthur is king of the old Britons and he is Welsh,' said Brent.

'And there's another thing. I saw him leave last night and I'm pretty sure he wasn't back this morning until later.' She regretted that she hadn't mentioned this earlier. 'What if he's a fifth columnist?'

He cursed. 'Then the bloody policeman didn't do his job properly.'

'Didn't he volunteer?'

He nodded then thought about it and turned to her. 'You must be my spy. Find an opportunity to ask him where he went and what his views are. If, as you suspect, he has told the Church hierarchy then he will have set in motion an avalanche of objections and we'll find out soon. But if he's told Nazi-sympathising connections then they are likely to stay quiet until the deed is done and we'll be able to tell where his sympathies lie. Now we must return.'

When they re-entered the Hall food was being set out in the refectory and Rosalyn asked if she might have it in her room, she did not want to be in the presence of Claff and Osgood. As expected, she was locked in again but managed to take a newspaper with her to pass the time.

*

Later that day she heard a light tap on the door. She went to it and quietly asked who was there. It was the Reverend Davies.

'I just wanted to thank you for not telling Greaves that I was in the cellar with you. Osgood told me that you explored it alone yesterday.'

'You can unlock the door and come and talk to me, it you like. I'm dressed and it's quite lonely up here,' said Rosalyn. The key turned and she opened the door to let the vicar in. She gestured him to the chair then went and sat on the bed, her head lowered and mouth downturned.

'Claff said he killed Farrell's dog this morning.' A tear escaped down her cheek and she blew her nose, giving the impression that she was only just holding herself together.

'You really mustn't blame yourself, my dear,' said Davies. 'Farrell was a grown man and he knew the risks he took.'

'You recognised the Welsh inscription, didn't you?'

'*Ein brenin unwaith a'r dyfodol.* Our once and future king.' He seemed smug, pleased with his translation.

'But what does it mean for us?' she asked.

'We shall be united behind a king who has the backing of the fae, my dear. One who had the power of Merlin behind him and now brings reconciliation between greyfolk and humans. You may be released from your role in this, as it will not be necessary to breed a new generation of fae/human. The racial purity of our two species will be maintained as God intended, and we will live in harmony as we did in the past. It will be a return to the old ways, of a nobler time.'

Rosalyn's heart sunk at the words 'racial purity'; it was too close to the Aryan ideal. She tried not to show her concern.

'What happens now?' she said.

'We must wait and see if Doctor Dee can live up to expectations. But this is not the creation of a zombie from a corpse, it is the waking of one who has been sleeping with this eventuality in mind.'

'But he's just a man. Is the Holy Grail or Excalibur in the coffin with him?'

'Well, that would be a fine thing,' said Davies. 'The Germans would think twice about invading if we had those artifacts, it might actually enable peace on earth. Peace in our time. Just think what a wonderful thing that would be. It is the best possible outcome my dear.'

'Peace with Hitler?'

'We are predestined to follow the road to our salvation. Bringing King Arthur here, now, whatever reason the fae had, this is our fate, it is irresistible.'

'Even if it means the end of Churchill and his government?' said Rosalyn.

'Well of course, we shall be saved at the eleventh hour and we must embrace it.'

She was shocked by his fatalism. 'But we have a choice. Mr Churchill says –'

'You cannot trust him. Look at Tonypandy, he betrayed the Welsh, and he will do it again. I can see you will never understand, you don't have the education, girl.'

She clenched her jaw but managed to control her voice. 'I saw you leave last night. Where did you go?'

His benign manner changed immediately. 'Quite the little spy, aren't you?' His voice was harsh.

'I thought you would get the Church to stop the abomination of raising the dead.'

'Not dead, just sleeping. Remember?'

'What did the bishops say?' she asked.

'That's enough Miss James.' He stood and moved to the door. 'You should stay out of the way from now on and keep your mouth shut lest it be permanently closed.'

He hesitated, and she felt his temptation to do her some violence. She stood, almost matching him in height, brought her fists to her sides and stuck out her jaw. He quickly left. Not so avuncular now, but Rosalyn also knew she'd failed and would have to wait until she saw Brent to tell him so. After barricading the door with a chair and table, she went to bed and slept, praying that her dreams would be of Farrell and not the hellish spectre of a dead king risen from the grave.

Wednesday 4 September 1940

Rosalyn woke early and looked eagerly out of her window. Being at the back of the house she would not see any new arrivals from the road and was keen to know when Doctor Dee arrived. But he would come in through the front door and out of her sight. The response of Osgood and Claff should be interesting. They hadn't known his identity when he lived in Pitdown Hall before. She had a long wait for breakfast and was disappointed when they sent it up on a tray. The cook's assistant was accompanied by Osgood, a precaution that he obviously resented.

As the boy bustled away, she sat on the bed and said, 'Osgood, don't go yet. Talk to me.'

He stood in the doorway and smiled down at her. She was tall but he was broad with a kind of ingrained sootiness like a chimney sweep. Perhaps there was the suggestion of hell and she thought she could detect a faint aroma of smoke. That sensation made her feel weak and it may have showed on her face because he stepped into the room, closed the door, and leaned on it. Rosalyn was afraid. She was dressed but had only stockinged feet. Why did his wife leave him? Perhaps he was used to having his way with women.

A big horse, that's what he is. The stroppy Cleveland Bay her uncle had bought to breed from before the war, full of attitude, prepared to crush you against a fence or a wall. But not vicious. She had to believe that. She was sure Brent would kill him if he harmed her.

'What are you going to do about Dee and the revenant if they bring it back to life?' she asked.

'None of your business. You only have one purpose.' He looked her up and down lasciviously and his voice, always deep, had taken on a husky edge, as though he was thinking what he might do with her. 'To spread your legs.' He adjusted his crotch.

Make him talk about it, control your voice, think how you managed the horse. They can sense fear. 'What do they need for magic like that?' she asked.

'Somebody will be sacrificed, or maybe more than one person. I know of several attempts by one man and you wouldn't want to meet him.' He was bragging now. 'Even he didn't succeed.'

'Aleister Crowley. I read about him in the newspaper. Do you think they'll use Farrell?' Masking her fear with confidence she said, 'He's still alive, isn't he? You didn't dislike him. Where are they keeping him?'

'So that's what this is about. Got a taste for it did you? I can give you what he did, bigger and better.'

She felt cold with fury, and it must have showed. He straightened up. He might have remembered what happened to Farrell.

'You shouldn't worry about him,' he said. 'Looks like one of your granddads tweaked John Dee's nose good and he's got it in for you. Maybe you'll be the sacrifice in the necromancy.'

Rosalyn smiled. 'If I were you, I'd be scared. You hexed him and he's a man who likes revenge. Don't think you'll be getting out Scot free.'

'That bastard had what was mine and I took revenge.' He stopped. 'Still, I look forward to meeting him, interesting old cove.' He opened the door. 'They'll be here about midday, so expect a long slow morning.' He closed the door and locked it.

'You may be able to forgive him for taking your wife, but your daughter is another matter,' she said through the door.

Rosalyn noticed that most of her jailors had taken out the key and stored it on a shelf nearby. Osgood failed to do that. She waited about an hour until she was sure the men had breakfasted and left for the day, then she slid the newspaper under the door and worked on the key to make it drop down. She didn't want it to fall too far away. It was not as easy as she had expected. In her schoolgirl stories it was always a foolproof way to escape.

Eventually it dropped. She drew it towards herself and almost lost it as it caught on the sill. She heard someone coming up the stairs and began to panic. In the nick of time she withdrew both the paper and key and hid the key under her pillow, throwing herself on the bed and casually continuing with the crossword.

It was Greaves and she heard him say, 'Where's the bloody key? Can you see it? That fool Osgood's put it somewhere out of sight or taken it with him. Go and get the spare it's hanging up in the office with the others.'

Someone walked away and Greaves spoke to her through the door. 'You're to come downstairs. Loveday wants to see you again. You can ask him any questions you want before the old man himself arrives. Are you dressed and ready to go?'

Rosalyn replied in the affirmative and tidied her room, hoping no one would search it for the key whilst she was out. The braid of hair was there too but they could not object to something so innocent, if they found it.

Greaves unlocked the door and escorted her through the house and the orangery to the office. Rosalyn entered cautiously. She saw Loveday, who had accompanied the box to the hall two days earlier and the female seolfor she had heard in the cellar. She took a long hard look at the creature. She was so unlike the ones she had met on her journey from Winchester to St Jude's Church. Tall and human-like and ageless, the seolfor did not smile and her expression was unreadable as she returned Rosalyn's stare equally coldly.

'You've met Miss James, Mr Loveday. She made a nuisance of herself in London and is still proving to be a handful, but I think you're aware of that,' said Greaves.

Loveday said, 'And this is the Lady Eoldrith.'

The seolfor studied her face and body, then touched her hair, examining her ears. A chill ran through Rosalyn, and the faint autumnal scent of mushrooms reminded her of that first morning at Pitdown when she had felt someone was watching her. Was it this creature or another?

Loveday still looked both old and young and in natural light the colour of his skin and hair were faded and made her think of dead things.

He smiled and beckoned her to sit, then stared at Greaves meaningfully.

'I'll leave you to it then,' Greaves said reluctantly and left the room.

Loveday sat behind the desk and, resting his chin on his hands, gazed at Rosalyn until she grew annoyed and stared back at him frowning.

'You fascinate me,' he said eventually.

'I don't know why, unless you knew my ancestor. The one who caused all these problems. Did he harm you in some way?'

'No he helped me and I think it is fair to say that I, in turn, helped him. I would never have met Doctor Dee if Robert McKinley hadn't come to the Ashmolean in 1848 to seek advice on the good doctor and his history.'

Rosalyn thought the doctor was anything but good. She said nothing.

Loveday said, 'You may as well know that McKinley's actions deprived the Doctor of some useful servants, a small group of old fae that had been with him for many years, by arrangement with Lord Faerie,'

'So this is a vendetta against our family. I suppose I should be glad my brothers have been spared.'

'Abducting serving men would attract too much attention. Besides you're the right age for the breeding programme and Lord Agremont is keen to begin the experiment.'

'I thought it had already begun,' said Rosalyn. Loveday and Eoldrith exchanged a look of surprise. 'I was midwife to Mrs Farrell and the poor creature she brought into the world - dead.'

He was surprised. 'A natural occurrence. A result of the intermingling of fae with humans at the house parties here at Pitdown Hall. Such decadence.'

Loveday's pale eyes stared at her own. He clearly suspected she knew more about the women held in London at the theatre, and their escape at the same time as her own.

'You let them out, didn't you?' he said.

'It was an accident. I stumbled on them quite by chance because I was afraid and ran away from Greaves and Brent. How was I to know they were prisoners? It was a London theatre after all. They might have been showgirls.'

Heavily pregnant showgirls. She smiled innocently.

He grimaced. 'You knew they were from this estate.'

'Didn't you enjoy the parties?' Rosalyn said spitefully, suspecting he would not have been favoured by the Pitdown women when more exotic and superhuman males were available.

He ignored this.

The seolfor female spoke to her for the first time. 'You will have no choice, Rosalyn James. They will mate you with a seolfor and your progeny, half-breeds, will be selected for their qualities. Any offspring that are of inadequate quality will be euthanised.' She observed her reaction with inquisitiveness.

'It's barbaric,' Rosalyn said.

'It isn't conventional to be sure. But if we accept the theories of your scientists, like the man Darwin and his survival of the fittest then it is logical. This will be the next step in our evolution and yours. An acceptance of the survival of the fittest. It will be an evolutionary step, the breeding of a master race, an 'ubermenschen'. Of course, a hybrid fae-human is likely to be 'uber alles' to borrow a phrase from your enemy.'

Man and superman, but there was a hint of bitterness on the exquisite face.

'I think you disapprove,' she said to Eoldrith.

Loveday shifted slightly and looked uncomfortable for the first time. She wondered if he had formed an attachment to the female seolfor.

'Why not breed human men with female seolfor?' Rosalyn said and knew from the hostile silence that it was a point of anger and sorrow.

Loveday winced.

Eoldrith said, 'Female seolfor are no longer fertile, and there are fewer of us. I think you're well matched with Lord Agremont, I believe he has seen you; you will find him handsome in a cold way.'

'She is no longer pure,' Loveday reminded Eoldrith.

With a movement Rosalyn did not see the seolfor was kneeling between her legs, pressing her hands against her stomach, and staring into her body.

'There is no fertilised seed in this belly.' The silvery voice said with what might have been regret.

The violation and physical contact with the pale creature shocked Rosalyn into immobility and she waited for her to move away, but Eoldrith remained studying her body with a cold curiosity. Eventually her face was close to Rosalyn's, and she stared into the silver-grey eyes and saw her own reflection.

'He will try hard to impregnate you. The things he will do.' Eoldrith's face changed, and she pulled away from her as quickly as she had come.

Was that sorrow?

'You love him, don't you?' Rosalyn had recognised the hopelessness of passion and jealousy on the pale beautiful face.

'If you don't conceive then he will give you to one of the lower orders. They are generally smaller and uglier, and many are unkind to humans, because they blame you for the loss of their homes. If that happens then you will have a miserable life until your spirit or your fertility is destroyed. The females will treat you most cruelly of all.' She smiled with satisfaction. 'Yes, I think Doctor Dee will have had satisfactory revenge.'

Rosalyn had a horrific vision of life in a prison with no human contact and only these creatures pawing her and raping her. But she would not give her the satisfaction of seeing this.

'Or I could give birth to a powerful king and become a, a …' she struggled for a suitable expression '… the founder of a dynasty.'

Loveday sniggered at her pathetic prediction, and she remembered the coffin in the cellar.

'And what about King Arthur?' said Rosalyn. 'How does he fit into this? If you raise him from the dead, won't he want to be king again?'

'Not dead,' said Eoldrith passionately. 'Just sleeping, and he is from an age when men and seolfor shared the land. You know Merlin was a child of mixed race, his father was not human. His wisdom protected Arthur until ...' She stopped.

Rosalyn knew very little about the legend of Arthur but she was certain that the fae were heavily involved and that in their dreamtime world, as Mariel called it, a thousand years could pass easily for those who chose its narcotic sleep. Was Arthur also a seolfor human hybrid or was he pure seolfor or pure human?

Loveday saw her mind working and realised they had said too much. He went to the door. 'Time to put you away, for now.'

Rosalyn had expected Greaves or one of the men to escort her to the attic but she was dismayed when Eoldrith took her roughly by the arm and marched her upstairs to her room.

She tried to speak to her, but this made Eoldrith stare at her wildly and grip Rosalyn's arm even more tightly with her vice-like hand.

Someone had replaced the key and she was again locked into the attic bedroom. She lay on the bed and went over the conversation from memory. It was imperative that Brent knew that Loveday, Davies and Eoldrith wanted to sabotage the cross breeding of human and fae. Davies to keep bloodlines pure, Eoldrith out of jealousy, and Loveday? Rosalyn thought the man might be in love with Eoldrith. That would leave only Dee and Agremont to support the breeding of a new race in exchange for assistance if the Germans invaded and it was something Churchill would be asked to consider as a last resort.

It was ironic that an ancient legend could be a weapon of sabotage in the twentieth century; an image of the perfect kingdom of Britain, embellished by centuries of fictive dreams. It was as unreal as the faerie glamour that had made old Gilgoreth look like a child as he led her through the woods in Hampshire.

The remains of Arthur had been brought to Pitdown Hall to be the focus of a fifth columnist insurrection against the government of Churchill and the King. They would settle a truce with Hitler and impose a new order on the British people, headed by a hero of old and gilded with the deceptive magic of the fae. It would be welcomed because war and bloodshed would be avoided, but at what cost to freedom?

8 A KING

Although the key was hidden in her room Rosalyn was afraid to escape, knowing that there were seolfor like Eoldrith in the house. But she had just enough courage to creep downstairs and leave a note in Brent's room saying they must talk. It was unsigned, but he would guess it came from her.

All the windows were open on the sultry day and she heard the telephone ring in the office. Doors were slammed. It became quiet and she paced the small room in frustration. Eventually there was a tap at the door and Brent let himself in.

It surprised her how pleased she was to see him.

He flopped onto the bed, a bit of an imposition she thought, as Brent crossed his ankles. He chuckled. 'Dee has refused to come down to the country, apparently he wants to stay in town and the circus will have to go to him.'

'Then the coffin will need to be moved.' Rosalyn thought about the procession of greyfolk and the draped casket when it arrived. 'Perhaps they'll carry it, at least part of the way.'

'Yes, I suppose so. We know they walked here with it but I don't know how they can manage that in town,' he said. 'I suppose they'll have to take it in a lorry. They seem to be reluctant to use mechanised transport.'

Rosalyn trusted him completely. She must tell him about Davies and Loveday and confirm his suspicion of their plan to activate the fifth column and negotiate with Hitler.

'Loveday and Davies both want to use the thing in the coffin to mount an attack on Churchill and bring down the government,' she said.

He sat up. After checking that no one was listening at the door he encouraged her to repeat everything she had learned.

'So that's why he volunteered,' said Brent. 'I wondered what his interest was. How disappointing. 'They'll take the casket to London and Dee will perform the raising of Arthur in the theatre in Soho. There are probably members of the government who would cooperate and who could be in contact with the conspirators. You say Loveday is not in favour of cross breeding seolfor and human?'

'I got the impression he wants to preserve the racial purity of humans and faerie folk, but it might be that he's jealous not to be part of it,' said Rosalyn. 'I heard someone arrive. Who was it?'

'A messenger from Dee, an elderly lady, some sort of servant I suppose. She went straight to the kitchen after handing over the letter. Loveday was beside himself with suppressed anger. I think Greaves was secretly relieved and now that strange female seolfor will accompany them to London.' As he said this he stood and took her hands. 'We have little time to prevent their treachery. I must speak to Greaves. Have courage Rosalyn.'

It was the first time he had used her given name and she flushed at the physical contact with him. She was reminded of Farrell holding her hand and for a moment she felt how weak she was. It must have shown because he withdrew his hands suddenly and spoke formally to her.

'Your information is important. I will persuade Greaves that our priority must be to prevent the formation of a movement to overthrow the government and replace it with fascist sympathisers. You've done well.'

He left her with a feeling of hope and loss. She so longed to be with people, and she was isolated and a prisoner in the stuffy attic room. Occasionally a warplane could be heard above, and she ran to the window and craned her neck to get a glimpse of it.

She read her newspaper from cover to cover irritated by the jingoistic journalism that tried to make Britain's plight into some sort of heroic stand. The country was standing alone against a ruthless ideology that had conquered western Europe in a stunning display of military prowess. She knew morale was important and that this was part of the propaganda. But she also knew that the British people were outwardly positive but feeling inwardly negative. If men were being trained to commit murder and sacrifice themselves, then these were desperate times.

About an hour later there was a tap on the door and Rosalyn thought Brent had returned and expected him to enter. Nothing happened and, when the tap was repeated, she went to the door.

'Who is it?' she said and stepped back as the key turned in the lock and the door opened a little and Mariel's slight form slid round it. She hugged her, almost in tears with relief that the older woman was safe. 'What are you doing here?'

Mariel carried a basket and she set out sandwiches and produced a bottle of beer.

'I don't have a glass I'm afraid,' said Rosalyn, regretting smashing it in her earlier temper. They drank from the bottle and after a long silence, she said, 'I expect you are disappointed that I didn't take up the generous offer to save myself and go with the fae.'

Mariel just smiled and patted her knee. When they had eaten, she carefully wiped her mouth and said, 'I must apologise to you for pushing you to run away. I'm afraid my maternal instinct got the better of me. I think more of you for coming back to face the enemy.'

'How are the pregnant women? Have any given birth yet?' Rosalyn was curious.

'Most of them have at least a month to go and Mrs Farrell's was premature. Or should I say *were* premature.' She looked sharply at Rosalyn. 'You didn't tell me everything, did you?'

It was clear that as the fae had taken the creature from her bed on the night of 27th August they would now have explained everything to Mariel.

'I thought I imagined it,' she said. 'I woke up with a bundle of sticks and a pinecone. I thought I was going mad. How could I explain that to you? But it means there is a baby made by Mrs Farrell and a seolfor that is still alive. Assuming it's still alive.'

Mariel nodded then stood up and walked to the window.

Fearing she would leave Rosalyn said, 'I have to get out of here. I can't stand being locked up and I don't think they intend to try to breed from me at least for now. They're planning on taking the remains of someone who might be King Arthur to London for resurrection.'

Mariel turned and looked intently at her.

'Then you will be safe,' she said.

'But the country will not. They intend to establish an alternative government to that of Churchill and the King and they will negotiate a truce with Hitler. After the fall of France and the defeat of so many countries in Europe a lot of ordinary people will support them. I'm sorry but I have to try and stop it.'

Mariel smiled slowly like a mischievous child and nodded. 'Come on then. Let's do it.'

*

Mariel made Rosalyn wait in the attic room whilst she returned the basket to the kitchen and scouted the great house to find out who was in residence. After what seemed an age, she reappeared and beckoned Rosalyn to follow her downstairs. Passing the understairs cupboard in the gloomy hall reminded Rosalyn of the hair braid that she still had hidden under the mattress. She must find somewhere safer to hide it. Cook and his assistant were busy in the kitchen with much chopping and cooking smells permeated the ground floor.

They tried the door to the cellar but was locked so they passed it and entered the chapel. Rosalyn was again struck by the coolness of the air and the odour of old books. The other woman began scrutinising the floor and the corners.

'Are you looking for something?' said Rosalyn.

'I'm hoping to find an old tomb or a grave that we can open.'

Her granddaughter stopped and looked at her in shock.

'We need to replace the remains of the king with something, preferably other bones.' She disappeared among the stacks of paper.

The idea made perfect sense. But how easy would it be to find old bones? It was likely that the noble people of the house had been interred in the chapel and the servants in the small cemetery.

Suddenly Mariel's voice exclaimed with delight.

'Behind these books there's a door. Help me move them.'

They carefully shifted the stacks of ancient documents and created a narrow entrance to a dark wall. Her eyesight must be exceptional thought Rosalyn but then she remembered her experience and a life spent with the fae. The wall was carved with figures that were not clear, but there was definitely at least one skull and what resembled a skeleton.

'A mausoleum,' Mariel whispered.

Rosalyn was unhappy at the idea of disturbing the dead. What they were going to do was worse. The door opened inward and between them they moved it to allow a six-inch gap. Mariel squeezed through but Rosalyn had a struggle to join her. They were in a very small tomb that housed the mortal remains of the Pitdown families. Coffins were laid on shelves. She could see them through her anointed eye. It was pitch black if she closed it. A cracking sound startled her but she saw Mariel prising the lid off a large coffin, then she grunted and pushed it to one side to reveal another older coffin further back.

'What's wrong with the first one?'

'Too fresh.'

Rosalyn shuddered and she caught the whiff of decay, but it may have been her imagination. The place had an oppressive atmosphere. She told herself what she had previously considered supernatural was, in fact, another natural dimension she had simply never encountered. Mariel seemed to have no qualms about the spirits of the dead resenting being disturbed.

'Help me with this one, will you?'

They hauled the old wooden box from its resting place and were grateful it held together. This was the advantage of being interred in a mausoleum rather than the damp earth where rot would soon claim the coffin and the corpse. A convenient pair of blocks enabled them to set it at waist level and Mariel immediately began prising it open, her small strong hands seemingly happy in their work. Rosalyn wondered how she had such energy and enthusiasm for a task of this kind. The older woman read her mind, or perhaps it was because she hung back squeamishly.

Mariel said, 'Let's hope this one is female. The other was male which would not do if we are to replace Arthur.'

'But surely you need to replace him with a male skeleton?'

'Then whatever is raised will be proclaimed Arthur, whoever he was originally. No, if they succeed in this profane experiment the result must not be someone they can use to gull a credulous population.'

In awe at the woman's logic and foresight Rosalyn joined in prying open the coffin and the lid soon parted from the sides, enabling them to slide it to the floor. The body was covered by a shroud and Mariel gently pulled it open to reveal a skeleton in a woman's dress.

'How long ago do you think she was buried?' asked Rosalyn.

'Last century judging by the clothes. She'll do very well. Help me undress her, or rather help me remove the bones from what's left of the garments. We'll need to collect them. The shroud is still sound, use that and don't worry about the order, we can sort it out when we replace Arthur, or whoever he is.'

It was with some revulsion that Rosalyn managed to extract the arm bones from the sleeves and the feet from the remains of the boots, but the bones of the torso were worst. Fortunately Mariel was familiar with the impediments of female Victorian dress and quickly ripped off the stays and tight buttons to reveal the remaining bones. The whole process had taken them but a few minutes and they wrapped the skeleton as gently as possible in the shroud.

'Now we switch it with whatever is in the casket in the cellar.'

Mariel slipped back through the gap and took the bones from Rosalyn who then joined her in the chapel. They concealed the door and replaced the books. Evidently that was the place they would hide the king. Would it be necessary to dress him in the frock? Rosalyn suppressed a giggle and realised her hair was standing on end.

They crept through the chapel; it was quiet and their activity seemed to have gone unnoticed. At the door Mariel signalled for Rosalyn to remain behind while she established the position in the hall. She closed the door behind her and waited, her ear pressed against the varnished wood. The bag of the Victorian woman's bones were clutched tightly, careful that nothing should fall and make a sound. The silence was comforting and gave her a chance to have another look at the small church built to nurture the spiritual well-being of the great family that had lived here.

She thought about their servants, they would be expected to attend chapel. The attic room Rosalyn occupied was probably the living space of several maids or men. They woke before dawn in the winter to set and light the fires to warm the Hall. The head of the household was responsible for their moral well-being as much as their physical health. How times had changed. The previous occupier had debauched every woman within his ambit.

She now knew the names of the gentry. The coffins in the mausoleum carried the brass plates with the family name of Genillard, but she didn't know if they had built the Hall in Tudor times or acquired it during the turbulent sixteenth and seventeenth centuries. How had it fallen into the hands of Doctor Dee in the twentieth century?

Her contemplation was interrupted by the door pushing against her and she let Mariel into the chapel.

'They're eating. The cellar is still locked, but you said there's another way to it?'

'Through Davies's bedroom. He may have pushed furniture in front of it but between us, we might be able to shift it, as long as we do it quietly.' Rosalyn thought. 'Won't they be looking for me?'

'They know I took you food earlier. Let's go.'

They tiptoed across the hall and were about to mount the stairs when the noise from the refectory increased as the door opened. Rosalyn quickly hid in the cupboard. She heard Mariel speak to someone, the tone of the interrogation sounded like Greaves, polite but imperious. Whatever she said he apologised and she heard his feet as he went upstairs. There was silence and she sat down, there could be a long wait before she was able to leave the cupboard. She tried not to think about the person whose remains she held in her arms. A woman who had laughed and cried in this house, perhaps been born, and almost certainly died here. Was she old? The insidious thought crept upon her. Had she died in childbirth? So many did and she could not stop the remembered screams and the smell of blood and tears that accompanied birthing and the sight of the woman upstairs with her strange offspring.

You need to think like a farmer, she told herself. Be pragmatic. Everything is normal except the deliberate cruelty of man. She had been obliged to read Thomas Hardy's 'Tess of the d'Urbervilles' and she hadn't liked it, thought it unnecessarily cruel. But sitting on the floor of the understairs cupboard she remembered many of the images and also Tess's fall from grace, her pregnancy and her mother's remark 'tis nature and what do please God'. If there is a God.

The door opened and Mariel entered. She put her finger to her lips and they heard footsteps walking down the stairs and moving into the refectory. They cautiously left the cupboard and made their way to the first floor and the room that Rosalyn indicated as Davies's. Mariel took out her knife. Fortunately for Davies the room was empty. They lifted the chest of drawers out of the way of the hidden door and opened it. There were no sounds coming from the cellar below and Rosalyn slowly navigated the steps as her elderly relative skipped down them like a teenager. She had to keep the bones quiet and intact.

By the time she emerged Mariel had removed the lid of the box and was carefully examining the coffin, then she began prising it open with her knife. As she broke the seal there was a sigh, and they looked at each other and then around the room. It had not been opened for many years, perhaps millennia. The gases must have been in there for hundreds of years, but the smell was neutral, perhaps a little like leather. Placing the female bones on the floor they both lifted the coffin lid and Rosalyn was surprised that in some part of her mind she still expected to find Farrell inside.

Feeling both relieved and disappointed, she peered into the gloom. It was another skeleton. He was clothed in rich robes that still glinted of gold and purple and wore a silver diadem on his brow. Rosalyn felt they should have been more respectful; he was a king after all. Immediately the robes changed colour. They became grey and silvery, like frosted leaves, and then they disintegrated.

'Do you think this could be the remains of a seolfor?' she whispered to Mariel.

They studied the skeleton. To their eyes the bones were grey and slightly luminous. They looked different to the ones from the Victorian woman's coffin, less porous and harder. Also, his shape and size was that of a tall well-built man.

'I can't see anything to suggest it, but the flesh has gone so the principal tell-tale signs have perished,' said Mariel. 'Let's take him out and see if there is anything else.'

Without speaking Mariel lifted the skull and they were shocked to see his long dark hair. 'Faerie magic,' said Mariel. The older woman did not seem shocked and smiled at Rosalyn's stricken face. The diadem remained intact and she wondered if they would be able to transfer it to the other body but no amount of prising and pulling would remove it from the king's smooth silvery skull.

'He's fae. Isn't he?' asked Rosalyn.

Mariel nodded. 'Or part fae.'

With unseemly haste they scooped the bones out of the coffin and replaced them with the unfortunate woman for whom Rosalyn had now created an imagined life story. She secretly hoped that if they succeeded in bringing her back to life, she would turn out to be a sharp-tongued harridan who would lambast Doctor Dee and his lackeys and with a special hatred for the Welsh and Davies in particular. Then she felt guilty as they had disturbed her in death.

All this took Rosalyn's mind off the gruesome deed they had carried out, and the coffin lid and box lid were replaced. Mariel had the ingenious idea of sealing the lid using a candle they found in the cellar and smearing the wax around the opening. They succeeded in replacing the furniture in front of the concealed door and prepared to go down to the chapel again. Mariel and Rosalyn closed the door to Davies's room and but before they could descend, they heard men leaving the dining room. They could not risk being seen together and Mariel would look odd carrying a shroud past the men's bedrooms, so Rosalyn took the king's bones up to her attic room and hid them under the bed. Mariel kissed her and locked her in for the night.

*

Thursday 5 September 1940

Lying above the mortal remains of Arthur, the legendary king of the Britons, one whose tale of love and valour had inspired poets for centuries, Rosalyn fell instantly asleep. She dreamed of swimming underwater, able to breathe, and looking at wonderful fish that were friendly and came to examine her. She was searching for something or someone and, if found, would be happy.

The pool became darker, the blue and green light patterns faded, and Rosalyn knew she was looking for her lover. A pike was guarding something and when she had driven it away, and brushed aside the weed, there was the child of Farrell's wife that she had taken to her cottage. Her only thought was to save it and take it to the surface to breathe and that was how she woke up. Perhaps the bones were just those of an old dead king and nothing magical, so she went back to sleep.

When Mariel brought up her breakfast early the following morning Rosalyn suggested smuggling the bones downstairs in a pile of bed sheets. She was certain that having a female servant at Pitdown Hall would be a relief to the men and they would make the most of it.

'You can say I've started my monthly,' she suggested. With Mariel's agreement she cut her third finger with the knife and smeared it on the sheet, diluted with water. They dragged the bones out from under the bed, still wrapped in the shroud and bundled them in the soiled bedsheet, making sure that blood showed. Menstrual blood was enough to repel most men. Mariel would hide them in the laundry until it was possible to transfer them into the chapel's mausoleum. Rosalyn's help would be necessary if they were to return everything to its original state, but she could not wander around the building without good reason.

When the opportunity presented itself, she would tell Brent but not the full involvement of Mariel. She explained this to her grandmother and tried to predict the reactions of Greaves and the others. She really was not sure that she knew them well enough. Davies was in favour of a change of government and there must be other fascist sympathisers in the country.

It was generally considered likely that the speedy fall of the Low Countries, Denmark and France must have meant the Germans had assistance from nationals working to that end. Norway had Quisling and Marshall Petain had sullied his own good name by surrendering France in exchange for Vichy. Brent would know what to do.

In order to further disguise their intentions, Mariel said she would launder all the sheets at Pitdown Hall and Rosalyn would help her. They traipsed around the building disturbing any remaining men. Attempts at ribaldry towards Rosalyn were quelled by a fierce stare from the older woman as she ferociously stripped the beds, tut-tutting at the dirty feet marks. She was stronger than she looked, wiry and determined when she should have been frail. Rosalyn's task was to carry the increasing pile of laundry as it was stacked onto her own sheets. Osgood and Claff headed off to their work.

When Greaves saw the bloody signs he said, 'Well at least you're not pregnant.'

Rosalyn was reminded of Eoldrith's actions and felt a surge of emotion at this. She wasn't sure if it was regret or relief, but it brought back the memory of Farrell's embrace and the thought that having his child would be the one thing that could make everything alright. She blushed and tears started and that was enough to drive away Greaves muttering about women and the time of the month.

Then he turned and said, 'We'll get out of your way. The seolfor female will be accompanying Brent to explore the railway…' he paused. 'Local places, she will use her powers to disguise them both so they cannot be seen, even in daylight.'

Rosalyn mouthed 'Davies' to Mariel.

'What about the Welshman?'

Greaves turned in surprise.

'I haven't got his sheets. His door's blocked.'

He walked to the door to Davies's room and pushed. The door swung in easily and he nearly fell through.

'Well it was when we tried it just now,' Mariel said.

It was clear that Davies had pushed furniture against it overnight and it was quite plausible that they had tried to open it. Mariel bustled to the bed and peeled back the candlewick cover.

'The Reverend Davies will be staying at the Hall to do some research with Mr Loveday. I'm sure they won't bother you.'

Greaves left them and they heard him going downstairs through the orangery to the office.

Rosalyn moved closer to Mariel and whispered, 'This is bad news. Greaves will be in the office, cook and his chap will be in the kitchen but Davies and Loveday are likely to be in the chapel where Doctor Dee's books are stored. We should have left the remains in my room. We'll be stuck in the laundry with Arthur's bones.'

'Well, let's get the copper on and start the wash, we'll need all the drying time available. When the sheets are hanging on the lines behind the wash house, we can explore with the excuse of searching for alternative ones for the beds.'

Rosalyn was used to hard work, but her grandmother was relentless. The boiling water created clouds of steam and the cook and his assistant stayed well away. She did everything she could to ensure that smells and steam found their way into the Hall. There was something depressing and sterilizing about the smell of Sunlight soap. Davies and Loveday came out of the chapel arguing. It was clear that the latter did not want to stay in there to work and he announced he would continue in the cellar.

Davies watched Loveday go, he was carrying a pile of documents. Then they saw him drift towards the source of the disturbance and they bustled about preparing to hang washing. As they began hanging the sheets, he announced that he might go for a walk to clear his head.

Mariel turned to Rosalyn. 'Carry on washing that mess from your sheets, girl. I'll see if I can find spares.' Then she marched off into the Hall. Rosalyn avoided Davies's eyes but went into the wash house to retrieve the remains of his hero, still wrapped in a bloody bundle. She hoped that Mariel would find a way to drive him out of the Hall altogether. As if in answer she heard a quavery soprano coming from the direction of the chapel, the doors were open and the elderly woman was clearly happy in her work, opening cupboards and any furniture that had been placed there in storage.

It did not take long for Davies to join Loveday in the cellar, well away from the chapel and allowing them the access they needed.

In the silence they bundled the bones in its shroud through the chapel and into the mausoleum.

'You must put everything back into place. I'll keep watch in case he returns. Can you manage?' Mariel said.

Rosalyn nodded. She would do it somehow and she carried it through the mausoleum door and Mariel closed it after her. So she was alone, and yet not alone she reminded herself, she was with the Genillard family and their ancestors. The empty dress of the woman they had stolen lay crumpled like an old skin. Would Loveday and Eoldrith find out about the deception before they were summoned to London for the ceremony of waking the dead king?

The air was cool and stale and she wished she had Mariel for company. The long bones fitted into the sleeves and into the skirt and she hid the torso behind the body of the dress. What to do about the crowned head? Rosalyn looked into the empty eye sockets and tried to imagine the person who had lived his life of thought, feelings, and imagination in this empty sphere. There is a whole world in one head and then it is gone as though it never existed. Scraps of a beard held the jaw in place and she hid it inside the ruffles at the neck and then wrapped a piece of lace around the diadem so it would not be noticeable if the coffin was opened.

Manhandling it back into place was awkward but she managed it and then replaced the more recent interment in front of it. That was a heavier and more substantial coffin. She dreaded the lid opening but took comfort from Mariel's matter of fact approach to death and corpses. When the room looked exactly as they had found it, she approached the door and looked for the handle. There was nothing to grasp to pull the door open into the room.

Rosalyn gasped. She could hear nothing, and the air was suddenly depleted of oxygen, though she knew it must be her imagination. Mariel had informed her that there was ventilation in places where the dead were left to rot above ground. Incidents where the gases of decomposition had created explosions were now much scarcer because provision had been made for the exchange of air with the outside. Her mind travelled around the building as she mentally searched for the vent in the chapel walls. Anything to take her mind off the fact that she was locked in a tomb. She sat on the blocks that had supported the coffin and thanked the gods that she had used the potion on her eye, because she could see in the dark. If she closed it the absence of that sense was overwhelming.

It made her think of the story of the faerie midwife. The midwife was human and she was at home one evening when there was a knock on the door. It was a man she didn't recognise, but he implored her to attend his wife who was in labour. She obliged and he took her to a part of the village that she'd never been to before and into a quaint house that she suspected might not be what it seemed. In the room there was a faerie woman in extreme pain and unable to conceal her species so the man also showed his true form and begged her to assist in any way she could.

The birthing was long and hard, but the baby was eventually born alive and the mother showed all the signs of a good recovery. The man paid the midwife handsomely and took her back to her own house. After this encounter she was never able to find that street and that house again. However, during the birthing process the midwife had wiped her eye whilst her hand was wet with fluid from the baby. It had stung but she thought no more about it. A few weeks after the event she was in the market and she saw the father going about his business. She stopped him and enquired how the mother and baby were doing. He was shocked and asked if she could see him and the midwife realised it was only through the eye that had received the fluid. If she closed it, he disappeared. Without hesitation the faerie man blinded her in that eye and vanished from her life forever.

How cruel he was, and ungrateful. Whether or not it was true she knew that these creatures did not have the same values as humans. They existed in a parallel world that was now rapidly diverging from the modern world as technology and science overwhelmed the human one. She realised they were not powerful, but weak and threatened with extinction. Whatever happens in London with the resurrection of Arthur, the seolfor would need to ensure their survival and if not by breeding with humans, then by subjugating them.

The Nazis were doing just that in Europe. Breeding pure Aryans and using the other races as slaves. She wondered why there were so many types of fae, from the tall seolfor so human-like, to the smaller ones she had met out in the countryside with their clever deceptions.

There was a light tap on the door. It opened and Rosalyn was pleased to squeeze through it, straight into the arms of Brent. He was wedged in the small space between the piles of documents and she was about to speak when he put a hand over her mouth.

For a second, she did not know whether to fight or comply but then heard Mariel arguing with Greaves outside the door of the chapel. Would they need to go back into the mausoleum? She hoped not. Mariel's voice was now an octave higher than usual and she must be having an effect because she was evidently moving away.

Brent put an arm around Rosalyn and led her through the chapel to the door. They left and took cover in the understairs cupboard. They didn't speak but as he was too tall to stand comfortably, he sat on the floor and Rosalyn joined him. She wanted to hug him for rescuing her but instead she sat next to him, their arms touching, and she became acutely aware of his presence.

She knew she still loved Farrell and had vivid memories of their night together, but there was comfort in this other masculine presence, his warmth, and his smell. She allowed herself to drift into a euphoric state where she felt safe and happy.

The door opened and Mariel beckoned sharply. 'Quick. You must go to your room before Loveday comes back as well.'

Reluctantly Rosalyn scrambled out of the cupboard and up the stairs arriving in her bedroom breathing heavily. What was happening to her? Was she falling in love with Brent? Was it some magic spell? There was a mystique about him. As she ran upstairs, she allowed herself a glance at him as he stood next to Mariel. He looked at her with curiosity but with none of the warmth she had seen in Farrell's eyes. He might guess, and she flushed with embarrassment. Was she a tart now that she'd lost her virginity? The girls at school used to say once you'd done it with a man you wanted more. Her mind was in turmoil.

*

Only as she lay on her bed and thought about what they had achieved, swapping the bones of King Arthur for some Victorian woman, did Rosalyn remember that Brent should have been on assignment with the men exploring railway tunnels. He had obviously returned early and Mariel had trusted him enough to tell him that she was trapped in the tomb of the Genillards. But how much did he know? She wanted Mariel to come and see her and explain what had happened. The bedroom door opened and Brent entered.

'That was close,' he said.

She nodded. 'You came back early.'

'We aborted the mission. The seolfor magic was effective in making us invisible as we walked through the station unseen, but as we approached the tracks, she became sick. It seemed to be a reaction to the railway lines.'

'Iron,' said Rosalyn. 'It's their Achilles heel.'

'Not a good quality in a modern warrior. I suppose they were fine in the bronze age.'

Rosalyn thought about this. 'Do you think iron is affecting their fertility?'

He shrugged.

'I have no idea,' Brent sat on the bed next to her and scratched the back of his neck with his thumb, a gesture she had noticed before.

'We have iron in our blood,' said Rosalyn. 'Perhaps they don't. I suppose it may be a weakness they hope to breed out of their race by mixing human blood into it.'

'I thought they were a different species,' said Brent. 'But I've been told there are hybrids of fae and humans already. I wonder how long there's been interbreeding.' He looked at her and shook his head. 'It makes no difference to the problems we have today. One way or another we must prevent a fifth column coup against our government. You agree?'

Exhausted she lay back on the bed and shut her eyes. He lay back too; the scarred side of his face was closest to her and she resisted the temptation to look. For the first time in a while she felt relaxed, and Rosalyn was just thinking how much they must resemble the effigies on a medieval tomb when sleep dragged her into its blissful state. She awoke some time later and he was gone. Had he looked at her? Had she snored? Was he tempted by her unconscious body? Damn it she was becoming obsessed with sex, and she thought of Farrell with a sharp stab of pain.

Everyone was summoned to the sitting room; Greaves came in when they were smoking and drinking coffee. A lorry would be arriving that day, and they were to travel in it to London with the coffin. That is, everyone except Eoldrith who would make her own way to the theatre. So it was going to happen, and there was a silence as each person thought what it might mean for them personally.

Eventually Osgood spoke up. 'Why do we have to go?'

Greaves said, 'It's a valuable cargo and you're needed to safeguard it.'

'He's afraid he might be sacrificed as part of the ritual,' said Claff.

Loveday stood up and addressed them with a degree of gravitas that Rosalyn had not noticed in him before.

'I have researched the process, and I can assure you there will be no need to sacrifice one of you to achieve the reawakening of King Arthur. You will be safe and more so than if you remain here when the Germans invade. Your government considers you as pawns to be sacrificed. We believe that our proposed course of action will prevent that happening and will bring peace to this country.'

Rosalyn watched the meaning of his words sink into their minds at different rates. Osgood and Claff eventually realised that Churchill's government would be overthrown and they saw that Greaves did not argue against it. Brent was grinding his teeth. Perhaps he thought the prospect of fighting the Nazis could be replaced by a civil war at home.

Davies stood and said, 'The country will unite behind Arthur and the seolfor will come out of the shadows and stand alongside us as warriors. Great Britain will be such a force that Hitler will sue for peace. If he doesn't, the whole of Europe will rise against him at the promise of the new kingdom of Camelot.'

His rousing speech did not have the effect he wanted but Claff and Osgood grunted and accepted the inevitable. Rosalyn reflected that Churchill's record so far was poor. The Norwegian venture had been a failure and the expedition that ended in Dunkirk was a pathetic defeat. With no allies in the European theatre it was only a matter of time before Britain was invaded or starved into submission as wolf-packs of U-Boats hunted merchant shipping off her coasts.

Rosalyn looked at Greaves and wondered what he would do. The conspiracy to raise Arthur was treasonous, surely he would not support it. She hoped he was waiting to see the outcome of the necromancy and, if possible, would attempt to salvage the cooperation of the seolfor as he had been instructed.

Rosalyn was allowed to eat an early dinner with the men in the refectory. Eoldrith, she was relieved to see, was absent and Mariel was in the kitchen with cook and his assistant, but Loveday had taken a place at the table and was eating the venison. She avoided his eye. Perhaps it was the buck that Farrell had shot when he was with her. She ate it anyway.

In the event the lorry did not arrive until after six and the driver wanted to start back immediately. In the blackout it would be a challenge to navigate the London streets so they were told to travel as far as possible whilst it was light and then bed down in the vehicle and wait for daylight. Rosalyn's heart sank at the prospect of spending a night in discomfort with the men and the same thought appeared to have occurred to Greaves.

He turned to Brent and said quietly, 'In view of Miss James's delicate condition it might be better if you bring her and the old woman to town on the train tomorrow. I'll make out passes for you.'

Rosalyn could have cheered. Her fake monthly had provided them with a chance to devise a strategy to prevent the seolfor plot. Instead she just looked suitably relieved and tired and made her excuses to find Mariel and tell her the plan. She found her working in the kitchen garden. Did the woman never stop? She had found wild blackberries and a few apples and was intending to create some sort of pudding with what ingredients were available.

Rosalyn watched the men carry the coffin up the cellar steps and carefully place it in the lorry. Then with their small bags they jumped in beside it, Greaves travelled with the driver. Loveday and Davies looked uncomfortable taking their places besides Claff and Osgood. The blacksmith scowled at her as they drove by, and she remembered that his wife and daughter were heavily pregnant prisoners held beneath the old theatre in Soho. Did he have some plan to wreak further revenge on Doctor Dee? Rosalyn hoped he did. She turned back to the Hall and joined Brent on the steps. Could they now speak safely?

'I think you've agreed to help Mariel prepare pudding for us,' he said in a neutral manner. 'She will be waiting for you in the kitchen.'

She nodded and meekly made her way to the kitchen to assist with the preparation of the blackberries and a quiet conversation with her grandmother.

'Your Private Brent will meet us in the chapel at seven thirty,' Mariel said.

'He isn't my Private Brent.'

Mariel smiled and Rosalyn blushed and said angrily, 'You never met Farrell. We loved each other. I miss him so much.' Her voice caught as she remembered their time together and she was ashamed to find herself weeping and having to stop sorting the blackberries and wiping her eyes and running nose. 'Now look at me.'

The cook was checking his stores and he noticed her emotional state and shook his head. Rosalyn felt even more frustrated and upset, they just thought it was her time of the month. She made her excuses and went up to the attic room and cried noisily into the pillow. When there were no more tears, she washed her face and looked out of the window at the darkening sky with a sense of hopelessness. She laid out her possessions on the bed then remembered and looked for the strange hair braid she had found in the secret stairwell. She stroked it fondly and it seemed to respond, like a cat, rising slightly to her hand, and made her smile. She braided her own dark hair and wrapped it around her head, adding the other to enhance its fullness so she felt quite regal.

It was not the fashion in wartime, so she covered it with a scarf tied at the front and then went down to meet Brent and Mariel in the chapel feeling stronger and more in control of her feelings.

*

The chapel was dark and quiet. The women sat in the first pew while Brent satisfied himself that they were alone. In the light of a few candles he set out what he wanted to achieve. They must prevent the resurrection of King Arthur and a change in government that would lead to a truce with Hitler.

'Whatever they manage to resurrect in London, the usurper 'king' will be a puppet of Dee and the seolfor,' said Brent. 'We have to stop it, whatever that takes.'

Mariel and Rosalyn exchanged glances.

Brent continued. 'I have access to explosives and I plan to blow up the theatre and everyone in it, myself included. I hope to spare you that sacrifice but I know Greaves is hoping the necromancy will fail and the plan of using seolfor to assist the sabotage of an invading force might still be feasible. Those are his orders after all. If they succeed in 'waking' Arthur then Greaves and I will take the necessary action.'

At Mariel's nod Rosalyn explained what they had been doing that morning, changing the remains, and placing the king into the mausoleum, and that the person they would resurrect would be a woman from the reign of Victoria.

She had never heard Brent laugh before, but he could, and did, seeming to relish their ingenuity and courage. Then he sobered.

'When they discover this, if they examine the bones, or when the magic fails, they'll know they've been deceived.'

'The skull still has a crown on it. We couldn't get it off, and …' Rosalyn hesitated. 'They aren't human bones.'

'We think this Arthur was seolfor,' said Mariel.

'Even worse,' said Brent. 'We still have to sabotage it. When they become aware of the deception, they'll return to Pitdown to find the bones of Arthur. We must move him to another place of hiding. He needs to be hidden far from here, where neither humans nor seolfor can find him. Can your friend from the fae help us?'

'Gilgoreth would be willing but it isn't fair to ask him to risk all to hide Arthur's bones,' Mariel said. 'The reach of Lord Faerie is immense and I think he would discover such a dark secret. No it is best to keep any of the fae from knowing the whereabouts of Arthur's remains.'

'Then who?' said Rosalyn despairingly.

Brent cleared his throat and reluctantly said, 'Let me make a phone call. Wait here.'

They watched him go.

Mariel took Rosalyn's hands. 'There's still a chance to prevent this.'

'And fight the Nazis,' said Rosalyn.

As she said this a shadow dropped from the roof and Eoldrith stood before them, her bright hair was standing on end so she looked about eight feet tall. Fury radiated from her. The women had no time to react as she came for Rosalyn. Mariel was instantly between them but was swept aside like a leaf. Desperately trying to find a weapon Rosalyn backed down the chapel aisle towards the door. She threw books at the creature, fighting a paralysis of fear that was instilled by the spectacle of a seolfor in her war glory.

She turned and tried to reach the door but Eoldrith was too fast and appeared in front of her with an inhuman speed. She looked at Rosalyn with anger and disgust. But that pause before delivering the killing blow enabled Rosalyn to drop to the hard floor and try to roll away. The hands grabbed her hair. But the scarf and the hairpiece came away and Rosalyn slid between the pews ignoring the pain as some of her own hair came out by the roots.

There was no time to think. The hard hands were reaching for her. Then there was a choking sound, a squeal and Rosalyn crawled forwards and saw the grabbing hands were reaching for Eoldrith's own throat. She was trying to tear away the dark plait that had wrapped itself there and was tightening in a stranglehold. She sat down hard.

A look of surprise on her face, Eoldrith clutched at the thing around her throat but was unable to loosen it. She fell onto her back, rocking right and left, but made no sound except the beating of her heels on the stone floor. After minutes of struggle Eoldrith lay in the aisle, energy fading and her face dark, engorged with blood. Mariel and Rosalyn stood against the door and watched in horror the slow strangulation. The braid was almost invisible now as it dug deep into her long neck, only the ends could be seen, bristling with excited energy as they wrung the life out of the seolfor. Eoldrith's eyes bulged and her tongue protruded. Mariel took out her knife and Rosalyn wondered if she would release her from the garrotting braid or from the agony of her death throes. She saw for the first time that the older woman was unable to act.

Rosalyn took the knife gently from her hand and went to Eoldrith. She knelt astride her and placed the blade above her heart, but then she too cowered from the act itself. The creature stopped clawing at her throat and grabbed Rosalyn's hands. Now she's going to overpower me and stab me thought Rosalyn. What a fool I am.

She looked into the silver bloodshot eyes and felt a force through her hands that drove the knife deep into Eoldrith's breast. She never knew if she had done it or if the creature was ending her own suffering, but the hands did not let go and she sat there as tremors raced through the strong body. There was no change in facial expression, no relaxation or closing of the eyes. They continued to stare at Rosalyn and when she tried to move, they followed her.

How will I know she's dead? Can she die? How long will I have to stay here looking at this horror?

Rosalyn was unaware how long she was sitting there until Mariel appeared at her side and began trying to loosen Eoldrith's hands. It was impossible. The older woman searched the body and eventually found a silver knife with a serrated edge. To Rosalyn's horror she inserted the knife below the braid and began to saw off the head. There was no change in the creature's expression so she must be dead and there was no spurting from the severed arteries so the heart must have stopped. But Rosalyn knew that Eoldrith was still inside the cadaver somewhere and it was not until the disfigured head was completely removed from the body that the hands around her own relaxed and she was able to crawl away. Then she started to shake.

After some time Rosalyn fought back the nausea and managed to stand. As she skirted the corpse of Eoldrith the braid of hair slid from its position around her neck, slick with blood. Mariel noticed the movement.

'You'd better pick that up,' she said.

Suppressing her revulsion Rosalyn hooked it out of the gore and placed it on the back of a pew. It was inert, seemingly dead, but she knew this was just pretence, it was possessed, and she should be grateful, because the thing had saved her life.

They sat it seemed an age, in shock. When Brent returned, he was cheerful but saw them huddled together and frowned. Then he saw the decapitated seolfor.

'Good God, what happened? Was that necessary? There'll be hell to pay.'

In a weak voice Rosalyn said, 'She would have killed us all and then told Loveday everything. She had to be silenced. Isn't that what you've been teaching us here? How to kill?'

Mariel walked over to the corpse and began dragging it towards the mausoleum.

'She wouldn't let go of me until her head was off,' said Rosalyn.

She went and helped Mariel move the body. They pulled her into the mausoleum and Brent helped them lift the headless corpse onto the table.

'She'll have to go in the coffin we took the bones from. I assume you've made arrangements to move Arthur somewhere else,' Mariel said to Brent.

'Somewhere that Loveday and Davies will not find. Where did you put him?'

'Rosalyn will show you,' Mariel left them.

They went through the process of dragging out the more recent interment again and she had to stop him from opening it as she indicated the older coffin set back. They lifted it out and they gazed at the white king in his diadem disguised by the long skirts and lace of a Victorian lady.

'You dressed him as a woman?' he said.

It did seem ridiculous, but she was stung by the implied criticism.

'They won't be looking for a woman.'

After they had lifted the clothes and bones out of the coffin, they struggled to fit in the large body of the seolfor. Rosalyn had been half expecting some magical transformation and she was disappointed to find the corpse as unwieldy and messy as that of any dead thing. Without its head it fitted snugly into the smaller woman's resting place and Rosalyn went back into the church to find the head. Mariel was cleaning the blood off the floor with a bucket and cloth. It was dark, almost black, but not silvery or green as she might have expected.

The head was in the font, a stone vessel that had been pushed out of the way behind the prayerbooks in a corner of the chapel. Light shone onto it from one of the stained-glass windows and in the setting sun Rosalyn thought it looked beautiful. Mariel had closed the eyes. It wore an expression more peaceful than anything she had seen in life, and she wondered how old Eoldrith had been. Mariel had told her that fae could live for hundreds of years if they conserved their energy and the use of their magical power. Rosalyn looked up.

'She dropped from the ceiling. Do you think she could fly?'

'Climbed up I expect. Some of them can make themselves light and if she sat still up among those hammer beams, it would have been difficult to see her. Not that we looked very hard when we came in,' Mariel said. 'Now take it into the mausoleum and reunite her please.'

It was necessary to place the head between her legs, an indignity she did not deserve. She had been infertile, and betrayed by her lover, Agremont, and Rosalyn felt sorry for her. When the grisly task was done, and Arthur's bones had been carried in his benefactor's best dress and set out near the altar, Brent and Rosalyn assisted with the floor cleaning. If he noticed that there was not a lot of blood for a decapitation, he said nothing, presumably he attributed it to the faerie woman's physiology. Rosalyn looked at the hair braid and noticed that it was thick with gore. She surreptitiously slipped it into a bucket and left to get more clean water. Once in the laundry room she rinsed the braid until it was its own sleek form. She wrapped it in her scarf and put it in her pocket. It had killed to save her, and although grateful she would treat it with respect and caution.

*

The chapel soon looked like its former self, all blood and evidence of disturbance of the books had been removed. They looked at the remains of Arthur, the Romano-British king or perhaps faerie, and his simple but impressive crown. He would always be a focal point for those with ulterior motives.

Brent said, 'We need to prepare for the journey tomorrow. The bones can remain in the chapel for now.'

They locked the door and went to clean themselves. When they were alone Mariel took Rosalyn's hand, 'Tell me about the braid. How did you come by it?'

She told her grandmother that she had found it at the top of the hidden staircase.

'Was that all you found? I saw nothing else in that stairwell.'

When Rosalyn explained about the strange skin and where she had left it, Mariel told part of Lily's story and her untimely end, so similar to that of Eoldrith. She wanted to her leave it at Pitdown Hall when they went to London, and Rosalyn nodded, but her mind was not completely made up.

In the sitting room Brent returned after about half an hour accompanied by the cook and his assistant, with a tray containing mugs of tea, and Mariel's summer pudding, full of blackberries and now cooked, with cream from a local farm to accompany it. In the morning they would have to leave and start the journey to London. Rosalyn noticed that Brent was avoiding looking at her. Such an odd man.

As Rosalyn sliced into the dome of dark bread the black juice flowed out reminding her of Eoldrith's blood. She stifled a sob and stood up. As she left the room cook muttered something about women's monthlies to the boy who expressed disgust. Mariel said something sharp and there was silence.

She raced upstairs to her bedroom and flung open the door. In the dusk she could see the silhouette of a man against the grey shape of the window. Her breath quickened, and her heart, already racing from the stairs, seemed to be trying to leave through her throat.

'Rosalyn.'

She knew that voice, loved that voice. But what if it was faerie glamour? Agremont here to deceive her. Then she caught the scent of him and knew it was Farrell, not dead, but returned to her. A sob as she moved to him and was covered by kisses. It was her lover; she could see and feel and taste him now. They stood in the window using the last glimmer of daylight to look as each undressed the other, breathing heavily and kissing each area of skin as it was exposed.

They stayed at the window as he entered her, and Rosalyn felt a joy that she thought would make her heart burst. Then he carried her to the bed. She thought briefly about the people downstairs but dismissed them from her mind with no shame, with defiance of convention and she was able to fully partake of the pleasure their lovemaking provided. He was back in her life, and she would never let him go, whatever the cost.

When they had finished, they lay talking in the darkness. She wanted to tell him everything that had happened, but he already knew about Eoldrith, that she had attacked them, and how she and Mariel had killed the creature. Would she tell him about the braid of hair and the part it had played in her defence? Somehow, she felt she couldn't. It was her secret strength, so she encouraged him to talk about himself and he told her how he'd been gagged and dragged down the stairs at the cottage, bundled into a car and taken to the barracks at Stoughton. They'd been pretty rough with him, treated him as a deserter and accepted the explanation that he'd been caught with a woman and that was why he was naked. Paperwork was promised but never delivered, and eventually the guards treated him well. He could tell them nothing, having signed the Official Secrets Act.

He caught her odd look and said, 'Yes, I can sign my name even if I couldn't read the document. Did you wade through all that legal stuff?'

She shook her head solemnly. 'At least I could tell it wasn't in German.'

He grinned then bit her shoulder.

'Ow. What happened yesterday?'

'I'd been interviewed by the CO before and every time had refused to tell him even my name, rank, and serial number. His frustration was compounded by the lack of any paperwork from Lieutenant Greaves then yesterday he got a phone call from a Captain whose name he recognised and was told to deliver me here, into the custody of Private Brent. He'd cooked up some precious paperwork so they could hand me over.'

Rosalyn stroked his face. 'How did you know …'

'Brent told me which room was yours.' He kissed her.

As they made love she thought of Brent and why he had not been able to look at her. It heightened her pleasure.

When Farrell slept, she tried to stay awake, delighting in his warmth and the scent of his body. Tucked against his chest she could feel his heart beat, then she realised by timing her breaths she could inhale the air he had exhaled from his lungs and so she breathed him in happily. Counting slowly would keep the morning at bay and make the night last longer.

Friday 6 September 1940

Something woke her and Rosalyn sat up in daylight and looked at the empty space in the bed. She touched where he had lain. The feeling of bereavement reminded her of the loss of the strange baby and finding only a pinecone and twigs. The door opened and she covered her breasts. Farrell came in with mugs of tea. He was dressed.

'You have to go to London today and I must carry out my duty,' he said when they had drunk their tea.

'Come back to bed.'

'You know I can't.' He kissed her, holding her stricken face between his hands. 'Don't cry Rosalyn. Don't let that be the memory I have of you. There will be enough tears shed in this war. There's hot water, have a bath.' He went to the door. 'I love you.'

In the water she lay submerged looking through it and holding her breath for a long as possible. If I can hold it for two minutes I won't cry and I'll go to London and play my part in stopping the overthrow of Churchill.'

Somehow, doing this and taking deep breaths when rising from the water made her feel renewed, and she went down to the hall with a determination that appeared to surprise both Brent and her grandmother. They expected a lovelorn girl and were greeted by a woman with the glint of battle in her eye.

9 DOCTOR DEE

At the stage door of the Hermitage Theatre the old doorman was nowhere to be found. Repeated knocking brought a tall man in an embroidered jacket to open it. His large eyes surveyed them quickly and he smiled with perfect teeth.

'Come in. My name's Wilson.'

When he spoke, his voice was deep but well-modulated and Rosalyn knew he must be an actor. He shook hands with Brent and bowed to the ladies extravagantly. Although he clearly recognised Mariel he did not remark on her presence. Rosalyn was fascinated to see that his dark eyes had received many drops of the oil that enabled the greyfolk to be seen. They were flecked with gold and sparkled in the dingy light of the corridor, he looked exotic and magical.

'You have been here before so I will spare you the tour and take you directly to our lower theatre. It's a studio really, many theatres have them as a rehearsal space. It only seats forty-four but the intimacy enables the audience to become involved in the performance. We expect to use it when the Germans come.'

Rosalyn wondered why they would be putting on shows during the occupation, but she had no chance to ask. Quickly, and with no idea how they had reached it, they were led through a small door into a red auditorium, slightly raked, with a stage to their right. The stage was lit and set for a play. A rock was at its centre with steps and paths to take the actors to the top or to various craggy points. The rock striations were visible, and someone had taken the trouble to paint fossilised creatures onto them.

In front and to the side of the stage there was a foreshore with painted starfish and crabs and in the middle of it was a crude throne encrusted with sea creatures. Rosalyn turned to Wilson.

'It's *The Tempest*, isn't it? It's a set for *The Tempest*. We did it at school. It's meant to be Prospero's Island.'

Wilson exclaimed in delight. 'Well done Miss James. We performed this in the main house earlier in the year and we could not bear to completely strike the set, so we brought it down here.'

He clapped his hands and from the wings there walked an elderly man with a grey beard. He wore a robe decorated with moons and stars and he raised his arms and declaimed in a voice powerful and yet weighted with age.

'Alas, the storm is come again!

My best way is to creep under his gaberdine;

There is no other shelter hereabout:

Misery acquaints a man with strange bedfellows.

I will here shroud till the dregs of the storm be past.'

Wilson dutifully applauded and Brent and Rosalyn joined in politely, she noted that Mariel had quietly left them and Wilson did not seem surprised. The applause jolted the old man and he pretended to be amazed to see them.

'I have an audience, Wilson!'

Wilson stepped forward and said, 'Act 2, Scene 2 of *The Tempest*. Very apposite don't you think? My master intends that the storm represents the second war with

Germany and it has come again, and he needs to shelter. They tell us this time we will be required to go underground to protect ourselves from the terrible bombs they will drop from the sky.'

Brent stepped forward.

He said, 'It certainly makes strange bedfellows and I believe that is why we are here, sir.'

'Who would have imagined such a thing?' The old man waved his hands. 'In my day war was fought between men, not machines.' He peered down at them. 'I don't recognise you. Bring them onto the stage Wilson so I can see them better.'

They mounted the ornate steps at the side of the stage and stood before him.

So this was Doctor Dee, alchemist and advisor to Queen Elizabeth, traveller and occultist to kings and nobles throughout Europe. She knew a little from her conversation with Mariel but they had not discussed again the matter of the braid and its murderous tendency. Rosalyn thought better of wrapping it round her body and now kept it in a cloth bag in her holdall with her personal things that men might prefer not to look into.

'May I present Private Brent and Miss James,' said Wilson.

If she expected any recognition of her name or her person Rosalyn received none and was relieved. They nodded.

'Now introduce me, Wilson.'

'May I present the mathematician, astronomer, teacher, occultist and alchemist Doctor John Dee, adviser to her glorious majesty Queen Elizabeth.'

Dee continued, 'I am an eminent scientist, an alumnus of Oxford University, a friend of queens, kings, and emperors. Or I was, once. They, of course, are now dead but I still live.'

Rosalyn stared at him. He evidently did not know who she was. Mariel had said he was senile and he was old, seemingly frail and yet there was a tension about him of energy but it was unreliable and, she feared, dangerous. Her involvement must be a mistake, then she remembered Loveday's interest and suspected he was the person who had initiated the request for Rosalyn personally.

While she was staring at him, he fussed about seating himself on the stage throne, and Brent looked at Wilson quizzically. He was met with a tolerant smile.

Doctor Dee continued his monologue. 'I once had my own faerie company who did my bidding and travelled the country with me. We performed the works of William Shakespeare.'

The eyes of the magus became glassy.

'I met Master Shakespeare, and I was the inspiration for his greatest work, *The Tempest;* I was his Prospero. My unsurpassed mathematical knowledge enabled me to advise on matters of navigation and I was a favourite of the beloved Elizabeth, Gloriana, the Virgin Queen. She and her Tudor forefathers were descended from Arthur - our once and future king. I proved it with genealogical tables and exhorted her to establish a navy that could once again rule the kingdom that had been Camelot.'

Rosalyn shuddered at the memory of the strong bones contained in the casket and what they had done to them. Dee appeared to sense this and turned his grey stone-like eyes on her. For the first time she registered the intelligence and strength that remained at the core of this frail old man, a man not quite human, whose soul had been stretched over four hundred years.

'I could have been her Merlin,' he said, and she heard the steely taint of bitterness. 'The Queen came to call at my house at Mortlake on the Thames, after I had recently lost my wife but I was not at home so I was unable to entertain her. Her spymaster Walsingham would have me spy for him but Edward, Kelley that is, Edward was so talented, he was my scrier, he wrote the words of angels in the Enochian language.

'Edward thought it best to establish ourselves with the nobles of the continent. I returned to England without him. Advising nobles is perilous business and the angels warned against it. But Edward continued, was knighted, and held high office. In the end, he fell from grace … Actually he fell from a high window whilst trying to escape and broke both his legs.' He smiled.

The familiar diatribe finished, his eyes closed, and he sat quite still. They waited for him to continue but he'd fallen asleep. Wilson indicated they should stay quiet, so nobody spoke. Rosalyn recalled that old people often remember events from the beginning of their lives but struggle to recall what happened last week. She was relieved that his most potent years were in the far distant past when he was Elizabeth's court magician with occult powers. He looked ill, perhaps the elixir of life had its limits. She wondered if Wilson was human and how long he had been with Doctor Dee.

Her thoughts were interrupted when the old man's head fell onto his chest and a loud snore erupted from his open mouth. As though waiting for the cue Loveday came onto the stage from the wings. A familiar revulsion swept through Rosalyn. He beckoned to them to follow, and she looked back to see Wilson pick the old man up as though he was a child and carry him into the wings on the opposite side of the stage.

*

The bare corridors leading to dressing rooms and technical stores seemed familiar from Rosalyn's flight on her previous visit, but she could not see anywhere that she recognised as leading to the imprisoned women. She stayed as close to Brent as possible; it would be abhorrent to find herself alone with Loveday. But where was Mariel?

'Where are you taking us Loveday?' asked Brent.

'The Green Room, of course,' he replied as though where else would they meet the seolfor or faeries or whatever.

Rosalyn had an image of a faerie glen, green and spring-like with delicate beams of sunshine and flowers. It would be a natural place like a faerie ring enhanced for being in London by the illusory faerie magic, what she now knew they called 'the glamour'. How like the theatre, she thought wryly.

She was almost looking forward to it when Loveday opened a door and ushered them into a large shabby room, painted green and furnished with an assortment of second-hand settees and chairs. There were no windows, and the odour was musty, with more than a hint of feet and old sweat. Seated morosely near a kettle on a spirit stove were Claff and Osgood.

Brent looked around the room. 'Where are Lieutenant Greaves and the Reverend? And what have they done with the remains of the so-called king?'

Osgood and Claff were uncharacteristically subdued. They sat, puppet-like, staring at the kettle and barely acknowledged the presence of Lovegood and their colleagues when they entered.

Rosalyn saw Osgood and Brent exchange a glance and she realised that the reason the men were here was so they could be killed if it went wrong. No tattle tales left to speak of the plot against Churchill. She kept her shock hidden and felt Loveday glide across the room.

'This Green Room is not what I expected,' she said to him.

'Ah, you were thinking no doubt of the Green Man, the forest God and remnant of pagan beliefs, to some still known as the devil. Sadly it has no connection. Every theatre has a Green Room where actors relax before going on stage. The colour was a relief for the eyes, damaged as they were by the 'lime' lights at the front of the stage. A cause of headaches, I believe.'

He sat on one of the settees and Rosalyn joined him, her newfound determination lending a calmness to her outward appearance. Brent occupied the men in talk about the journey up and listened as they complained of the lack of facilities.

'You interest me, Mr Loveday.'

As though surprised, a small amount of colour appeared in his pale cheeks and perhaps moisture in his strange eyes. Rosalyn knew he had not received much flattery and she was going to use all her charms to find out what was intended tonight.

'I'm glad you are going to be reasonable,' he said.

Rosalyn smiled and nodded. She was close to him, and his breath was strange, it smelled of almonds. Marzipan and Christmas she thought, and she felt a twinge of regret at the memories of her family and past Christmas festivities. He appeared to sense this.

'I find your human weakness attractive,' he continued. 'You were correct about my feelings for Eoldrith but she cares only for Agremont. The fae have such power; you would not believe the beauty of their world. Their food is incomparable ... I see you are surprised, we are told not to eat it, but it's fine to eat and drink with them. You'll find that out when he takes you to bed.'

'But that won't be necessary if we can unite the country behind its true king.'

Rosalyn kept her face neutral; she must be simply interested in what he was telling her.

As hoped, he continued, moving closer and whispering. 'I would like to tell you everything, but it must be kept secret. If humans were aware that it is possible, they would be summoning the souls of their dead loved ones and there will be so many in the forthcoming months and years. Even now the mediums are holding seances to contact the dead and find out what is happening in the world. Can you think of any surer sign that people are unhappy with the way things are? Our brave young airman dying in a futile battle against a larger airforce and so many bombs still to come unless we see sense.'

'Camelot reborn,' Rosalyn said, her eyes sparkling.

'A return to the days of chivalry and romance,' he said.

'No more guns and bombs.'

'No more trains or cars or damnable planes.'

'How exactly are you going to do that?' she said.

'The seolfor will take care of it. All over the world.'

The whispered conversation had drawn the attention of the others and they were no longer talking so Loveday stopped. Rosalyn fought her revulsion and put a hand on his arm. He looked at it and she thought he might pull away, so she smiled gently.

'I'm worried,' she whispered. 'Is Doctor Dee capable of doing this thing? He seemed distracted.'

'With my help. I am his amanuensis,' he said proudly. 'I am his right hand. We can, and will, awaken Arthur from his long sleep.'

'When?'

'Soon, Miss James, Rosalyn. You don't have long to wait.'

'Shall be part of the ritual? May I watch?'

His face was close to hers and she could smell him. He did not smell like a man and she was grateful that congress with him was not proposed, but then what did the seolfor smell like? Eoldrith had produced a citrus odour as blood oozed from her body. Rosalyn tried not to think about Eoldrith but something like disgust must have shown on her face because Loveday pulled back.

Brent was sitting with Osgood and Claff and he noticed the change in mood and called out. 'Who do I have to sleep with around here to get a meal.'

Loveday stood and darted a suspicious look at Rosalyn, who smiled as sweetly as she could.

'I will have provisions sent down to you.' At the door he turned. 'Tonight you will see a miracle of life and magic.' Then he left.

*

Brent moved to the door.

'No use. It's locked. There's a toilet and a tap. If you want to kip, it'll have to be on a settee,' said Claff.

Brent turned to Rosalyn. 'Did you learn anything new?'

'The resurrection will be soon and it seems we are expected to watch so it may be in the little theatre. Assuming it is to be here.'

'We would have taken the remains to another site if it was to be carried out somewhere else,' said Claff. 'I can't see that old man we met earlier being able to summon a waiter in a restaurant, let alone a spirit.'

'Have you met him?' said Osgood. 'We haven't seen anyone apart from Loveday. There are no shows running and all the staff have been sent away. Occasionally we hear some sounds, but it's difficult to make out what they are.'

They listened, but the silence was leaden.

'Don't let them hear you speak disrespectfully of Arthur,' said Claff. 'Anyway what are we doing here? They don't need us for their magic. I don't like this theatre, it's creepy and the air's bad. I want to be in the countryside.'

Brent turned to Osgood. 'You're a warlock. What's involved in communicating with the dead?'

He rubbed his stubbly chin. 'This isn't divination, that would be using a dead soul as a conduit to information or knowledge. Not that I ever practised such a thing. I did use a sacrifice to confound the old man's noddle in revenge for taking my wife and my sweet girl.'

'So there will be sacrifice in this ritual?'

'Very likely and maybe more than one. That's why they've got us here, I reckon.'

Rosalyn said, 'Why didn't you attack Loveday when he came in? We could have fought our way out.' She was amazed at their meekness.

'We can't move, otherwise I'd have stood when you joined us, my lady,' Osgood said sarcastically.

Brent moved Claff's legs. They were a dead weight. They could talk and move their arms, but little else.

Horrified, Rosalyn said, 'You should have warned us. Did you drink something or was it a spell?'

'Don't know and it's too late for us. Why should we save you?' said Claff. 'The more of us there are the less likely we'll be sacrificed. It might be you.'

He pointed at Rosalyn and there was an uncomfortable silence.

Eventually Osgood said, 'They keep saying Arthur isn't dead but sleeping. So this isn't the usual necromancy. It's possible he'll chose a body to occupy so they'll give him as wide a choice as possible.'

Rosalyn looked at Brent as she remembered they had replaced the bones with those of a woman. The soul might choose her body.

'We can't just sit here,' said Rosalyn. 'Is there anything in your bag that might open the door?'

They searched the room looking for possible escape routes.

Brent said nothing and she remembered he had brought explosives. It was lucky they hadn't searched them when they came in; he would no doubt have a gun and his knife. He must have the gun into his jacket and the knife in his sock. The explosives had been concealed.

Out of sight of Claff and Osgood he hid the holdall in a cupboard. Rosalyn strapped her knife to her waist and covered it with her jacket. She also had her secret and magical weapon, a murderous length of dark hair tied in a braid. She removed it from her bag, restored to its original lustre and was tempted to add it to her own hair as she had at Pitdown. But the thought of it being so close to her neck recalled Mariel's words about its history, and she decided to wrap it around her left arm instead. Brent was clearly puzzled at this, but then he did not know what havoc it had wreaked in its past.

While they waited, Rosalyn and Brent made Claff and Osgood as comfortable as possible. Their talk was of revenge against Davies in particular and it became clear that the spell or drug was wearing off the men. By the time the door opened again they were able to totter about like old men.

Greaves entered; his face taut with stress.

'What in hell's name is happening?' said Brent, any military protocol forgotten.

'I'm sorry you were incapacitated,' Greaves apologised to Claff and Osgood. Then to everyone, 'The ritual will take place tonight, at midnight, and high ranking seolfor will attend. They're worried because Eoldrith should be here and has not arrived. Did you see her before you left?'

Brent lied, 'I haven't seen her since you left with Arthur's bones yesterday. What about you Miss James?'

Rosalyn shook her head, not quite able to trust her voice.

'I suppose it will have to proceed without her. The stage is being prepared.' Greaves sat heavily and put his head in his hands. 'I hope it fails. If it succeeds the seolfor intend to unite behind him, using their most powerful magic, and invite the King to stand down, perhaps remove himself and his family to Canada. They have promised me no deaths. Tomorrow the Prime Minister and the key cabinet ministers have been invited to meet with Agremont and Lord Faerie. I have seen terrible things done by humans to each other, but that creature frightens me.'

Brent was furious. 'So if King Arthur is in living human form you hope Churchill will embrace him as a leader, and if not, you propose to assassinate him and overthrow the government.' He faced Greaves. 'The Prime Minister will not countenance any negotiations with the enemy. You're doing Hitler's job you know.'

Greaves could not look at him and became even more pale.

'If the resurrection fails then Churchill attends a meeting with Agremont and Faerie as planned. Has he met them before?' Brent said.

Greaves said, 'He's met Agremont and thinks they want a small area of land where they can exist in peace. The breeding programme hasn't been mentioned but I have reason to believe he would not oppose interspecies unions, provided the women were willing.'

Rosalyn asked, 'Why do you think that?'

'He supported eugenics in 1913 as a way to improve the quality of humankind. As well as the seolfor wanting to increase their numbers we have a way to improve the abilities of future humans.'

'What do you mean, he supported eugenics?' she asked.

'He wants to improve the British race,' said Greaves. 'Eliminate mental deficiency. You can see the reasoning surely. Your own tribe ensures its racial purity quite fastidiously.' He spoke coldly but did not look at Rosalyn directly.

So this is a war about race after all, or perhaps about the next evolutionary step in the human species. Not about religion as so many have been before, but a competition for superiority. Having seolfor blood might give us an advantage. Did Greaves know that the Pitdown women were somewhere in this building, waiting to give birth? She assumed they had not yet done so and wondered when Mariel would be able to update her on the situation.

'If you overthrow the government and sue for peace you will be throwing in your lot with the ideologies of the Nazis.'

'I don't like it any more than you do,' said Greaves unhappily. 'Anyway it may not work.'

Rosalyn thought of the woman whose bones would be subject to the ritual and wondered what they would see tonight. She knew that Osgood's wife and daughter were held at the theatre, assuming they hadn't been moved to a more secure location. Did he really have no idea? What would he do if he found out? She must ask Brent when they were alone. Osgood might have regained his strength by then and she felt a fear and sense of despair at the idea that a similar fate could affect them all and render them unable to resist whatever horror awaited. Where was Mariel? Could she intervene in some way?

It was the middle of the afternoon. Rosalyn needed to occupy herself for hours. Greaves told them there was food in the cupboards and Osgood confirmed they had not eaten it. The possible cause of their paralysis was a bottle of whisky they had found in the little kitchen, unless it was a seolfor spell that had been cast on them when they arrived. She made and ate a sandwich then waited to see what effect it would have. After half an hour she declared the bread, butter, and cheese to be safe, so they helped themselves and trusted the tea as well.

The room was an area where actors waited before they went onto the stage so it was comfortable, and before long Claff and Osgood were snoring. Even Greaves drifted off in the quiet and warmth. Brent was twitchy and chain smoking. She would hate to see him if they ran out of cigarettes. They dared not speak so she found an old newspaper and looked at what had been in the news on 19th June.

Timings of the blackout were prominent on the first page, and below that, a seemingly ridiculous advertisement for 'British Made' Imperial Typewriters. She wondered what the factory was making now. Weapons hopefully. The banner headline read 'Battle of Britain: R.A.F. on offensive' but there was no detail. It was an attempt at morale-boosting propaganda. A photograph of smiling children being evacuated took up much of the page, justification of the struggle, no doubt. The inside pages had instructions on what to do if the enemy came but Rosalyn found the advertisements more distracting than the old news. News that had been supplanted many times in the theatre of war since June.

In the way of propaganda some adverts were intended to be reassuring but it was sad to think that familiar images of cocoa and indigestion relief might fade into the carnage of war. Then she saw an advertisement for scent and a drawing of a couple dancing, she in a ball gown and he in military uniform. The strapline was 'She's always certain of romance' because she wears 'Evening in Paris'. How awful. She'd just read that the Nazi Command had established their headquarters at the Ritz Hotel in Paris.

It was the sight of the lovers embracing that really upset her. His arms around the woman, like Farrell's had been around her last night. The euphoria of their time together was overwhelming and she raised the newspaper to cover the flow of tears down her cheeks. She made no sound and when the crying stopped just let them dry and breathed as naturally as possible. Eventually her eyes settled on the radio guide and she felt able to ask if anyone had seen a wireless. From his brisk reaction she could tell that Brent knew she'd been upset and he set about searching for it, probably relieved to be active.

When the machine had been switched on and warmed up, he tuned it to the Home Service and they listened to children's hour until the news at six o'clock. The signal was poor but better than nothing and even Claff and Osgood became engrossed in the storytelling and cheered when a baddie was defeated by the hero. Then newsreader Alvar Liddell's refined tones updated them on the latest bombing raids on British towns and they knew that the airfields were still the primary targets.

In the doldrums of the hour of gramophone records, the door opened and Mariel brought beef paste sandwiches and bottles of beer. Rosalyn moved to the door and whispered to her as she made to leave. Greaves coughed.

'Women's matters,' she said and Mariel nodded.

He waved them out with a warning to be back soon.

They walked along a corridor and Rosalyn could hear snatches of conversation as they passed what was evidently access to the stage.

Turning into a dressing room and closing the door, her grandmother spoke quietly. 'We don't have much time. There is another way out of the Green Room but it's difficult to find unless you know about it. Next to the kitchen is a vent to allow air into the room. It seems small but there is a catch to the right that opens a larger door. It's still only a crawl space but better than nothing. You will find yourself in the alley next to the theatre. Please use it, if you get the chance.'

'Have you discovered any information on Davies's network of Fifthcolumnists?'

'I'm sorry,' Mariel shook her head. 'He has a radio and has been talking to one contact on that but they have stayed away from the theatre. Davies has seen greyfolk and they have not. He believes in magic, but I imagine his counterparts would be sceptical. They might think he's gone crazy, so they'll wait for the outcome of tonight's experiment.'

'Are the women still here?'

'Yes. They have been kept malleable with the use of some magic potions and are quite happy to be visited regularly by seolfor who treat them like royalty and provide extravagant food and drink.'

'Will it harm the babies?' asked Rosalyn, thinking of the horror of the birth she had witnessed.

'Only a few of the seolfor now care. Many are focussed on the raising of Arthur, and we know how that will end. It's a shame that our only plan tonight is the destruction of everything.'

The theatre will be destroyed if Brent succeeds, no doubt blamed by the authorities on an errant bomb or something similar. Rosalyn would have liked to save the women if she could.

'Tell me how to find the women's room and how to release them. Please.'

'I don't think that would be a good idea.'

'I must try. One of the men in the Green Room is a husband and a father to two of them, at the very least I can take him to them.'

Mariel regarded her and eventually gave her directions. They returned to the Green Room and Rosalyn entered alone. When she was sure no one was looking she surreptitiously studied the vent near the kitchen. She would only use it if absolutely necessary.

10 ABOMINATION

As the hour of necromancy approached the group became more tense. At about eleven o'clock Loveday opened the door and beckoned to them. Osgood and Claff, now fully restored, rose and crowded him at the door demanding to be released.

Greaves spoke quietly to Brent.

'Churchill is coming here tomorrow. I have warned my contacts and if the creature is successfully resurrected, he will be informed, but I fear he may rashly ignore advice and still venture to see if it is really King Arthur. You know how curious he is about England's history.' Before Brent could reply he said, 'I intend to kill whatever abomination they produce. I expect you to have my back.' He ignored Rosalyn.

There was no chance to speak further because two seolfor entered the room and compelled Osgood and Claff away from the door. They were armed with spears and a touch from a weapon was enough to make Claff cry out in pain. Apart from Eoldrith they were the first she had seen up close and Rosalyn thought how grey they looked in the flat light of the electric bulbs but the touch of the spear sent a rainbow flare down its length and she felt their power. The braid on her arm tightened slightly and she shivered. Rosalyn and Brent were ushered out of the Green Room by the guards and Loveday.

They were taken to the pink and white room at the top of the building where Mariel had recounted the incredible history of her family. Loveday entered with them and the guards waited outside. Black-out meant that they could not see the city but the room was bright with a warm glow and Lord Agremont was at the centre of it.

He came forward and took Rosalyn's hand. 'My bride, I believe. Let me introduce myself: Agremont, Lord of the Northern counties of this once beautiful country.' He kissed her hand and she looked down at her shabby land girl trousers and shirt. He noticed and waved a hand so that she appeared to be dressed in fine fabrics, still trousered but bright and glamorous. Clever, and she was surprised how grateful she felt. A weakness the seolfor had long experience of exploiting. The braid on her arm was quiet, waiting. He might have sensed it because he stroked the sleeve of that arm and looked at her curiously but said nothing.

He led her to a seat and turned his attention to Brent, thin and scarred, reeking of the foreign tobacco he smoked. Rosalyn was able to study the seolfor. He was shorter than Brent, but still about six foot and slim but powerful looking. He had long black hair swept back and partly braided. His ears were pointed as was his nose and his eyes long and attractive but it was difficult to describe the colour. She decided the changing hue was part of their glamour. She closed one eye and then the other, but he was visible to both. His mouth was sensual and cruel despite the smile he had treated her to. Rosalyn was ashamed to feel attracted to him.

'Where is Eoldrith?'

The question surprised her and hot blood suffused her neck but Agremont was looking directly at Brent and Rosalyn felt the air thicken. It became hard to breathe but it gave her time to gather strength before he turned that gaze at her.

'My lovely lady. Where is Eoldrith?'

She stood and, unable to control the flush on her face, she cast her mind back to that morning when Farrell had left her, and she had lain under the water in the old-fashioned bathroom at Pitdown. She held her breath, didn't need to breathe, relaxed to make it last. She thought of all this as she stared into those golden eyes and it was as though a sheet of water separated her from him. Water in which she had swum with Farrell. Water that had washed every trace of Eoldrith's blood from her. The braid trembled.

At last in a steady voice she said, 'The Lady Eoldrith is in love with you.'

After what seemed a long time, perhaps moments, perhaps minutes, he pulled back and said, 'You feel sympathy for her. Perhaps she has her own plans. We will continue without her presence.'

Brent fell to his knees and Rosalyn sat down heavily.

'Who was the other that travelled with them?'

Loveday replied, 'An old servant woman.'

'I must speak with her too. Find her and bring her here.'

The seolfor guards took the arms of Brent and Rosalyn and pulled them from the room and back down to the Green Room. Mariel would know how to deal with Agremont, she really must not worry.

*

The red curtains were closed and the house lights up as the human party was ushered by Loveday and the Reverend Davies into their seats in the front row. Rosalyn tried to catch the vicar's eye, but he avoided looking at her. He appeared more unctuous than usual as he led Greaves, stiff with anger, to his seat. She tried to sit at the end of their little party, but Loveday put her firmly between Brent and Greaves.

It was unpleasant to be between their rough khaki uniforms. The glamour of the encounter with Agremont had worn off and she was even more aware that her own trousers were shabby and her linen not particularly clean. An evening at the theatre would usually warrant lipstick and a hairdo, perhaps perfume. Appalled at her feminine weakness and vanity she tried not to think about the scent advert in the newspaper and its effect on her emotions. This was not an evening at the theatre but an abomination of unnatural sorcery.

The seats were old plush velvet and were worn flat. Many of the arm rests were frayed and the carpet was not clean. A door opened and about half a dozen seolfor walked in and sat in the middle of the auditorium. Immediately the house brightened, and all the surface looked new and clean. Glamour. It's what they are good at - illusion.

They waited what seemed an age so that the two groups became restless. Greaves looked at his watch and Rosalyn saw it was nearly midnight. All were impatient and a strong tenor voice behind them rang out, 'Get on with it Dee. I want to know what you've got for me before I change my plans.' Rosalyn tried to see who had spoken.

'What plans?' said Osgood. 'Does he mean the breeding with humans?'

'Shut up,' said the voice and each of the humans found their mouths closed and unable to turn in their seats. Brent grasped her hand and Rosalyn felt comforted. That voice was not Agremont and she supposed it must be Lord Faerie.

The curtains opened onto a scene that might have been take from Macbeth. Clouds appeared to pass on a moonlit night behind the alchemist in his most dramatic robes, long white beard flowing. Typical of Dee to make it a show. He was really just a charlatan, what a relief, nothing would happen. There was a table draped in red and black cloth and on it something covered with a silver sheet. Presumably the bones they had brought from Pitdown were there.

Davies appeared on the stage with a bowl, and they heard a sound like that a cat. He's going to sacrifice a cat. It mewled again and an arm waved, and Rosalyn realised it was a baby. A living baby in a bowl. If she had been able, she would have screamed but her stifled sob made Brent hold her hand more tightly, and on the other side Greaves trembled with rage. The trauma in the front row was matched with a murmur of approval further back. This was a serious attempt at necromancy and all attention focussed on Dee. How could he do this evil thing?

He took the bowl and the crying increased then stopped suddenly as he did something to the contents. Nausea flooded her and she put her head between her legs. I will kill you Davies she thought as her sight became white then red and then returned to normal. I will rip your rotten heart out. Through tear-filled eyes she saw the contents of the bowl drained onto the silver sheet splashing it red. The men were each moaning at the horror, even the seolfor were silent. Davies took back the bowl with the child's remains.

During this abomination Doctor Dee had been murmuring incomprehensible words that now grew louder. One of the greyfolk behind Rosalyn gasped and she could see that the silver cloth moved. The bones beneath it had wakened. Loveday and Davies stood on each side and held the sheet so that whatever was forming underneath could fully manifest. There appeared to be a long struggle and eventually they tacitly agreed to look at what was happening. It shocked them. Loveday was clearly disgusted and stood away from the thing. Davies drew closer then cast a confused glance at Dee and shook his head.

At Dee's indication they threw aside the sheet and everyone saw the thing that lay upon the covered altar. It was a white-skinned woman in her mid-fifties. Rosalyn and Brent had to fake their surprise. The naked body was convulsing and then it stopped. Davies prodded it. Dee pulled back the long hair to look at her face. Dead. Yet another stillbirth for the stable of Doctor Dee, thought Rosalyn.

Davies replaced the cloth. Nobody wanted to speak. Each wanted another to take responsibility.

'What is this? What have you done?' said the voice of Faerie.

Eventually Davies said, 'I'm sorry Lord Faerie, but it appears the bones were those of a woman, and not of King Arthur.'

There was a gasp and Agremont said, 'What has Eoldrith done?'

'Where's the crown?' said Dee. 'There should be a crown upon his head. Where is it?'

'I saw no crown,' said Loveday. 'Eoldrith was the finder of the cache, she can vouch ... but she's not here.'

'I will summon her,' said Lord Faerie.

When they saw the owner of that voice Brent gripped her hand tighter. Faerie walked onto the stage, he was bright like moonlight and sharp like frost. He was a hundred times more frightening than Agremont but there was a familial resemblance. They were related, she was sure. He looked with disgust at the body exposed to their gaze, then raised his arms. Dee began to giggle. It must be dementia; this is not the time to laugh. No one else made a sound.

The brightness increased and every other part of the theatre dimmed, he could suck light from all its sources and focussed it on the corpse. He was going to use it to summon Eoldrith and Rosalyn realised she might respond from beyond her hastily found grave. They would have to move and she squeezed Brent's hand. He signalled her to be patient, they would move if Eoldrith appeared.

The incantation was interminable, but the humans regained their voices. The naked woman was pulsating, her heels drumming, and in a reverse acting of Eoldrith's death she sat up, clutching her throat. The braid vibrated on Rosalyn's arm. Faerie continued his rant as Eoldrith struggled back to life through the same pain and horror as she had experienced in death.

At last she found a terrible voice, pointed at Rosalyn and rasped, 'She killed me with her magic.'

Then her head fell back, the body collapsed, and both dissolved until only bones and dust remained. There was shouting and confusion among the seolfor and the humans.

Greaves took out his pistol and fired at the people on the stage. Loveday and Davies dived for cover. Faerie signalled his bodyguard, but a lighting bar fell onto the stage knocking him over and showering the theatre with sparks.

Brent had pulled Rosalyn to the floor and in the chaos, they crawled along the row of seats towards the door. They reached it as the seolfor guards descended on Greaves and he kept shooting until the sounds were replaced by screams and followed them along the corridor. Without looking back they fled as far as they could go.

'We don't know the way out,' Brent said.

Claff and Osgood caught up with them.

'Follow me.' Rosalyn led them to the room where the women were housed. It was deeper and not the way out, but she wanted Osgood to see what had become of his wife and daughter. Perhaps the sacrificed baby had been a newborn Pitdown child.

When Rosalyn, Brent, Osgood, and Claff entered the large well-appointed room, it was clear that the women had been either drugged or put under a spell. They sat in the hazy light in various states of undress. Some were clothed in satin robes of the sort Rosalyn had only seen in American films. Most were open to show their distended bellies. Swollen feet were thrust into mules fluffy with ostrich feathers. The most exotic perfume fragranced the air and each woman had her own dressing table with bottles and powder puffs. Silk stockings hung on chairs.

Rosalyn wondered if Mariel did their washing. There was no evidence that they had used their own hands for any menial work and most had painted nails. Her thoughts were interrupted by a groan. Osgood had recognised his wife.

'Amy,' he said grabbing her shoulders. 'You look like a common tart.' He shook her. 'She's pissed and in her condition.' He looked about and spied his daughter. This time the reaction was grief. 'What have they done to you, my darling girl?' He knelt in front of a pretty fair-haired girl of about seventeen. Her face was as made up as that of her mother, her hair in a permanent wave, as most of them were. Film magazines lay scattered around and it was clear that beautifying themselves was their principal occupation.

Rosalyn remembered what Loveday had said about visits and she thought the bedrooms must be elsewhere. There were two other women and Claff grunted at one. When he caught her quizzical look he just said, 'Barmaid at my local. And the other one's a farmer's daughter.'

'Look for outdoor clothes,' Rosalyn instructed the men. 'We have to get them out of here – before we blow it up.'

Brent said, 'I have to get back to the Green Room somehow. Can you help them find a way out.'

Rosalyn nodded.

'Where's the little Indian woman?' he continued.

She said, 'Who do you think was responsible for the lighting bar dropping onto them? My guess is she was up in the fly tower, pulling strings. Or in this case cutting ropes.'

The women were encouraged to gather their most respectable clothes and put on shoes and hats. Fortunately they were inclined to be compliant and cooperated with every request and eventually Brent, Rosalyn, Osgood and Claff each had a heavily pregnant woman at their side ready to flee the strange prison they had known for so many months. Of course she had no idea where to take them and, as they wandered around, hoped to avoid the room of cages. There must be a staircase going downwards.

Mariel appeared, like a guardian angel, but her right arm hung uselessly at her side. 'He almost got me,' she said. 'This way.'

She led the group down rough-hewn stairs until they were in a more orderly set of tunnels. It was deep.

Brent said, 'I have to go back. Things to do.' He handed off his female charge to Mariel who could barely manage with her good arm.

'I'll take her,' said Osgood. 'She's my wife.' His daughter was on the other side of him and he was strong enough to manage both.

'Good luck,' Rosalyn hugged Brent and watched him turn back. 'Is it much further?'

Mariel said, 'It's a long way down. If it wasn't the middle of the night, you'd hear the trains.'

'The underground?'

'We're heading for the Central Line. It's deep but there are plenty of old lift shafts for ventilation and unused stairs for emergencies. They rely on the escalators now. Which is fine as long as there's electricity.'

They continued downwards. Rosalyn heard a commotion behind them. They were being followed. She hoped Brent would be alright, he was armed. But surely the seolfor are comfortable underground and they would be trapped. Even if they made it to the platforms there was nowhere to run. She said this to Mariel.

Her grandmother chuckled. 'There is a lot of iron down here. The fae don't like iron, it weakens them and makes them ill, though they will never admit it. They hate London, the air carries so many particles that are poisonous to seolfor.'

Rosalyn recalled Eoldrith's reaction to the training exercise of exploring the Guildford rail tunnels. It was the reason they aborted the mission and indicated the first real problem the auxiliaries might experience if they worked with greyfolk. The pregnant women were slowly coming out of whatever trance they were in and began complaining about their feet and more plaintively, their bladders.

'Let them pee but otherwise keep moving,' Rosalyn said. 'I can hear them catching up.' To Mariel she said, 'What happened on the stage?'

'The bullets didn't do much damage, unfortunately. Loveday was injured but I saw Wilson whisking Dee away and Davies escaped unharmed.'

'Lord Faerie?'

'He went upwards through the fly tower. He'll be long gone, out into the woods and hills. Agremont and the guards are our most likely pursuers. They killed your Lieutenant Greaves,' Mariel turned. 'You must carry on, I'll stay here and hold them off.'

'No, you'll be killed.'

'Faerie recognised me as he ascended. I'm as good as dead anyway. This right arm is just the beginning of the hex he's brought down upon me. Death by degrees. I'm just glad I've helped to get you on the way out. Don't let it be in vain, Rosalyn.' She kissed her then said to the others. 'As quick as you can now, iron will protect you, lie between the rails if you must.'

Rosalyn saw her slight form, now limping badly as she retraced her steps. She grabbed the whining woman at her side. 'Stop grizzling. This is war. If you want to live get a move on.' She dragged the girl down the steps and eventually hurried them onto a platform. It was dark and empty. They had relied on the faerie oil and night vision to get them this far.

Claff said, 'What do we do now?' He turned to Rosalyn.

'Over the platform onto the rails and pray that a train doesn't come through,' she said. 'There should be enough iron here to confound their magic.'

He nodded at her and they helped the women onto the tracks, some openly crying and complaining.

They hunkered down and waited for the seolfor to appear. The sound of a person's footsteps got closer and Rosalyn heard Davies exhorting his comrades.

'Come on. What are you hanging back for? I can hear the blasted women. They're here, I tell you. Where are you going? Come back, you grey skinned cowards, damn you.'

There was silence and Rosalyn realised how polluted the air was. It stank of sulphur and soot stalely pushed around by carriages whenever a train passed, but never replaced with what passed as fresh air in this polluted city. No wonder the fae couldn't stand it. They were infinitely more sensitive than humans.

Davies walked past them along the platform and for once the women kept quiet. When he had gone by, Osgood and then Claff quietly mounted the platform. They did not need to speak and approached with the stealth of assassins. The time had come for their revenge. They had seen him with the baby in a bowl and knew of his betrayal; he was not going to get out of this station alive.

Mrs Osgood, now mostly returned to her senses, held her daughter in her arms and Rosalyn held the hands of the other two girls as they listened to the horror of a man being beaten to death. They did not need knives or bullets to send him to whatever hell awaited him, and it was not quick. When it was over, they threw his body onto the railway line for the first train of the day to mangle and helped the five women onto the platform.

Rosalyn said, 'I'm going back. I must know what has happened to Mariel and Brent.' They nodded. 'Take them to the station and find a hospital. They'll need all the medical help they can get when the time to give birth arrives.'

The seolfor guards had not returned while Davies was being killed, and there was a good chance they'd gone back to whatever route they used to come and go from the theatre. She hoped so but unwrapped the braid of hair from her arm. It had helped her against Eoldrith so there was a possibility that it hated fae and might be useful again. She put it in her pocket and cautiously began the climb back up the steps.

*

As they had hurried down with the struggling women there had been no chance to look around, but now Rosalyn was able to see that these steps were not seolfor made. They had been built by men in the last century when the dirty and dangerous job of digging out the London underground railway system had begun. Years of steam trains had covered every surface with soot, but underneath there was evidence of tiling and the elaborate decoration the Victorians had added to everything they built. Rosalyn was running out of breath when she saw something at a turn in the stairs. It was a shoe and she recognised it as one of Mariel's.

There was no evidence of a struggle, and no blood that she could distinguish in the half-light that her one enchanted eye could see, so they must have taken her, probably for interrogation. Could Mariel withstand torture and what sort of techniques did the fae use when they had potions and magic at hand? She picked up the shoe and continued upwards, always listening for any sounds ahead.

The climb seemed interminable. An occasional smell of urine indicated where someone had pissed on the way down. There was a movement to her right and she saw a small black mouse skittering away. This might mean she was near the top of the stairs where the little creatures could forage for food among the debris of the actors in their dressing rooms. Her pace slowed and a final turn brought her to the door they had used to enter this stairwell. In the silence she could hear her heart thudding and struggled to control her breathing. There was no sound from the dingy corridor but what if she opened the door and was faced with the seolfor guards or one of their lords?

The auxiliary unit training kicked in and she took out her knife, cracked the door a fraction and listened. There were no sounds and a cautious look showed that the corridor was empty. The enemy had not expected anyone to return. If they'd captured Mariel and Brent, they would be even now interrogating them for information about Eoldrith and might discover that the remains of Arthur had been stolen and replaced. But where was the interrogation taking place? She thought the seolfor would probably leave the theatre and go somewhere healthier. London was evidently not a place for the fae, its new technology epitomised the industrial revolution, the change that had increased the rate of their decline in the world and was now reaching a monstrous climax of iron and steel machines.

The theatre was a maze of corridors even above the tunnels that connected it to the underground network. Despite wanting to find Brent and her grandmother Rosalyn felt obliged to do whatever was best for her country. The dilemma was knowing what that was. Brent had wanted to blow up the whole nest of vipers but there might be information about traitors that could help in the war effort. Perhaps Davies should have been taken alive - too late now. Mariel had said that Davies's wireless only provided one contact and it was likely the authorities had a good idea who the internal enemy comprised, most of Oswald Moseley's blackshirts were now in prison or under observation.

Greaves's action in shooting at Dee and Faerie must mean that the arrangement with seolfor for their help against an invading army was likely to be unachievable and Rosalyn wondered how useful they would really be in a war of iron-based weapons. Individual fae like Gilgoreth might be persuaded to provide information on enemy movements of troops and supplies. But it would be against the policy of his lords. How she would miss Mariel. She thought this as she retraced her steps to the Green Room. She stopped dead at the door. There was a faint odour of mushrooms and she heard a man cry out.

Walking slowly backwards Rosalyn found the way into the stage wings. A dull light illuminated the auditorium and on the stage she could see the detritus from the fallen lighting bar. She picked up a smashed lantern. It was a heavy metal cylinder. She picked up another and armed with these went back to the Green Room with the only weapon that might prove useful against seolfor magic.

Agremont was standing over Brent with his back to the door and Loveday was watching from the kitchen, a bloody stain on his leg. Rosalyn did not hesitate but ran towards Agremont with both lanterns held in front of her. Whatever he propelled towards her was enough to knock her off her feet but she felt no pain and no paralysis. He must have received some blowback from the lights' metal because he grunted and did not attack again immediately. This gave her time to get up and charge him using her improvised shield. The closeness meant the second blast was concertinaed and appeared to have a greater effect on Agremont than it did on Rosalyn. He began to vanish and she clubbed him with a lamp, looking up too late to avoid being hit by a walking stick wielded by Loveday.

Blood filled her mouth and she lay on her back trying to recover her senses and keep fighting. She threw the braid at his face but it fell short and she raised her arm to protect herself from another blow as he approached. Loveday suddenly dropped to the floor: the braid had wrapped itself around his legs. He cried out in shock and then horror as, like a snake, it slithered up to his throat and he shrieked as it began to strangle him. But Agremont was rising.

'Here!' shouted Brent, holding out a hand. Rosalyn gave him her knife, he threw it and it stuck out of Agremont's chest. He looked shocked then sat down hard. Brent crawled to him and began to beat him with the lantern, brutally over and over. When Agremont was unconscious he used the cable attached to the lamp to bind his hands behind his back.

Loveday was also not moving and the braid came away easily for Rosalyn. She bound his hands with cable as well. Then she looked for Mariel and found her curled like a child on the floor behind a settee. She was not breathing.

'I'm sorry,' said Brent. 'There's nothing we can do for her.'

Rosalyn stroked her grandmother's face, hardly able to breathe from grief. Brent was examining the explosives and the timer. She turned when she heard him curse.

He said, 'You should go now. The timer's damaged. I'll detonate it when you're clear.'

A small brown hand closed over hers. Mariel was conscious, terribly hurt but with a determination in her eyes that Rosalyn would never forget. She helped her to Brent's side.

'Tell me what to do.'

He argued but she insisted that he still had work to do and he reluctantly agreed, pressed by her strength of spirit.

While he explained the workings of the device Rosalyn went to the ventilation panel and pulled it away revealing the exit. Then she ran back and kissed her grandmother and helped Brent across the room. She looked back. Mariel smiled and nodded. 'You go.' That was the last time she saw her grandmother's grandmother from the last century, and every ounce of energy was taken dragging her own body and that of Brent through the tiny crawl space.

They found themselves against a grid and kicked it out so they fell into a dark alley way and heard the all clear being given from the night's air raid warnings. As they struggled up the dirty path the blast came from deep inside the Hermitage theatre, the brick walls remained but the fly tower was blown off above them and no doubt damage had been done to the internal structure. Apart from lights and other technical equipment the theatre was mostly a thing of wood, canvas, and paint.

An ARP warden came along on a bicycle, alerted by the noise, and helped them to a safe distance. The alarms during the night had been mostly false ones but fire crews were out in force, and they did what they could to save the historic façade of the old building. When asked if anyone was inside Rosalyn and Brent pretended they had no knowledge of the place. They were just canoodling in the alley when the explosion happened. The warden professed himself puzzled as no bombs had fallen on this area as far as he was aware.

An ambulance took them to Westminster Hospital. Brent was barely conscious and in pain from injuries to his chest. The scars on his face were vivid from the torture he'd endured at

Agremont's hands, and no doubt confused the young medic who seemed to decide they were fresh burns caused by the explosion.

Brent told Rosalyn in a whisper, 'The real damage is internal. When A was torturing me, it felt as though a hand was inside my body squeezing my heart.'

Their heads were so close together she splattered him with blood from a damaged tooth and bitten lip as the old Morris went over craters in the road.

'I understand.' Then louder to the attendant, 'I think he's having a heart attack. Crushing pains in the chest.'

The hospital was quiet and prepared for casualties and Brent was taken away while Rosalyn's superficial injuries were treated. Liberally applied iodine turned her skin yellow, the tooth was pushed back into place and a stitch applied to her lip. Eventually she was allowed to rest in a side room while waiting to be interviewed by the police.

Mariel was dead she was sure and probably Loveday and Agremont, but she did not know about the seolfor and Doctor Dee and his servant. There may have been other people in the building; but according to their cover story they could have no knowledge of that. She would have to decide on a believable scenario. Had they just met and where? Casual lovers were becoming more common in war and, in her land girl clothes she could not pass as a prostitute, more's the pity she thought. Rosalyn decided to pretend the blow she had suffered had impaired her memory. They could get their stories straight when Brent regained consciousness. If he ever did.

A strong sweet cup of tea and some aspirin were enough to allow sleep and only a few sad dreams that caused her to cry.

11 BLITZ

Saturday 7 September 1940

Some time later Rosalyn was sitting on the edge of Brent's bed, and she whispered, 'What's your first name?' She thought he said Julian but couldn't be sure, so she rifled through his papers and found the information she needed. The identity card gave his occupation category as 'I' and working at a place she didn't recognise. It took a few seconds to remember that 'I' stood for inmate. Looking at his battered face and body she then wondered where he'd been before the auxiliary units had recruited him and offered him a commission that he had turned down on principle. Perhaps it was a hospital, but then they would have described him as a patient. The only explanation was that he had been in prison or a lunatic asylum.

Eventually a police constable arrived and asked to see their papers. Rosalyn told him they had met in a pub and taken shelter when the air raid siren had sounded. No she could not remember which pub, nor where exactly the shelter was. They must have fallen asleep because when they decided to leave it was nearly morning and the all clear sounded. Then they were walking up that alley when a huge explosion knocked them off their feet and poor Julian had had a heart attack.

The policeman was a middle-aged man and obviously decided they had been having sex somewhere but the girl did not look like a tart so he would have to accept her explanation. He too had noted the description of Brent as an inmate. When he quizzed her Rosalyn said she had no knowledge of his background, which she realised, was startlingly true. Somehow, she must get word to the woman who had recruited her or to another member of the auxiliary units.

'There was another chap with him in the pub, an officer. His name was Lieutenant Greaves. I think something awful might have happened to him.'

'What was that?'

'He went into a building after he heard a cry for help. Then it collapsed. Near the theatre. I can't say exactly where because it was so dark and then there was the explosion. Must have been an unexploded bomb from earlier, don't you think?'

Despite Rosalyn's vagueness, being given an officer's name provided impetus for the policeman to try and contact Greaves's superiors. He went away and Rosalyn sat looking at the man in the bed and wondered about his previous life. What institution had Brent been in and why was he so cynical?

'Get me a cigarette, will you?'

'I thought you were asleep. You seemed to be fast off when the constable was here.'

He grunted. 'I'm gasping. Light it for me, can you?'

The packet of Gauloises was crushed but she managed to reshape one of the cigarettes and lit it, knowing she would be in trouble if Sister caught her. He inhaled deeply and a spark appeared in those dark brown eyes, in the blue-black face.

'You look terrible,' she said.

'You're no oil painting yourself, darling. I may call you that now we're courting.'

Rosalyn snorted.

'What had we been up to, by the way? I missed the saucy details. I was awake for part of the interview but not all of it.'

She gave him the gist of her fabrication but said she hoped the mention of Greaves would bring them to the attention of Special Forces so they could report more fully.

'I have a number. If you call it, they'll send someone quickly.' He gave her a four-digit Westminster number and she found a pay phone in the main concourse. Rosalyn was uncertain how much she should say so she mentioned Pitdown Hall, Greaves and Brent in the hope that the message of which hospital they were in would reach the right person. When she returned to his room, he had tidied away his identity card. There was an awkward silence.

'I expect you wonder why I was locked away in a prison,' Brent said and indicated he wanted another cigarette. He only had one working hand, the other was bandaged.

'I assumed it was a lunatic asylum,' said Rosalyn, trying for a joke.

He did not laugh. 'It might have been Broadmoor, but I had a good brief. I'm sure it won't surprise you to discover I killed someone.'

'Then I'm surprised they didn't hang you.'

'It was self-defence.'

'So you're not a murderer.'

'Oh I fully intended to kill her, in fact I stalked her, hunted her down.'

Rosalyn was shocked to learn that he'd killed a woman. She had imagined a brutal man attacking Brent and being beaten by the better fighter.

'I intended to execute her, in cold blood, but I wanted her to know why the sentence, my death sentence on her, was being carried out.' He paused but she said nothing. 'She was in my unit in Spain and she betrayed us, for money.'

'When was this?' asked Rosalyn.

'A little under three years ago. I pleaded guilty but there were witnesses who'd seen her shoot at me first. She missed. So I shot her between the eyes.'

Rosalyn said, 'Well Julian, I always knew you were a killer so it comes as no real surprise. You were the perfect recruit for the auxiliaries, but why were you assigned to the Pitdown Hall operation? We were never going to be conventional, with half the women in the village missing and the stain of Dee's riotous parties on the estate itself. Not to mention the recognition of greyfolk.'

'They were never sure about Pitdown, whether it was a Fifthcolumn nest. Some of the aristos who frequented the house were inclined to Moseley's way of thinking. I was basically a cleaner. If the seolfor and Fifthcolumnists looked like being a problem I was to draw a line under everything.'

'How would you get away with that?'

'An accident whilst training on explosives. It does happen. And I can assure you I would have done it to wipe out fascists,' Brent said.

'Poor Lieutenant Greaves,' said Rosalyn. She felt exhausted. 'Will you be sent back to jail now?'

'Doubt it. There's still plenty of dirty work to do. What happened to the pregnant women?' he asked.

'Oh Lord, I clean forgot about them. I'll go and scout around, see if I can find out if they were brought here.' Rosalyn jumped up but then staggered to the door, dizzy. She looked back at Brent but his eyes were closed as he relished the last puff of his cigarette.

*

A few enquiries brought her to a maternity unit but it was locked down. A nurse explained that most pregnant women had been evacuated or gave birth at home. Only the worst cases were being admitted.

Rosalyn explained that these would be very bad cases, premature labour brought on by bombing and in the vicinity of Tottenham Court Road underground station. That sounded familiar and the nurse directed her to the emergency unit where ambulances had brought four pregnant women, one of whom was in labour, and two surly men who refused to leave their sides.

Good men, thought Rosalyn, and hurried along to the ward. She knew she was getting close because she heard screaming and there were soldiers pulling Osgood into a corridor. Claff was already sitting on the floor, white faced and angry. She waited until the soldiers had backed off them and stood, guns at the ready.

'Is that how you treat anxious fathers?' she addressed a Corporal.

He turned to her. 'They mustn't interfere with the doctors and nurses. And anyway, it's not allowed for men to watch their wives give birth. And they can't all be their wives, can they? It's perverted, that's what it is.'

'They look quite peaceful now, Corporal. Perhaps you can take their word that they won't interfere anymore.'

Osgood said, 'I give you my word that I won't do anything against the doctor's wishes.'

'Me too,' said Claff.

'Come and sit in the waiting room,' said Rosalyn in as motherly a way as she could manage. She thought she sounded more like a head girl but they meekly complied and the soldiers stood down, relieved to be rid of one problem.

It was morning and they were easily persuaded to go to the canteen where they managed to scrounge tea and toast. She asked them what had happened and if anyone had mentioned the vicar.

'We threw his body on the line so I doubt if they'll find it easy to recognise him and we got up to the station on the escalators when they came on this morning. None of them had gone into labour then. My wife was the first,' Osgood said. His face was a poorly concealed mask of agony. Claff put a hand on his shoulder. 'She's screaming now and the others are terrified they'll be next.'

'Do they know what happened to Mrs Farrell?' asked Rosalyn.

'I think they're starting to suspect it's not going to be straight forward,' Osgood said to her. 'Can you talk to the doctors and tell them there might be complications? I'm afraid for my wife. If she's the first she might die before they realise.'

What could she say to convince them a caesarean section would be needed? She had to try. She memorised the women's names and then Rosalyn left the men and returned to the emergency ward. She grabbed a bunch of flowers from a nurse's desk and followed a suited man into the ward as though she was his wife. She didn't get far. The man was a consultant and it took all of Rosalyn's persuasive ability to talk her way into the area where the women were kept. She described them in detail, knew their names and convinced the doctor that her familiarity with them would be a help.

When she entered the ward, they did recognise her but associated her with the seolfor and the hideous journey away from what they still perceived as their place of safety. The young girl she knew as Osgood's daughter, her name was Sally, started to wail.

'It's alright Sally, it's only me. Your dad asked me to look in on you,' said Rosalyn.

This and the look of distress on Rosalyn's face must have convinced the barmaid, she now knew as Flo, that she was here to help and she reassured Sally. Eventually they managed to smile and welcomed her so the nurses left them alone.

'How's my mum doing?' asked Sally.

'I don't know,' said Rosalyn. 'But I was there when Mrs Farrell gave birth.'

'She's dead ain't she?' said Flo.

Rosalyn decided to tell them the truth. 'She died giving birth. Mrs Osgood is in labour now I believe, are any of you experiencing contractions, or have your waters broken?'

They shook their heads. They were all young. Sally could not have been more than eighteen and Flo and her friend Edie were perhaps early twenties. Rosalyn hoped that the call to Brent's private number would bring a particular type of help that knew what had been going on, and could be relied on to treat these women with special care.

'Stay as calm as you can. I'll see if I can persuade the doctors to give Mrs Osgood a caesarean section so she doesn't have the difficulties that Mrs Farrell experienced.' She could hardly bring herself to say the name again and it brought her up with a jolt.

Rosalyn left their ward and went in search of a midwife, someone who might be sympathetic. The corridor was empty but she could hear sounds of a woman in pain from a room so she crept in and watched the proceedings. An older severe looking woman approached her with the clear intention of ejecting her.

Rosalyn said, 'I was present at a birth recently from the same village as these women and the baby was horribly deformed and caused the woman to bleed to death. It is suspected that some chemical has been used in the vicinity that will produce this abnormality and the only way to save the woman is to perform a Caesar operation.' She was well spoken and tried to sound like someone in authority. The nurse hesitated then went and spoke to the doctor.

Rosalyn repeated her story to him and he nodded. He instructed his team to take Mrs Osgood to surgery and asked for Rosalyn's name and credentials. She could only tell him the name of Pitdown Hall and when he asked more questions stated that the Official Secrets Act prevented her from answering them. She hoped that any enquiry would be stopped when that place was mentioned. They hurried away to the lifts and she went back to the girls and told them.

The glamour of their captivity by the fae had almost worn off and they seemed to be suffering withdrawal symptoms, alternately reminiscing about the wonderful things they had experienced and then crying when they were given tea or any food. They complained that it tasted of nothing and Rosalyn feared they had been cursed by eating faerie food.

In the middle of the afternoon a doctor came and told them that Mrs Osgood was very weak but had been delivered of a baby boy. She would need to stay in hospital or a nursing home for a long while.

Sally started crying, whether from gratitude or fear was uncertain.

Rosalyn said, 'How is the baby?'

The doctor gave her an odd look. 'He's jaundiced and will need considerable care.'

'May I see him?'

The women became quiet at this, fear in their eyes at what it might mean for them.

Rosalyn said, 'On behalf of his father of course. Mr Osgood is here in the hospital and it might be better if I prepare him for the sight of his son.'

The doctor agreed and Rosalyn accompanied him to a small room in which a cot lay near the window. He was well wrapped, and she straightway opened the wrappings and counted the fingers and toes and examined his ears carefully. They were slightly pointed and his body was covered in a fine hair. She stroked it and he smiled. Babies of this age can't smile, she reminded herself, but he was similar to the little one she had taken to her cottage. She turned to the doctor.

'Was there anything else?'

It was evident there had been something else and while he hesitated, she said, 'A deformed twin?'

He nodded. 'It was a stone baby, luckily we saw it and removed it. Best not to mention it to mother. It has been disposed of.'

Rosalyn walked to the door.

'Oh there is one other thing,' said the doctor. 'He has a full set of teeth. Rather more than usual in fact.'

Rosalyn looked back at the cot with horror. Her lasting impression of Lord Faerie was that he had too many teeth. Could this be his progeny? She would not think of it. The agents from whoever in government knew about the experiment must arrive soon and proper arrangements made. Mrs Osgood was doing well, she rehearsed as she left the ward, and the baby was jaundiced but probably will recover in good time.

Where the pregnant Pitdown women had been the room was empty. Rosalyn turned to be confronted by a man in a suit who took her arm and led her to the hospital entrance, brooking no discussion. A private ambulance was waiting and he forced her into the back of it. The pregnant girls and Brent sat morosely on the beds.

'They came for us then,' said Rosalyn to Brent when the doors were closed and no one else could overhear them. There was no sign of Osgood and Claff, but then she had forgotten to mention them when she called the number.

'What will happen to us?' asked Flo.

'How much do you remember of the fathers of your babies?'

'We danced, he was handsome, we fell in love,' she stopped. 'I can't quite remember what he looked like. He gave me a picture though and jewellery.' She rooted around in her handbag and brought out some fine silver bracelets and a photograph. She looked at it and frowned. There was no image. It was grey.

'Let me see,' said Edie and grabbed it. Then she brought out hers and it too was blank.

Sally started crying. 'I want my Mum.'

Rosalyn said, 'Your mother is going to be alright but will need lots of care and may have to stay in hospital.'

'What about the baby?' said Flo.

'A boy and he'll be alright too. He must stay with his mother obviously.'

'Where are they taking us?'

Rosalyn looked at Brent. He said nothing and shook his head.

'I expect they're taking us out of London to a hospital that specialises in maternity care,' she said.

Flo persisted, 'So why are you coming? And 'im? Why have they brought you? And who are they? They behave like coppers but they're not, are they?'

This barmaid was bright and she was right to suspect some underhand reason for their abduction. Rosalyn wondered what they would do with Mrs Osgood, but she would probably turn up at some point. If she or Brent told them the truth it might be signing their death warrants. Best to keep them ignorant.

'What do you think, Flo?' Rosalyn asked her.

She rubbed her swollen belly for a few minutes then said, 'I thought those men were actors, friends of the old man in the Hall. They never said anything about the Germans to us but now I think they were Fifthcolumnists, like that blackshirt fella. We're being arrested, aren't we? Because we're having Nazi babies?'

Sally wailed and Edie said, 'It's your fault Flo. You took me to them parties and they gave us stuff to drink. I hardly remember any of it. They must have drugged us.'

Flo said, 'We don't know anything and we didn't do anything so we're not in trouble, right? And if they take the babies away then we can cope with that can't we?' She looked at the other two and they nodded. Sally was weeping.

That seemed to settle them, and Rosalyn wondered where they were being taken. She felt it must be out of town but had no idea in which direction. After about an hour the women began to ask for a toilet break and the ambulance stopped in a lay-by. They were helped out and lumbered off into the bushes. Brent somehow found a cigarette and begged a light.

Rosalyn was stretching her legs and looking southwards when she saw them in the sky on the horizon; a mass of small black shapes. As they approached, she realised there were hundreds of German bombers and they were heading for London. It was a terrifying sight, in daylight and in so many numbers, and then the noise drowned out the birdsong and soon the sky was thick with them. Even the driver and the guard who were escorting them looked shocked and the girls stared upwards when they returned.

'There must be three hundred bombers,' said Brent, 'And there'll twice as many fighters protecting them.' He pointed to the east. 'Look, our Spitfires and Hurricanes are coming in but the ME 109s will engage them. We don't have enough. Most of the bombers will get through.'

Rosalyn moved over to him and said quietly, 'Any idea where they're taking us?'

'To meet someone in government who knows about the deal with the seolfor I would imagine. We're going southeast so perhaps Chartwell.'

'Churchill's home?'

'It depends who's there and who's expected, but I imagine he's in London now and unlikely to get away except to Chequers. We'll be down the priority list. They might send another War Office representative. Someone who knows what we've been about at Pitdown.'

The disappointment at not meeting the Prime Minister was swiftly replaced by fear for the people of London and the devastation about to be inflicted upon them. The guard shouted for everyone to get back into the ambulance and they moved off, stopping at a village for the man to use a telephone. He returned grumbling and spoke to the driver.

'Change of plan, I think,' muttered Brent.

He was right. The ambulance turned around and headed west.

*

It was getting dark and the fires that burned London were just a glare reflected in the evening sky. The raid had not lasted long but the devastation was evident. It was difficult to drop bombs on London without hitting something, or someone.

The ambulance did not have enough petrol for this additional journey and after almost two hours they were transferred onto a military truck at a barracks. There was more room, but it wasn't so comfortable. Rosalyn was worried about Brent, he kept falling asleep or becoming unconscious, she was not sure which. She told the guard and he shrugged.

'All I know is you're going to a military hospital. He'll be taken care of.'

'What are you going to do with the women?' she asked.

But he ignored her and got into the cab. She was worried that if the deal with the seolfor fell apart the government would not want anyone to know that it had been considered. The ramifications would be huge. A hidden world made public. If the government did not silence them then the seolfor may take it upon themselves. She wouldn't blame them after what happened to Eoldrith.

'What's to stop us escaping?' she whispered to Brent.

'Three heavily pregnant women.'

'We could leave them. They don't know anything.'

'We can hear you, you know,' said Flo.

'I'm sorry, but the less you know, the better,' said Rosalyn. Would they be safer with the seolfor than with their own people? 'The seolfor will want the children, you can be sure of that.'

'Who are they, these seolfor?' said Edie. 'Are they Nazis or not?'

Brent groaned. He was evidently in pain but Rosalyn was not sure if it was a comment on the turn in the conversation. She decided to come clean.

'Mrs Farrell's baby – the one that lived – was taken by the seolfor and they're bringing her up as one of their own.'

Brent chuckled. 'You kept that secret.'

'We were told it died,' said Flo.

'One of them did but the twin survived, and I kept it from the humans. I've seen her and she's thriving.'

The girls were open mouthed.

'They're not human?' said Edie.

'You've done it now,' said Brent.

'The men you've been consorting with are greyfolk, faeries, magical people, whatever you want to call them. Your babies will be mixed species.'

Sally started to wail.

'Shut up,' said Flo. She sat and thought about it. 'My nan always put a piece of bread in her pocket when she went into the woods looking for mushrooms. I asked if she was feeding the birds, but she said it was to ward off the faeries as she was taking their food. Maybe she was right. I don't walk under ladders.'

'I throw a pinch of salt over me left shoulder if I spill some,' said Edie.

'I touch wood,' said Sally.

'What'll happen to us?'

Rosalyn had no idea what the fae would do with them, she was certain they would only want the babies, but the government was another matter. The country's morale was critical, and crazy women talking about greyfolk would not help a fragile situation. The worst case would be a secret grave in the woods, or the story of a random bomb dropping on a house they were all in. They might be incarcerated in a lunatic asylum as Victorian husbands did with troublesome wives.

Putting a smile on her face Rosalyn reached out to the girls, and they all held hands. 'Let's wait and see. If we stand together, I'm sure we can weather this.' She didn't look at Brent but could imagine the sceptical expression. They settled into a fatalistic silence with Sally weeping softly. The other people who were involved, Sally's mother, Osgood and Claff, would be dealt with in the same way, she was sure.

In the late evening the lorry stopped and the men in the cab jumped out and could be heard speaking to others. The back doors opened and the women were asked to climb down. They needed help and each was allocated a soldier to assist her. Brent was taken on a stretcher and they walked forward through a wooded entrance to what Rosalyn was expecting to be a hospital, even a temporary one. In the dim light she could see a large flint faced doorway and her first thought was that it was a church or cathedral, but inside it became clear that this was a cave. They were being imprisoned in a cave.

Their panic and Sally's renewed wailing prompted the guard who had been with them since London to say, 'Don't worry. These caves are going to be used if the Germans bomb this area, which they haven't yet. You'll be safe in here and there are some beds further along, and lavatories.'

'Is there a doctor?' said Rosalyn quietly to the man. 'These women are near full term and the deliveries will not be straightforward.' She dreaded having to go through another birth like Mrs Farrell's.

Immediately she saw from his face that it had not been considered. A suspicion. They were all going to die there, so it wasn't necessary. He looked guilty, although the deed had yet to be done. Who could murder four English women and perhaps Brent, in cold blood? Rosalyn realised she had been trained to do exactly that. She wanted to scream but controlled it enough to say, 'Please send out for a doctor as soon as you can.' She smiled at him and turned away, lest he see the real fear in her eyes.

When they had settled into the dormitory areas and been provided with tea and toast and a little cheese, Rosalyn sat on Brent's bed. He knew. She lit a cigarette for him and one for herself. There was nothing to be done. Alone she would not be able to escape armed trained men, and there would be no point in fighting them. These men were on her side and doing the dirty little jobs that war forced upon otherwise civilised people. They were going to die. A wave of acceptance flooded her. When the cigarette was done, she climbed into the bed with him, under the blankets and held him in her arms. Someone turned out the light and she slept.

12 RECKONING

Sunday 8 September 1940

From a sleep deeper than any she could remember since a child, Rosalyn was shaken awake and led quietly from the room, her bag brought along by a soldier. She was given a few minutes to freshen up before being taken through the cathedral-like door into a cold Autumn morning. Surely they wouldn't have encouraged her to wash if she was going to be shot?

She asked what time it was; 0400 hours. There was a jeep and an officer and two more soldiers waiting for her, and she was put into the back of the vehicle with no explanation and driven off. So no assassination here, and perhaps a chance to explain to someone with knowledge.

'May I ask where you are taking me?' she said to the officer.

'You're being taken to Chequers.'

He refused to say anything more until they were parking in front of the house. It was still dark, but she had the impression of a large Tudor building not dissimilar to Pitdown Hall with steps to an imposing square door.

'The Prime Minister wishes to speak with you.'

Rosalyn felt a flush of excitement and embarrassment. As they took her to a reception room, she could only think how grubby she must look. A quick splash of cold water had not been enough. Her long hair was loose, and she was combing it with her fingers when a young woman came in. She smiled as she saw Rosalyn's anxiety and offered to take her to a bathroom and provide a hairbrush. The officer took her bag, and a soldier searched her thoroughly for weapons. And so it was in a relatively tidy condition, although clad in dirty clothes, that Rosalyn was shown into the office of Winston Churchill.

He said, 'Sit down Miss James.'

Then he studied her carefully and seemed, she thought, quite benign. It was strange to be looking at a face so familiar and not be seeing it in a newspaper.

'I warn you I have very little time this morning. You may know that London has been bombed.' That voice was familiar too.

Rosalyn said, 'We saw them coming over in the afternoon.'

'The attack was not aimed at military targets, but at the common people. Regrettably the people will bear the cost of this war. Today I must go and see that cost for myself.'

He was not a young man but there was an energy about him. She noticed the people who worked closely with him carried an air of calmness and confidence. Rosalyn was certain she could speak her mind and receive a fair hearing.

He said, 'I have known the seolfor, the 'greyfolk', for only a short time, and understand little about them. I want you to tell me what you know and whether you think they should remain hidden.'

'I haven't known them for long either,' Rosalyn said, 'but I met someone who has known them and lived with them and she didn't trust them. They seem to have little in the way of a moral compass and have no respect for humans. Deception is the weapon they use most effectively. They operate a caste system among their own kind, and the lower orders seem sympathetic, but the nobility are cold and ruthless.'

Rosalyn told him about the attempt to bring back the old King Arthur of legend. That was clearly a surprise, the lack of success meant that his advisers had kept it secret. He was fascinated, especially when she mentioned that Arthur's bones did not appear to be human, and he had probably been seolfor.

'You saw the bones?' the Prime Minister interrupted.

'My grandmother and I stole them and replaced them with others. Don't ask me where they are now. I have no idea.' Rosalyn would not mention Farrell.

She set out as succinctly as possible the events of the last three days and had the pleasure of seeing his eyes light up, then fill with tears at the death of her grandmother.

'Brave, self-sacrificing lady,' he said.

Her story ended with the situation of Brent and the women who were now imprisoned in some caves.

'The Hellfire Caves.' When she looked confused, he said, 'Caves at West Wycombe used for satanic rites and orgies, or so we're led to believe.'

'There is also the matter of a woman who gave birth in Westminster hospital to a mixed species baby and the two men of our auxiliary unit, last seen in that hospital.'

'Ah yes. The special auxiliary unit. So you've signed the Official Secrets Act and know that you can't tell anyone of this.'

'The other women haven't signed it, and they didn't know whose babies they were carrying until they were abducted yesterday.'

'I think you'll find they were abducted a long time ago, and not by our forces.'

'Sorry,' Rosalyn blushed. 'What will happen to us?'

The Prime Minister rolled a cigar in his stubby fingers. Surely, he was not going to smoke it at five in the morning.

When he did not reply she said, 'I think the seolfor will settle for having the children.'

He said, 'Their mothers are willing to give them up?'

'In the circumstances, yes.' Rosalyn hoped that was true. The baby she had taken from Mrs Farrell was oddly appealing, but the one she had seen at the hospital, with a full set of teeth, less so.

The secretary she met earlier put her head around the door.

'The car is ready Prime Minister.'

He stood and so did Rosalyn. Dawn was beginning to break, and he looked out of the window at the preparations for his journey and the cloud-streaked sky.

'You're lucky, young lady. If this was Nazi Europe, you would all be in a mass grave or a concentration camp. However, that is not the way we do things.' He turned to her. 'Unless it is absolutely necessary.' She knew the truth of that. 'You will be taken to Wales and settled in a remote area, under guard. I cannot afford to be at war with another enemy and the seolfor will have the children if that is their desire. I hold you personally responsible for the behaviour of the mothers.'

'Thank you, sir.'

'You can also thank a man who appeared at the foot of my bed this morning at three am and woke me to plead your case. He had infiltrated the most closely guarded of my residences and managed not to kill anyone in the process.'

Rosalyn's breath caught.

'I assumed he was intending to assassinate me and I reached for my revolver. Don't bother, he said, and held up the weapon. If he's an example of our auxiliary units, then I almost feel sorry for the Nazis.' The Prime Minister smiled. 'In fact, I was reminded of myself at his age.'

Before she could ask him questions the door opened and Rosalyn was led out of the room in a rush of activity as Winston Churchill and his papers and accoutrements were tidied up and whisked off to London to survey the damage from the previous night's bombing raid. She later read that he'd wept when he saw the destruction inflicted upon the poorest of East End homes. People knew how much he cared and that he would lead them as well as he could, committing his body and soul to the fight.

It was in a fervour of hope and pleasure that Rosalyn descended to the kitchens of Chequers for a quick breakfast. Had the intruder been Farrell? She heard the chatter of servants before entering the room and then looked anxiously at the faces of strangers until she recognised his broad shoulders standing with his back to her as he helped with the washing up. Sleeves rolled up, braces, no collar, hair neat as always; she could see the soft skin on the back of his neck and longed to kiss it.

How scruffy she must look. Thankful she had at least been able to brush her hair, Rosalyn stood in the middle of the kitchen as the chatter faded and he turned slowly. Then the smile lines appeared, and he dried his hands and approached and hugged her, burying her face in his shoulder as she wept.

*

22 December 1940
'I've finished this book.'

'That was quick,' said Rosalyn. 'It's the last one. Father said he'd drop off some more next time he visits.'

'Please ask him, no more Enid Blyton,' said Farrell. 'Nor Biggles. I would prefer something more like the Rider Haggard now.'

She laughed and reached under the vegetables she was preparing. 'Here's a newspaper. It's a bit old but I don't think you've read it.'

The cottage was small, dark, and sometimes cosy and situated near a hamlet called Goginan on the side of a mountain. Farrell had declared that he would learn Welsh as soon as he had mastered the skills of reading and writing in English. Rosalyn knew it would have to wait. She didn't want him to become literate. He could be called up and had already been earmarked by Churchill's own recommendation to serve in the Commandos. It was almost Christmas in 1940. The Germans had not invaded Britain yet, and if they did, it would be in Springtime. They had a few more months together.

After the Prime Minister and his entourage had left Chequers, Rosalyn and Farrell were shown into an office and interviewed by the woman who had visited her uncle's farm. Formal and businesslike as usual she asked them where they wanted to go.

The choices seemed to be her uncle's farm, her father in Wales or London. She had held Farrell's hand tightly and knew that London would not suit him. Pitdown was to be occupied by the army and returning to the farm would raise too many questions. She asked about the women and was told they were being transferred to a hospital so Rosalyn suggested they could all be relocated to Wales, near her father but in a remote area.

She frequently wondered what had happened to Brent. Her last memory of him was holding his thin body as they slept in the West Wycombe caves. Perhaps he was dead. Claff and Osgood were deployed as farm hands in the Welsh mountains looking after sheep and game and keeping the women in order. They had now signed the Official Secrets Act and it had been impressed on them that speaking of their experiences would result in a charge of treason and potential hanging. In fact, their deaths would certainly be quicker and less public.

Flo and Edie were the most sensible and could be relocated when it was safe, but Sally and her mother would remain with Osgood. The girl was vulnerable and needed her parents. Claff seemed happy to tag along with the blacksmith. Rosalyn thought he felt safe with a man whose skills involved the working of iron. The metal might protect them from the harmful intentions of any seolfor who harboured resentment for the frustration of their plans and for the death of Eoldrith.

The babies had been safely delivered in a military hospital and a death certificate was given to each mother. The children had passed into the hands of their other families, their futures unknown. Rosalyn had supervised the arrangements, liaising with Gilgoreth and a small group of human-looking female seolfor who immediately cooed over the little creatures. She was glad to be rid of them and wondered what the repercussions would be, and when. For there would be consequences she felt sure, but the greyfolk had largely disappeared. Faerie, last seen exiting the fly tower of the Hermitage Theatre, had not reopened discussions with the government of a people engaged in a war of iron and steel. Their weakness in the presence of iron was now widely understood.

Rosalyn suspected most of the greyfolk had entered a period of stasis, their dream world, at least until this conflict was over. Perhaps they hoped for total human destruction enabling them to reclaim a world in which they could thrive, as it was before the industrial revolution and the time of iron. She hoped that John Dee and Wilson, if they survived, were with them, and that she would never see them again. Looking at Farrell as he drew his finger across the old newspaper print, she knew that faerie blood was already mixed with human.

He refused to tell her where he had hidden the remains of Arthur and had told only the Prime Minister. Feeling her gaze, he looked up and they smiled. Their baby was due in May. Rosalyn hoped he would be there for the birth, but no one knew what the world would be like in May 1941.

BOOKS BY THIS AUTHOR

www.vickyfox-alchemy.com

Opened Ground

Sarah Madeley has a secret when she is summoned to a deconsecrated church to investigate the ancient stones found beneath it. St Jude's has a history of unquiet spirits and has suffered the collapse of part of its graveyard. Torrential rain and a new farm road have caused the ground to open. Each member of the team of archaeologists responds differently to the arcane power of the site.

Cut off by the storm, they are disturbed to find evidence of a long history of blood sacrifice and murder. The past is revealed through the ghosts of victims and by research into historical documents that tell the story of a ruthless killer.

In a high-risk battle of wits Sarah must discover who began the spiral of death and what has been unleashed on this ancient hill and had been suppressed by the presence of the church for a millennium.

Fallen Angels

It is 1848 and Robert McKinley has fallen in love with an actress from a travelling company. There is something magical about the world of the players, but they disappear without trace.

He is torn between the search for her and joining fellow pre-Raphaelite painters to form an artist's community. They long for the idealized simplicity of medieval art, aware that a desperate struggle is beginning in the English countryside. Industry wraps iron bonds on its people as surely as the railway spreads through the landscape, but they are not the only creatures caught up in the great web of technology.

Others have lived in this realm far longer, gods and lords of the old order, under and over hills, possessing magic and longevity, in harmony with nature. McKinley must battle an unholy alliance of men and these creatures to find the woman he loves. This is a bloody story of passion and the mystical.

Printed in Great Britain
by Amazon